Praise for
I'll Be Seeing You

'I devoured this story in one greedy, glorious gulp. Oh, the women! I love them. I love their families and their voices and their stories. I bet you'll love them, too.'
—Marisa de los Santos, bestselling author of *Love Walked In*

'A delight! *I'll Be Seeing You* made me want to get out a pen and paper and write a friend a good old-fashioned letter.'
—Sarah Jio, author of *The Violets of March*

'Original and heartfelt... Set in World War II, yet somehow timeless, this novel is as beautifully written as it is captivating. An absolutely terrific debut.'
—Sarah Pekkanen, author of *The Opposite of Me*

'Women on the WWII home front faced loneliness and terrible fears. But *I'll Be Seeing You* tells the compelling story of two women who endured, bolstered by duty, love and, most important, friendship. I read this sweet, compassionate novel with my heart in my throat.'
—Kelly O'Connor McNees, author of
The Lost Summer of Louisa May Alcott

'Vivid and well-crafted, *I'll Be Seeing You* poignantly illustrates the hopes and struggles of life on the home front. Readers will laugh, cry and [...] of frie[...]
—Pam Jenoff, best[...] *irl*

D0813152

I'LL BE SEEING YOU

SUZANNE HAYES & LORETTA NYHAN

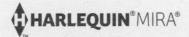

First published in Great Britain 2013
Harlequin MIRA, an imprint of Harlequin (UK) Limited,
Eton House, 18-24 Paradise Road,
Richmond, Surrey, TW9 1SR

© Suzanne Hayes & Loretta Nyhan 2013

ISBN 978 1 848 45258 9

60-0913

Harlequin's policy is to use papers that are natural, renewable and recyclable products and made from wood grown in sustainable forests. The logging and manufacturing processes conform to the legal environmental regulations of the country of origin.

Printed and bound by
CPI Group (UK) Ltd, Croydon, CR0 4YY

Suzanne Hayes is the author of the novel *The Witch of Little Italy* (under the name Suzanne Palmieri) and her essays have been published in *Life Learning Magazine* and *Full of Crow: On the Wing* edition. She lives with her husband and three daughters in New Haven, Connecticut.

Loretta Nyhan has worked as a journalist and copywriter, and currently teaches college writing and humanities. She lives in the Chicago area with her husband and family. *I'll Be Seeing You* is her first novel.

To all the women who have waited...
and to those who continue to wait

January 19, 1943

Dear "Garden Witch,"

I've stained my fingers blue trying to do this right.

Tonight, though, I'm feeling rather lonesome and overwhelmed, so I'm throwing caution to the wind and finally writing to you, a woman I do not know, with the honest understanding that you might not have the time (or desire) to write back in return.

I guess the best place to begin is at the beginning, right?

There's a ladies' 4-H group that meets at the church hall on Wednesday afternoons. I don't really fit in, but I'm trying to pass the time. Anyway, they didn't give out real names, only these addresses, you know? And said if we felt lonesome (which I do) or desperate (which I didn't…but I feel it creeping in on me day by day) or anything, we could sit down and write a letter to another girl who might be in the same situation. The situation. I just loved the way Old Lady Moldyflower (Mrs. Moldenhauer) said it. What does she know about our "situation"?

They passed a hat around that held pieces of paper with fake names and real addresses. I suppose the purpose is anonymity, but I figured if we are going to write, why not know each other? The paper slips hadn't been folded, and the girls were sifting through, picking whichever struck their fancy. The whole exercise felt silly and impractical, to tell you the truth. I wasn't going to take a name at all, but Mrs. Moldenhauer nudged me so hard I believe she left a bruise on my upper arm. To spite her, I picked last. I guess the other girls skipped over you because you have "witch" in your fake name. I feel lucky I got you. I could use a little magic these days. I'm seven months along now, and Robbie, Jr. is only just two. He's a holy terror.

Well…here's hoping you get this and you feel like writing back. It'll be good to run to the mailbox looking for a letter without an army seal on it.

My name is Gloria Whitehall. I'm twenty-three years old. My husband is First Sergeant Robert Whitehall in the Second Infantry.

Nice to make your acquaintance.

With fondest regards,
Glory

February 1, 1943

IOWA CITY, IOWA

Dear Glory,

I hope this letter finds you well.

I apologize for its lateness, but to be honest I spent a week debating whether or not to pass your letter along to Mrs. Kleinschmidt, my next-door neighbor. She dragged me to the Christmas party for the 4-H, which is when we war wives scrawled our phony names on those slips of pink paper. I was in an awful mood, hence my choice of pseudonym. I do, however, have a lovely garden from late spring through early fall. I can't say it's magical, but it definitely has personality. I planted sunflowers last year and they grew to enormous heights, nearly reaching our gutters. Mrs. Kleinschmidt pronounced them "vulgar" and claimed that staring at their round, pockmarked faces gave her headaches. Of course, this is only incentive to plant more this year.

Now, lest you think I truly am a witch, I should tell you about my "situation," as your Rockport version of Mrs. K. so quaintly puts it.

My husband, Sal, is too old to fight in a war but signed up, anyway, right after Pearl Harbor. Until then he'd been teaching biology at the university here. He spent some years working in a hospital when we lived in Chicago, so they placed him as a medic with the 34th Infantry. Last I read, his division was in Tunisia. I had to look it up on a map.

My boy, Toby, turned eighteen on Halloween. By Christmas he was in Maryland starting his basic training for the navy. On the day he left I was still making his bed and pressing out his clothes, so I'm worried sick about how he's going to manage. I can't imagine the drill sergeants are patient.

Toby also looks young for his age. His cheeks are still rosy, and his hair is the color of the corn that grows on every square foot of this state. My parents were from Munich, so I've filled him with schnitzel and potato dumplings since he was as old as your Robbie. I'm hoping if he's spotted by the Germans they'll take one look and mistake him for one of their own. The Führer's dream!

Your boy sounds like a rascal. Toby was always quiet, but I do remember those toddler years—chasing him around the backyard, up the stairs, down the street. I didn't treasure them. I couldn't wait until he grew old enough to talk to me while we ate lunch. When he did, all he wanted to do was stick his nose in a book.

I also understand about loneliness and not fitting in. I've lived in this town for ten years and only have one woman I can call a true friend. Her name is Irene and she works at the university library. We met at a weekday matinee showing of *The Thin Man* back in '35 at the Englert Theater here in Iowa City. I was dead sick of sitting by myself at the pictures, so I walked up to Irene and said her pretty dark hair made her look just like Myrna Loy. (It doesn't, not even if you squint.) She laughed at the empty compliment and we've been friends ever since.

Irene is a few years younger than me, shy and unmarried, but I've come to realize those types of differences become mere trivialities with the passing of time. She and I meet for lunch almost every afternoon, freezing our behinds off on a metal picnic bench because the navy shut the cafeterias down for aviator training. I would think that kind of instruction would mostly take place in the air, but what do I know? We moan and groan, but I honestly don't mind the chill. In fact, the lunch hour is the highlight of my day.

So that's me. Marguerite Vincenzo. Almost forty-one years old. Garden Witch.

It's nice to meet you over these many miles, Glory. You said you need some magic? Well, I need something glorious. This town doesn't provide much in the way of that.

Sincerely,
Rita

P.S. The people here call me Margie. I hate it. Sal calls me Rita sometimes, so I'd like to go by that. I hope you don't mind.

February 14, 1943

ROCKPORT, MASSACHUSETTS

Dear Rita,

Rita? Like Rita Hayworth? Oh, gosh, I love that name. Do you have red hair? Oh, Rita, I'm so glad you wrote back. I was scared I might have chased you away.

And then I read your letter every night. Thinking about your boy and your husband, Sal. He's Italian? I wish I was. I think it would be very romantic to be Italian. I spent some time in Italy when I was growing up. Sometimes now, when I think about this war, I wonder about the beautiful places I've been, the people I met, and worry. What will the world look like after all this violence?

Your words gave me a much needed respite from worry. Thank you for that. I laughed and laughed about the sunflowers. I want to learn to do something with this rocky patch of land I have here behind the house. It's falling down due to a lack of upkeep, but lovely just the same. Robert wants me to move in with his mother who lives in Beverly, but I can't leave this place. It was my family's summerhouse (though since I married Robert, we've called it our permanent home). It's so soothing, with the sea on one side and the woods on the other. I'm only ten minutes from town and the bus stops right at the end of our road. I wish he wouldn't worry so much. I've been independent all my life.

So, your Sal is in Tunisia? How exciting! My Robert is in Sparta, Wisconsin, training. I guess it's going to be cold over in Europe. Funny, I always remember it being warm there. I find myself thinking more and more about the past the bigger my belly gets with this baby. Isn't that strange? But I suppose this war makes thinking about the future too difficult.

Tell me more about you, Rita. Tell me what else you grow in your garden and how you grow it. Should I be doing anything now in my yard? Tell me what it's like to have a grown-up boy. Robbie might just kill me. He already hates the baby. I'm trying to tell him everything will be all right, but how can I say it with a straight face? My son's no idiot. He knows when I'm lying.

The medicine won't taste bad.

The bath is not hot.

Daddy will be safe.

Lies.

I'm so big now I can't do much. And the snow…it falls and there isn't any relief. I go to the market once a week and then come home.

So thank you, Rita. Thank you for writing back. Because life is so closed up…and now it feels more open, like a wide, wide field in Iowa.

I'm enclosing a sketch of my square bit of earth here on the cliffs that I call a backyard. It's sunny. Tell me what I should plant in my victory garden, Garden Witch.

And tell me a better lie to tell my son so he grows up as good and open and pure as yours seems to be.

With great newfound affection,

Glory

February 19, 1943

IOWA CITY, IOWA

Dear Glory,

I wish I had red hair! Once my hair was as vibrant as Toby's, but now it's faded and pale. I wear bright coral lipstick all the time so people have something else to look at. Thank heavens for Mr. Max Factor.

Anyway, your letter came just before lunch yesterday. I read it while picking at a hamburger plate in a dark leather booth at the Capitol Café. Irene is in Omaha visiting family, so I'd planned on staying inside with some egg salad and a cup of tea. Then the postman arrived and I got ants in my pants so I grabbed what he brought and hoofed it into town.

The emptiness is hard to get used to. It's the middle of the academic term, yet I could roll a bowling ball down Washington Street and not hit a soul. I'm sure the weather has something to do with it (a whopping eight degrees at noontime), but more likely it's this war. With so many boys gone overseas the university might as well rename itself Sister Josephine's School for Educating Ladies. And those gals have no time for meandering—they are busy bees indeed.

It sounds like you have your hands full as well. Robbie will come around, but he is at a tough age. Now that I think about it, all the ages are difficult, even after they leave the house. Take my Toby, for instance. Turns out you were slightly mistaken in your assessment of him—he isn't quite on the shortlist for sainthood.

I had just returned from the café yesterday when someone knocked on the front door. My heart nearly stopped beating—the unannounced visitor is about as welcome as the devil these days—and I ran to the window to see if a government vehicle sat in our driveway. I wanted to start dancing when I saw it was a girl standing on the porch. She was a colorless, skinny thing, mewling like a cat, and when I ushered her inside she started crying, tears so big and fat I worried she'd drown.

Her name is Roylene.

"My daddy owns Roy's Tavern? On Clinton Street? By the co-op grocery?"

Everything is a question with this girl, like she doesn't trust herself enough for the declarative. I took her coat and snuck a sly glance at her tummy (flat as a pancake, thank God), and poured a cup for her. She slurped at it like a Chinaman.

Apparently when my Toby turned eighteen he headed straight for the enlistment office, and then took a detour through Roy's Tavern on his way home. Instead of going to class last November he sat on a bar stool writing in his notebooks and spouting poetry to Roylene. "My daddy says I'm no good behind the bar? So I work in the kitchen? Toby sits between the sacks of flour and potatoes and keeps me company?"

At that last question she started crying again. I swear, Glory, I did not know what to do. I patted her hand, which was all bone. That girl might work in a kitchen but she sure isn't doing any eating.

"Have you tried writing to him, hon?" She cried harder at this, her small frame racking over my kitchen table.

"I'm no good at it? I thought I'd just wait until he came back? But I can't wait anymore?"

"Do you want me to include a message from you when I write to him?"

Her face lit up, and for a few short seconds I could see what kept Toby interested.

"Please?"

So she's coming back next Monday, her day off. I have no idea what Toby really thinks of her. I'm tempted to write him a letter first, to ask, but now that just seems mean.

I have been giving some thought to your garden. I'm spoiled—Iowa's soil is rich and loamy. I was stumped, so I asked Irene. She said to think about the rocky places we're reading about in the newspapers—the shores of Italy, the mountains of Greece. What do they grow there? Oregano? Lemon balm?

Or, you could simply throw down a few inches of compost and fake it. That's what we do, isn't it? Do the best with what we have? It's not lying, dear. Don't look at it that way. It's hopeful pretending. Consider it your patriotic duty.

Sincerely,
Rita

———————

February 20, 1943

V-mail from Marguerite Vincenzo
to Pfc. Salvatore Vincenzo

Sal,

I can fit exactly fifteen lines on these damn things. Sixteen if I don't sign my name. You'll know who it's from, wontcha? Maybe I'll seal it with a kiss and the censor can get lipstick all over his fingers.

I miss you. The nights are quiet, but the mornings are worse—this town seems cleared out, like everyone snuck off without saying goodbye. I know what you're thinking and I am trying to keep myself busy. Promise. I have a war wife pen pal (surprise, surprise) and Mrs. Kleinschmidt has me down at the American Legion rolling bandages. I hate the look of them. Bandages have only one use, you know?

I guess you do know. But I'm not supposed to write about things like that so I won't. The thought of you getting a letter with the words blacked out is just too depressing.

Anyway, Toby wrote last week. He said the air in Maryland smells like fish soup and his bunkmate's name is Howard. He neglected to mention anything about the girl who came looking for him a few days ago, some scrawny thing named Roylene. Ring a bell for you? Didn't for me. I suppose she's harmless enough.

Now I've done it. Only one line to say I love you. And I do. Be safe. XO Rita

March 1, 1943

ROCKPORT, MASSACHUSETTS

Dear Rita,

I'm so glad you are good at telling stories. I haven't curled up with a good book in a long time, since before Robbie was born. When I was a girl, I'd spend the day at the beach with only a blanket and the latest Nancy Drew mystery. I loved her outspokenness. She was never afraid. I admired that so.

And what a mysterious situation you find yourself in. I wonder what your boy is up to. Do you like her, this girl? I couldn't tell from your letter. I guess it doesn't matter. At least you have something to take your mind off Sal.

My Robert's mother, Claire Whitehall, doesn't like me. Never did. She thinks I'm "new money" because my mother wasn't technically part of the New England aristocracy. Imagine. I was brought up summering right here on these rocks in this town. I'd barely even kissed a boy until Robert. And even though I've known her my whole life, I can't seem to get her to accept me. I've almost stopped trying. Almost.

An herb garden sounds lovely. I've ordered seeds from the Sears Roebuck catalog and my dear friend Levi Miller is going to fix up a big square like you said with all that good soil. Then I'll put in all kinds of things. And some big sunflowers just for you.

Levi can't fight. He's got a bad heart or something. You'd never know it from looking at him. As children, we played on the beaches together every summer right here in Rockport. He never seemed to have any difficulty keeping up with Robert when we were small. Or me, for that matter—have I told you I was considered a tomboy? Still am, in some ways, though you'd never suspect it if you saw me. It's Levi who plays with Robbie now that I can't run around anymore. I'm almost due. Any day now, actually. I'm not even a bit scared of the pain. Does that convince you? It doesn't convince me.

As I write this letter I'm watching Robbie, my little love, play in the snow. My heart aches for Robert. Rita, will it ever stop? The missing? I just don't know. Everything is the same, and then new, and then the same again (only not really the same). The best thing for me is to keep on going about my day as if my sweet husband were to walk in the door any moment, picking up Robbie with one strong arm, and folding me close to him with the other.

I still cook for him. I know it sounds crazy. I've been making this recipe every week. It's so easy, and doesn't touch the sugar ration. Enjoy.

Beer Bread! (So simple and good.)
Mix one bottle of beer, three cups of self-rising flour and 1/2 cup corn syrup. Bake at 375°F for 45 minutes.

Let me know if you like it.

Warm wishes,
Glory

March 9, 1943

IOWA CITY, IOWA

Dear Glory,

You would think Iowa would be oozing with corn syrup—corn grows everywhere here. Would you believe I once saw a stalk shooting up through a crack in the sidewalk? Our grocery was all out, though, so I borrowed some from Mrs. Kleinschmidt. She'll probably lord it over me, but the bread was worth it. Completely delicious.

My heart goes out to Levi. The men left here walk around town like they forgot where they parked their cars. Do you know that look? Something's missing, and probably will be for their entire lives. Are they the lucky ones? I don't know. I am glad you're giving Levi something to do. Have him get that soil in fast so you can let it set a bit before you plant. Treat new soil like a newborn babe—lots of rest, lots of food, lots of love.

Roylene came back, scratching at the door again like a stray. She wanted to add something to the note I was writing to Toby. "Well?" I said as we sat down at the kitchen table. She jammed one dirty fingernail in her mouth and bit down. Her eyes looked everywhere but at me.

Patience is indeed a virtue, but I had dishes to wash and wasn't feeling particularly virtuous. "Spit it out," I said.

She flinched. "Tell him I finally got the potato soup right?"

So I used one of my precious lines of V-mail for an update on Roylene's cooking skills. I didn't ask her to stay for dinner. Heck, I didn't even pour her some tea. Maybe this war is making me mean. I haven't heard from Sal. Not a word, Glory, and it's driving me nuts. To answer your question, the missing never stops. For me, the wondering is even worse. We've been married for twenty-one years. I'd like to think I'd know if he died. I'd feel it, right?

When I stepped onto the porch to see Roylene out, Mrs. Kleinschmidt stood on her front lawn, staring hard at both of us. I watched her look down her ski slope nose at the girl's tatty coat and men's galoshes. My conscience started poking at me.

"Roylene," I called out as she latched my front gate.

"Yes, ma'am?"

"I'll come to the tavern and read you Toby's letter when it comes."

She smiled, the little bit of brightness in that girl coming out. I waved and Roylene shuffled down the road, head hanging low between her bony shoulders. She was barely out of earshot when Mrs. Kleinschmidt started in about Okies and vagabonds and the progeny of Mr. Roosevelt's handouts. I stuck my tongue out at her haughty face and she put a cork in it, stomping up her porch steps without another word. I felt guilty later so I wrapped up half the loaf of beer bread and brought it over as a peace offering. She knew right off it was a day old, and her complaints followed me all the way home. It was good the second day, and the third, too. Irene even said so when I brought her some for lunch. We ate it with stew made from every leftover vegetable I had in my icebox, along with some Spam I chopped up and added to the mix. Cook that stuff with an onion and you might as well be eating filet mignon!

Take care of yourself, hon, and let me know when that baby comes.

Sincerely,
Rita

March 16, 1943

ROCKPORT, MASSACHUSETTS

Dear Rita,

This baby will NEVER come. The doctor predicted I'd have it two weeks ago. I know these things can't be rushed or even speculated about. But with each passing day I get heavier and more sluggish. Like a big fat slug in the garden.

Also, my temper is short. This adorable little girl ran up to me in the market yesterday and said, "Is that a baby in your tummy?"

and I snapped back, "What do you think it is? Do you suppose I've swallowed a watermelon?"

Her sweet little eyes filled up with tears and I thought her mother might yell at me or glare, even. But no…she looked at me with soft forgiving eyes that told me she understood. She'd been there, too. Women know one another, don't we? We can peer into our deepest, hidden places.

Well, maybe not all women.

I grew up around fancy things, Rita. Nurseries and nannies. My mother? Well, let's put it this way—she was a side dish more than a main course in the banquet of my youth.

Father and Mother traveled a lot. It's funny, I don't remember missing them. Mostly I was excited to see what presents they brought me from wherever they went. Swiss chocolate, Spanish flamenco dancer dolls, music boxes.

Gosh, sitting here doing nothing but growing large is making me remember strange, forgotten things. And I'm noticing things, too.

Like the way I sway back and forth even if I'm not holding Robbie. I see other mothers do this, as well. You swing, lulling them to sleep even if they're not in your arms.

My mother never swayed. She stood up so tall it was as if a string held her up from heaven. "Don't slouch, Gloria. If you slouch like that the world will treat you like a pack mule. Good posture is the key to independence."

I have to admit I still slouch sometimes.

And also, her hands. My mother's hands were always perfect. She wore gloves when she went out, but when at home she kept a pot of hand cream (rosewater and glycerin) near her at all times. Rubbing it in methodically. Cuticles first, then nails. The backs of her hands and then up each finger. I believe her hands were soft like rose petals. But I hardly ever felt them.

She died three years ago, my mother. From the cancer. I miss her every day.

I've been thinking of her hands a lot. I can't imagine having such perfect hands. Mine are rough, but strong. And my son knows them well.

I suppose this is all nonsense. Nonsense written by a woman very tired of carrying this weight. (And who might be at the end of her rope!)

I suppose my childhood was lonesome, too. I've promised that my own children will never feel alone.

But there's a funny thing about promises. It's easier to keep them before you make them.

Love,
Glory

P.S. I'll write as SOON as this baby makes his or her appearance. I promise!

April 1, 1943

V-mail from Marguerite Vincenzo
to Pfc. Salvatore Vincenzo

(Got your letter yesterday. How's that for a turnaround?)

Husband of mine,

Happy April Fool's Day! (Though I don't feel much like foolin'.) Remember the time I hid all of your underwear in the freezer? You sure got me back. I'm fairly certain Mrs. K. is still not recovered from the sight of my brassieres hanging from the fence posts.

I did give her that boy's name from your squad. I can't imagine being so far away with no one to write to. Mrs. K. grumbled a bit, but snatched the address up so quickly I will now pay even less attention to her rheumatism complaints. When it comes to the war effort, it seems that woman has nothing but time. She's got at least a dozen soldiers on her V-mail list, and manages to post her letters twice a week. God knows what she tells them. Still, something is better than nothing, even if that something concerns the fine points of making wienerschnitzel or crocheting a dickey.

And…about that other stuff. I'd be a fool to expect hearts and flowers all the time. Please continue to write about what you are really seeing, without worrying about what might be upsetting to me. If I'm in this war, too, then I should be upset. You know I'm not the type to think collecting bacon grease and scrap metal will keep anyone from dying. How about you give me the words so you don't have to hold them in? It's the least I can do.

If I sound like a broken record, so be it—take care of yourself. Irene says you should keep your feet dry. She came across some articles about trench foot, but given her filing skills they could have been from the *last* war. And, no, I won't set her up with Roland. He's half her height and twice her width. Come up with someone better.

Love you,
Rita

P.S. You'll probably need a magnifying glass to read this letter, but I can get twenty-two lines on these things if I shrink my handwriting to Lilliputian proportions. I believe I've developed a permanent squint.

April 4, 1943

Dear Rita,

As I write this letter I sneak glances at my sleeping baby in her Moses basket. The sun is pouring in through the window. Spring's come early in many ways.

Robert came to the hospital after she was born. He was granted a leave and he came. I swear, Rita, I thought I was dreaming when I woke up and saw his face.

Labor was harder this time around. I thought it was supposed to get easier? This one was plain stubborn and turned all upside down. They had to pull her out by her feet. I don't remember it because they put me out. Thank God.

But when I woke up there he was. My shining man. Holding our baby in his arms.

And for a moment I thought we were all dead. And it was heaven. Heaven through a field of yellow tulips. How Robert managed to get those tulips with such short notice is nothing less than a miracle. This whole thing feels miraculous. She's here, my sweet baby. And she got to meet her father. That's more than many, many women can say these days.

As I woke, Robert leaned over me, his mouth against my ear. "You fought for this one. You're a tough gal. I'd go to battle with you at my side any day," he murmured.

We named her Corrine. After my mother. I was so glad he didn't want to name her Claire, after *his* mother. But I think my dear old mother-in-law was angry about it. She left the hospital in a huff when we told her.

"Don't worry, she'll get over it," he said as he smiled down at Corrine.

"Oh, I'm not worried,"

"No, you wouldn't be." He laughed. "You don't worry about things even when you should."

I smiled at him and reached up to take off his hat so I could run my fingers through his thick, golden hair. Only, Rita, he doesn't have any! His hair is cut so short. He's a true soldier now.

"Do you like it, Glory?" he asked.

"Well, it reminds me of when we were little, in the summer. When your mother made you crop your hair."

"I can't tell if that means you like it or not. You play unfair, Mrs. Whitehall!"

"Ah, it is my job to remain enigmatic so you will remain forever in love with me," I said.

I meant it as a joke, Rita. But then he looked deep into my eyes and pulled my face toward him with his free hand.

"I will never love anyone else. You're my girl. You always have been," he said.

When Robert left the hospital I promised him I'd be brave. That I wouldn't cry. And I didn't…until he left. Then I cried a river.

For my mother.

For my husband.

For my little boy who now has the big-boy responsibility of being a big brother.

Things are slowly getting back to normal. Levi, my childhood friend who helped with the garden, has also turned out to be a help with Robbie. You should see how he's transforming my yard. I told him what you said on how to treat the soil. He said you were wise and a good friend to have. He's right.

And Mrs. Moldenhauer, that woman who dragged me to the 4-H what seems like ages ago, has been a great comfort as well (even though I make fun of her). I've employed her "roommate," Marie, to nanny for me. Robert insisted. She's much younger than Mrs. Moldenhauer. Nicer, too. She cares for me and fusses over us. She's been cooking meals and bringing them over still piping hot from her own stove.

But I have to admit I'm also warming to Mrs. Moldenhauer herself. She's written short stories featuring Robbie as the main character to keep him entertained. And she has this powder-white hair piled up on top of her head. I think she's a liberal Democrat. And guess what? She's also some sort of preacher! Keeps trying to get me to come to her church in Gloucester. But I steer clear of religion and politics.

I only wish Marie cooked better, but thankfully I'll be up and around and off this stupid "REST" soon. Robbie misses my chicken soup. Keeps asking for it, the sweetheart. I've been making it with chicken feet lately. I really have. It tastes better, I think.

What about you? I took your last letter with me to the hospital and read it over and over.

When I close my eyes I can see your place. So open. Almost like the ocean.

With love (And peace soon?),
Glory

April 11, 1943

IOWA CITY, IOWA

Dear Glory,

Congratulations on the birth of Corrine! How blessed you are, and how brave.

The thought of you waking up to your husband holding his new daughter had me smiling for days. I don't believe in miracles, Glory, but sometimes there are moments when everything seems to line up in the right order. I'm so happy your family was together for such a momentous occasion.

The blanket that accompanies this letter was knitted with Mrs. Kleinschmidt's best light wool. I told her it was for the Red Cross, so she didn't give me the business about using it. Don't worry about the lie—I did my penance by sitting with Mrs. K. while she wrote her twelve daily V-mails to enlisted men who would probably rather receive letters from Mussolini. In between missives she told me, quite frequently, that I hold the yarn incorrectly and my shoddy technique would give me arthritis in my old age.

I hope Corrine likes it, even if it is green.

So, Miss Glory, I have some news myself. A letter from Toby came yesterday! He's still stateside, but will ship off to the Pacific soon. Yes, he'll be halfway around the world from Sal. I think Toby naively assumed Uncle Sam would drop him into his father's lap in North Africa. To be honest, I was hoping that, too.

Toby predicts he'll be granted some form of leave before shipping out, possibly as much as three days. He plans on coming home, even if for just a few hours. I told Toby I'd meet him halfway if it meant we could spend more time together. And what else is there to do in Ohio but drink coffee and chew the fat?

At the bottom of Toby's letter was a message for Roylene. It said: "Send me the recipe." That's it. At first I thought, maybe he doesn't know her all that well. And if he did, why wouldn't he write to her on his own? But then it hit me—it's a code! Maybe I've been going to the movies too much, but I'm his mother and I know when something's up. I'm going down to see Roylene at the tavern this week to see what this business is all about. Don't worry, I'll be real sly—a regular Sam Spade.

Well, I can't wait to hear all about your victory garden. Digging in the dirt will help you reclaim your figure in no time. I'm about to head out to give my soil a good flip. I just saw Mrs. K. leave, and I want to get it done before she returns or I'll be pulling double-duty.

Take care of yourself,
Rita

P.S. I've taped a dime to this letter so Robbie can go to the drug-store to buy a candy bar or two with his OWN money. Big brothers need their sustenance!

April 25, 1943

ROCKPORT, MASSACHUSETTS

Oh, dearest Rita,

Thank you so much for the lovely blanket. I wrap Corrine in it every day and think of you. And Robbie loved having money of his own. It went straight into his piggy bank (he's so like his father!)

When I was a little girl, I used to cherish having money of my own, too. My father's family was and still is very wealthy. My father was probably the smartest man in America during the crash. He was smart all around. I wish I'd known him better. But money can do that to a family, make them strangers. There's something closer about a family that struggles together. A bond. I watched the difference between me and Robert and then Levi, growing up. Robert and I came from another world.

We were summer people in this town. Wealthy and comfortable. And then there was Levi. Working-class and a year-round resident. But his family was so, so close. I used to wish his mother was my own. She never sat back on the shores and watched us from a distance under lace umbrellas. She always jumped into the waves next to us. And she collected "mermaid toes" (little peach-colored glittery shells shaped like toenails). Her name was Lucy and she died when we were all eleven years old. I try to be like her every day.

This war has been what I like to call "the great equalizer." I feel comfortable living here in our summerhouse. And I don't feel above or below anyone. Women and men, too, are acting as if they both have things to give to society. Everyone has a straight back as they walk through town, as if we are all carrying the pride of a country. It's good to feel like that.

Enough about the war. Let's talk about my garden!

My garden is just lovely. I have all sorts of herbs and vegetables starting. Lettuce is already coming up. I can't wait to see it in full bloom. My hands are fairly caked with dirt each day and my apron, too. I love it. I love feeling the earth on my skin.

Now, your mystery girl and Toby are obviously saying something in code to each other. But what? Oh, it's like reading a novel. Keep me posted on this!

With hope of peace in the near future,
Glory

May 2, 1943

V-mail from Marguerite Vincenzo
to Seaman Tobias Vincenzo

Only Son,

I think there is a distinct possibility surrounding yourself with all that water has done something to your Midwestern brain waves. She's a stranger, Toby. The thought of being stuck in a train car with someone incapable of making declarative sentences is enough to send me running for your father's bourbon.

But...fine. If it's really important to you, then I will ask her to come along. If we end up staying at a motel, she will bunk with me and I'll pay for your very separate room. Am I making myself clear?

I don't feel comfortable doing any of this without speaking to her father first. Yes, yes, I do realize you are both adults, but crossing a birthday marker doesn't require anything but the ability to wait for time to pass. It doesn't prove much.

See you in Ohio.

I love you.
Your ma

P.S. I am not a carrier pigeon. If you want to write to this girl, then write to her, and vice versa.

May 9, 1943

IOWA CITY, IOWA

Dear Glory,

I've just returned home after a lovely Mother's Day mass at the aptly named St. Mary's. As I watched the darling young schoolgirls bring their floral offerings to the statue of Our Lady, I thought of you. I hope you are adjusting well to a new baby in the house, and this letter finds you well. If the world can't be at peace, then maybe you can find a little in your living room.

Now...I have so much to share—hold on to your hat....

First, I finally received a letter from Sal! Large sections were blacked out, but I was able to piece together enough of it to know that he is fine. Sal's primary responsibility is sewing up wounds (which is pretty funny, as he grew up in the back of his family's tailor shop on the west side of Chicago). Some of the other guys wrote *Stitch* on his helmet, and the nickname has stuck. At least, he told me, they didn't write *Old Man*.

Getting his letter was like Christmas morning and my wedding day rolled into one. It's amazing what a few lines on a V-mail can do for a person. The worry doesn't stop, but, to borrow a military phrase, it retreats in the face of its enemy, which I guess is hope. Sal's taking care of himself, and besides the end of this war, that's the most I can ask for.

I've heard from Toby, as well. I'll be seeing him next month, when his leave is granted. We're meeting halfway, in Columbus, and it looks like he'll have a full forty-eight hours to visit.

If you sense a certain lack of enthusiasm in my words, then you really are starting to get to know me through these letters. I am remarkably unenthused. Toby requested I bring Roylene with me to Ohio, and—believe it or not—I've agreed. Yes, I will be sending my son off to war with that skinny gal standing next to me blubbering away. I was about to refuse, but this is what my son wrote in his last letter: "Ma, don't you always say to never walk away from an opportunity to do a kindness? Well, here's a golden one. Be nice to Roylene."

The thing is, I don't always say that. *Sal* does.

I have no idea if Toby's interested in this girl or if she's his charity case du jour. My husband and son have always been suckers for the underdog. Not me. We'll see what happens.

Give those little ones a kiss,
Rita

———

May 11, 1943

IOWA CITY, IOWA

Dear Glory,

I'm in a mood today. Writing to you probably isn't the best idea, but I'm going to do it, anyway. Will you still write back if I reveal a few blemishes on my character?

I've just finished picking slugs from my garden. Most satisfying thing I've done in a while, watching those vile things drown in a cup full of sudsy water. I'm a menace to all the living today. The reason for my destructive state? Guilt. It makes me mean. And I've been feeling guilty as hell all morning.

Yesterday I finally got around to visiting Roy's Tavern. I did try once before, when Toby's first message for Roylene came. That evening, she was taking the garbage out when I approached, and I flattened my back against the wall so she wouldn't see me. I watched her struggle with the bin's lid. A bottle fell out and hit the pavement, bits of glass rolling every which way, but I stayed where I was while she ran back into the tavern for a dustpan and broom.

Roylene cleaned up every shard, slowly and methodically, as though the act was the only thing in the world she was meant to accomplish, as though she'd been placed on God's green earth to do that, and only that. She had no reason to hurry. Her life is set. She could have been eighteen or eighty.

The sight of her filled me first with sadness and then a strong sense of revulsion. There should not be a place for Toby in such a life. If he hadn't been about to ship off to war, would my son have reached out to someone like her? Shouldn't their relationship—or whatever it is—be another casualty of history? I practically ran from the tavern that night, with no intention of going back.

I do realize how this sounds. I suppose I am a snob, but please see me as a mother who wants the best for her child. If it makes any difference, I did make a genuine attempt yesterday to discuss the Ohio trip with her father.

I talked Irene into going with me, figuring she'd keep me from changing my mind. We arrived at the tavern at the lunch hour, and only a few older men sat drinking their meals at the bar. The interior was a picture of gloom, none of the early-spring sun filtered through the dirty windows. Irene gave me the eye, but I made a quick peace with the mission to accomplish, and nudged her forward. We scooted our bottoms onto a pair of bar stools and ordered two ginger ales and a corned beef to split. The barman, short and skinny with a shock of white hair atop his head, gave us the once-over.

"Who're you?" he demanded.

I figured this was the eponymous Roy. I introduced myself and mentioned Toby's admiration of his establishment and my acquaintance with his daughter. The man leaned over the wooden bar, his clay-colored eyes boring into mine.

"We don't serve Krauts," he growled. "I told your son as much."

My mouth fell open so hard my chin nearly landed in my lap.

"Pardon me?" I asked.

"You heard me," he said. "Get the hell out."

Irene yanked me off my seat and we did leave—not too fast, mind you, and with our heads held high. We stood on the sidewalk outside Roy's for a minute, our shock rendering us momentarily speechless.

Irene wanted to take a walk around campus to clear our heads and find something to eat. "Wait," I told her, and I marched right back in that tavern and up to that horrendous man. "My son the Kraut is fighting for you," I said, and, oh, boy, was it hard to keep my voice level. "You should be thankful." And then I did get the hell out of there because my legs were shaking like gelatin.

By the time I got home, Irene and I had rehashed the experience so many times it stopped making my heart pound and I could just laugh. What a creep!

I put my key in the door, and all I could think about was what a kick Sal would get when I told him the story. Then I stepped into my living room and realized I was alone. I wanted to cry. Instead,

I turned right around and headed over to Mrs. Kleinschmidt's. A fellow German, I figured she'd appreciate the story and, I figured, if she ever ran into Roy he'd rue the day.

Mrs. K. sat at her kitchen table, with approximately one million V-mail letters open in front of her, painstakingly copying the same message on each one. It struck me as ridiculous, and though I shouldn't have, I said, "Why do you make yourself crazy over this? You do enough for the war effort."

Glory, her look could have froze a lake in the middle of summer. *"Ich bin Deutscher,"* she said.

"My family is German, too," I countered. "What does that have to do with it?"

She returned to her letter writing. "You have an enlisted husband and son to secure your reputation as a good American. I do not."

"You can't be serious," I said.

Mrs. K. drew herself to standing and slammed one hand on the table, sending the papers in all directions. *"Du bist eine dumme Frau!"* she spat.

And you know, she was right. I am a stupid woman. I saw Mrs. Kleinschmidt every day, yet I never recognized her fear, so distracted I've been with my own petty concerns.

I helped her clean up the kitchen floor, and then I let myself out. I went to bed that night feeling shamed. Is my quickness to judge the sign of a small mind? How little I understand of the world. Why haven't I been paying attention?

This afternoon I'm going to purchase two train tickets for Columbus, Ohio. Adjoining seats. Lord help me.

Love,
Rita

May 13, 1943

V-mail from Gloria Whitehall
to Sgt. Robert Whitehall

Darling Robert,

How are you doing? I miss you like crazy. And the baby? She misses you, too. Even though I know you won't believe me. Babies know...they do! Anyway, I'm taking lots of pictures like you asked. Robbie told me to tell you that Corrine spit up on his favorite bear. I'll let him know you think it's tragic. I was happy to read, in your last letter, that you've come to your senses and admitted that I was right. It's better for us all in the Rockport house. And I know you like us being closer to Levi. And thank you for that bit of romance you gave me. We certainly do belong near the beaches where we fell in love. I cried and cried when I read those words. (Happy tears.) I told Levi to fix the latch on the gate as you asked. And you were right. Robbie is wild now that Corrine is born. He would have run straight into the ocean. Thank you for always taking good care of us.

Love,
Your Ladygirl

May 16, 1943

ROCKPORT, MASSACHUSETTS

Dear Rita,

Two letters from you in one day! They feel so solid in my hands. That's such a nice feeling with everything so faint and weightless around me now. And the truth is, I'm beginning to wait for your letters with bated breath. They are like talismans for me.

How awful, being treated like that. I can't imagine. I'm not German but, it seems to me, American is American. That man should be punished.

I told Mrs. Moldenhauer all about it. She's been coming over even more since Corrine was born, and I'm growing quite fond of her. She said, "Obstinate thinkers will be the ruination of Freedom." I remember it verbatim because it was just so...profound. I'm not political at all. Or religious. Is that terrible? I suppose I should begin to believe in something, so I can give tradition to my children. I simply haven't decided what to believe in. I went from debutante to war bride. Maybe Mrs. Moldenhauer can teach me a thing or two.

She even convinced me to go to that church of hers last Sunday. I took Robbie, but Corrine stayed with Levi because Marie was at the "service," too. He's been such a help around here. When Robert left for Sparta, we saw him off together at the station. It seemed only fitting. I mean, the three of us have been thick as thieves for as long as any of us can remember. And Robert's last words before he left were to Levi, not to me. "Take care of my family, Lee," he said. "You know I will," said Levi. And so far, he's made good on his promise. Anyway, Mrs. Moldenhauer's church isn't like any church I've ever been to, Rita. It's full of women talking about peace and love. More like a movement than a sermon. Mrs. Moldenhauer is a feminist! Can you believe it? An old lady like her? And a member of some sort of socialist party. I have to admit I felt a little guilty as my heart rose with her words. My father was a staunch Republican whose favorite saying was "Damn the Democrats!"

I might go again.

I'm glad you got V-mail from Sal. I just got one from Robert, too! Maybe everyone is getting letters this month. That would be nice. There's so much blocked out on them, though. I don't know if he's still stateside or not. It kills me.

I have to tell you that I'm so happy you will bring that skinny girl with you to see Toby. Though I understand your reservations. I look at my sweet Robbie and wonder how I'll feel when he takes to a girl. Then again, Claire Whitehall doesn't like me. I think I've told you that. But what you don't know is that she hasn't liked me since I was a little girl. It has less to do with ME and more to do with my own mother, who she deemed inappropriate. New money and all that.

The mystery part about your boy and that Roylene is the fascinating thing. What are those two up to? I was listening to *I Love a Mystery* the other evening (I try to catch it every night, but it's hard with the baby) and I was thinking your story would be a great plot. Better than theirs.

Keep strong, Rita. I'm happy to hear I'm not alone in my growing fondness to old-lady neighbors. Don't let anyone else bully you or I might just have to take a train and wave my wild little son around. "Take THAT!" I'd say.

He's been so naughty he'd send any bigot running.

Yours in true friendship,
Glory

May 21, 1943

Dear Glory,

I'm sitting on our patio this early morning, with a cup of tea to warm me before the sun makes its appearance. My garden is doing well, though I think if I eat any more spinach I'll turn into Popeye. How is yours coming along?

I got a kick out of your last letter. That Mrs. Moldenhauer sounds like a suffragette. I'm old enough to remember those. My father called them "dirty birdies." I think our pops would have gotten along.

I also think you should go back to the church meetings. What could it hurt? Sal always says it's our responsibility as human beings to never lose our curiosity. He is absolutely right. And let's face it, we're not the ones doing the heavy lifting in this war. The least we can do is not let our brains atrophy. Get in there and see what these gals are all about. New ideas leave the old ones shaking in their shoes, don't they?

Then again, those most eager to tell people what to do are often those most in need of guidance. You are getting advice from a hypocrite, my dear. I haven't talked to Mrs. K. since that incident in her kitchen. Not a word. She peers at me over her blinds, but I look away. I'm a big chicken, afraid of an old woman. Squawk! Squawk!

The situation with Roylene is even worse. I did buy those tickets, just as I promised. They sat atop my dresser gathering dust for days, a constant reminder of a mission unaccomplished. Oh, but how

Toby's expectations gnawed at my conscience! When I couldn't stand it anymore, I squared my shoulders and planned another visit to Roy's Tavern. Irene refused to go back—she claims Roy is a madman—so I was flying solo. I got all gussied up in my most expensive-looking suit, and applied my makeup with the precision of a surgeon. I pulled on my baby-pink day gloves and shoved my feet into a pair of tan pumps with ankle straps. (I still have decent ankles, kiddo.) I was ready to take on that mean little man.

Only I never made it past the front gate.

A few mornings later, Roylene showed up on my porch, wearing a flour-sack dress and a hand-knit sweater the color of wet sand. I was mortified that it was *she* who came to *me*.

"I saw you at the tavern?" was all she said.

The morning still held the chill of spring, but I didn't invite her in. "Wait here," I said, and dashed into the house to retrieve the train tickets. I gave her one of them and explained the departure and arrival schedule. "You'll need to get permission from your father," I stuck on to the end of my lecture. "I don't think he'd appreciate you running off."

She stared at me, blank as a barn door. Her eyes are a dull hazel, unable to decide between brown and green.

"You're very welcome," I snapped. I hadn't meant to sound overly harsh, but maybe I did because a crimson flush crept down the steep slopes of her cheeks. She opened her mouth, then decided fleeing was her best option. Roylene nearly tripped down the steps trying to get away from me. I would have hightailed it for the safety of my living room as well, but a moth hole on the back of her sweater caught my attention—it had frayed into a crater.

"Roylene!" My tone brought her to a halt.

She turned, slowly, a look of complete terror on her face.

"Give me your cardigan."

Her fear slid into confusion. "It's my only warm-weather sweater, Mrs. Vincenzo? Don't you own a bunch already?"

"I want to repair it," I said, struggling to soften my voice. "Don't you want to look your best for our trip?"

She handed the decrepit sweater over like she was giving me one of her kidneys, and then ran down the street without a backward glance.

We leave for Ohio in five days. Wish me luck.

Rita

May 26, 1943

ROCKPORT, MASSACHUSETTS

Dear Rita,

How nice of you to offer to fix Roylene's sweater. I've been getting handy these days, too. Marie is teaching me to knit and crochet. And I've picked up some embroidery on my own. Sometimes I wonder about my mother and what she did with her free time. As far as I know she never cooked, cleaned or made anything with her hands. I'd feel robbed if I couldn't do these things. There's such a sense of accomplishment.

The days are slow and soft with a new baby. Marie has moved in for the moment, so I can better care for Corrine. As I've said, Robbie is full of energy and more than a little attention deprived since her birth.

A few days ago, we were all sitting on the porch having breakfast and something terrible happened. Marie and I were talking about the war, Mrs. M.'s sermons and ration cards. Robbie was trying to get my attention but I insisted he stay quiet. I had little Corrine at my breast. (I decided to breast-feed her. Mrs. M. said it was my patriotic duty. I'm enjoying the closeness. I didn't breast-feed Robbie. Claire Whitehall, the mother-in-law of all mother-in-laws, told me it was a disgusting habit and gave me a jar of some powdered milk.) Anyway, Robbie walked right up to me and smacked the baby on her head!

I wanted to hit him, Rita. I wanted to throw him right over the railing of the porch. And that feeling…the rage that rose up so suddenly made me remember another time. The only other time I've ever felt violence surge in my blood.

Robert, Levi and I were about twelve years old. We'd just reunited on the beaches here in Rockport and the day started out lovely. Then Levi started to tease me about how my body was changing. I didn't want to become a woman, so I was sensitive to it. I was so afraid that if I changed too much, we wouldn't be best friends anymore.

"Stop looking at me like that, Levi," I shouted.

"He can't help it, Glory. You're turning into a Ladygirl right in front of us. What are we supposed to do?" asked Robert.

Somehow, Robert saying that made it so much worse. And I noticed they'd changed, too. They looked like young men. And they were both so handsome in their different ways. Robert light, Levi dark.

Levi elbowed Robert. "Hey, leave her be. Race you to the sandbar!"

And the two of them took off without me. When they returned to shore, falling on the sand laughing and out of breath, I walked right over to them with my hands on my hips. I wanted to bury them both in the sand and leave them for dead. So I did something that I'm not proud of…and it's worse than you not inviting Roylene into your home. I kicked Robert in his side. Hard.

I didn't know what my foot was going to do until it did it. Moved by the anger, not by my own will. I wanted to make both those boys suffer the way I'd suffered. But I learned that all I did was create a great chasm between us. (And I hurt my foot rather badly!)

And that's war, right, Rita? Two sides hurting each other, acting out in violence, before trying to resolve any feelings? Or maybe that's too simple. I'd like to think that America is like Levi's mother. The grand negotiator.

Robert didn't speak to me for an entire week. In the end, Levi was the one who brought us all back together. Making jokes and reminding us that no matter who we became, we'd always be friends. He was probably taking the advice of his wise, wise mother. But it worked.

So, there I was, sitting on the porch, my hand encircling Robbie's wrists in a fierce grip. But instead of walloping him, I got up, gave my cherub-cheeked baby to Marie and brought Robbie inside. I went to his room and let him pick out some books.

"Let's read, just you and me," I said.

He climbed up on my lap and I read to him, one hand pushing his hair from his brow and placing kisses on his head between pages. After the first book he said, "I'm sorry, Mama."

I gave him one more kiss. "I know, Robbie. Sometimes we do things when we are mad and scared, and we don't mean them at all."

I was so glad I'd kicked Robert that day, and remembered what it felt like, because if that hadn't happened…I would have spanked my poor boy.

Anyway, I have a lot of time on my hands these days. I love being domestic. Robbie's helped me roll up all these balls of tinfoil to bring to the local junk man who does something with them for the war effort. We've even got as far as peeling the foil from gum wrappers! And we've begun collecting milkweed pods. Mrs. M. says there's a factory out in Michigan that's turning the silk from the pods into parachutes. Can you imagine?

Oh, and I'll leave you with a ration book idea:

Take the lard you've bought and put it in a bowl. Mix it with yellow food coloring and you can almost fool your taste buds into thinking it's butter!

Love, love, love,
Glory

May 26, 1943

SOMEWHERE IN WESTERN OHIO

Dear Glory,

Greetings from the (rail) road!

We switched trains in Indianapolis about two hours ago. There are so many uniformed boys in our car, I feel like I'm heading off to war as well. They joke and play cards and drink from small, cheap bottles of whiskey. One rather inebriated fellow squeezed between Roylene and myself as we returned from the dining car and said he was caught between two slices of heaven. I laughed—how could I not? A little fun is in order. They mightn't have any idea what's in store overseas, but my Sal's letters have given me enough of an impression. I wanted to buy them all steak dinners and kiss their ruddy cheeks. Instead, I sat across from Roylene and busied myself extracting pen and paper from my bag. I kept one eye on her. She bit her fingernails and wiped the cuttings on her seat when she thought I wasn't looking. A moment ago, I offered her my *Women's Day* to give her hands something to do. She's flipping through to be respectful, but I don't think she's reading.

We've exhausted the standard small-talk topics. During the interminable journey from Des Moines to Indianapolis, I learned the following, and not much else: 1. Mrs. K. was right—Roylene is from Oklahoma. Roy went north to escape the dust when everyone else, including his wife, went West. The poor thing hasn't seen her mother in years. 2. Roylene slaves away at the tavern six days a week. 3. She doesn't like egg salad (too spongy), but blueberry pie suits her fine.

Fascinating stuff. My boy likes Whitman and Poe. What in the world are they going to talk about? I guess it doesn't make any difference. I have a lot to say to my son before he ships off to God knows where. The girl won't get a word in edgewise.

I must admit, ragged fingernails aside, Roylene's taken a smidge more concern with her appearance. She's rolled her hair for the trip, and she's wearing a clean dress and the summer sweater I mended. I found a ruby-red doily I crocheted ages ago and cut it up to trim the collar and cuffs. It offsets the odd yarn color, giving it a rich maple hue. A dab of scarlet lipstick would seal the deal but that's probably asking too much.

The magazine lies open on her lap, but Roylene's eyes are closing. The soldier boys have also quieted, settling into a drunken snooze. They still have quite a trip ahead. Our stop is only an hour away at this point, give or take. There is a chance Toby will be waiting for us at the station.

Oh, Glory, I can't wait to see him.

Love
Rita

May 27, 1943
(3 or 4 o'clock in the damn morning)

SANDY PINES ROADSIDE MOTEL,
OUTSIDE OF COLUMBUS, OHIO

Glory,

There is neither sand nor pine trees in the vicinity of this motel, only a deserted gravel parking lot lit by the dull blue glow of a Pabst Blue Ribbon sign. It's not the middle of the night but close enough. Even the earliest risers are still tucked in their beds.

Except Roylene. Her bed is empty. The coverlet lies in a crumpled heap. She didn't have the decency to tuck a few pillows under it to trick my sleepy eyes.

Honestly, it is preferable to think some maniac broke into our room and stole her in the dead of night than give a second's thought to what is really going on.

I've spent the past twenty minutes trying to decide whether or not I should march over to Toby's room and bang on the door. I'm tempted, I'll tell you that. But to be truthful, my motivation is not to break up their tryst but to assuage my loneliness. I came here to see my boy. I haven't gotten my chance with him yet.

The man who picked us up at the train station was barely recognizable. After they cut Toby's hair, they must have taken a chisel to the rest of him, chipping away at the boyish layers, sharpening his features as though his face was one more weapon to ready for battle. He waved at us, and I could hardly raise my hand in return. Roylene yelped and jumped on him like a bedbug.

"You look pretty," Toby said, his fingers drifting from her face to the doily collar. "This sweater suits you."

I sewed it! I wanted to shout. *Don't you recognize your mother's handiwork?* Instead, I forced a smile and said, "Isn't she, though?"

"Smart, too," Toby added, keeping his eyes on Roylene. He wrapped his hands around her narrow face. "Did you bring it?"

Her skinny hand dove into the front of her dress, and she pulled a crumpled sheet of paper from her nonexistent bosom. "It's not that good?" she whispered.

"Good enough to earn my girl her high school diploma," he murmured, then briefly turned his bright eyes to me. "She wrote an essay about how to make potato soup for the high school equivalency."

I should have complimented her, but my brain froze after the words *my girl.* I was supposed to hand *my boy* over to her? Oh, Glory, I've always been protective of Toby, overly so, to be honest, but I don't think you'd have blamed me if I pushed her back on that train and sent her off to Timbuktu. Before I knew it, he'd thrown his arm over her shoulders and they were walking down the platform, away from where I stood. "Come on, Ma," Toby called, and I scurried to catch up.

Today we spent most of our time wandering the city, playing

tourist and ignoring the inevitable. I didn't feel like a third wheel so much as a souvenir, a postcard from a past life.

And here I sit, alone. I was mistaken about Toby's leave—he doesn't have a full forty-eight hours. His train leaves in an hour or two. He said goodbye to me last night, told me not to bother getting up to see him off, that it was too early and I should get my beauty rest.

I'm not going to sleep through his departure. I'm going to get dressed and walk over to the train station. Then I'm going to kiss him on the crown of his head and imagine his fine, golden hair tickling my nose.

I'm going to say goodbye to my son.

Rita

———————

June 5, 1943

ROCKPORT, MASSACHUSETTS

Dear Rita,

How my heart ached for you when I received your letters. I can only imagine my Robbie all grown up and walking down the street in front of me, hand in hand with another girl. Right now I'm his best girl...and I don't want that to change anytime soon. I suppose it's good that Toby has a girl. And perhaps it wasn't as scandalous as you think...their night together. Couldn't it be that they were taking a walk under the stars? I wonder if having another person waiting for him won't give him even more reason to make it home unharmed? I know I'm waxing enthusiastic, but I'm turning into quite the optimist lately!

I must admit, after I read your letter I pushed back the coffee table in the living room and put on the radio. I held my Robbie close and danced with him. How I cried. I whispered into his ear, "Stay just the way you are."

And I do want him to stay how he is. I'd like a little snapshot of this time to keep in my heart forever. The only thing missing is Robert. Like a throbbing hollowness that won't go away. A splinter I can't find. A toothache. His absence is always right behind me.

Anyway...my life has become one big whirl of busy. It seems like I go from the garden to the tub and then pull on some stockings (Do you have any left? I'm completely out of silk but have some nylons stocked up if you want me to send you some. Shh! Don't tell!) and run out the door and down the road to Mrs. M.'s so we can go to one of her meetings. I run so fast the hairpins come out and I have to wear my hair wild. Claire Whitehall would KILL me. Marie has been kind enough to stay home from the meetings and stay with the kids. She said, "I've had my turn, now you go have yours." I swear I'm falling more in love with Mrs. M. and Marie every day.

I feel like a sparrow flitting around landing here or there. It feels good. Weightless.

The kids are doing well, though I've noticed that Robbie isn't asking for Robert anymore. He's taken to calling Levi "Papa." I'm worried about that and know I should put the kibosh on it. Maybe I should encourage Robbie to call him Uncle Levi? He's so like a brother to Robert, anyway....

Those meetings, though, with Mrs. M....leave me breathless. I never knew how much power we have as a people, a government. There have been some ingenious women in our history, Rita. Wouldn't it be nice to join the ranks of Abigail Adams, Lucretia Mott or even Elizabeth Cady Stanton?

"We hold these truths to be self-evident, that all men AND WOMEN are created equal." Imagine! See what they don't teach us in school? I swear Corrine will grow up knowing what she's made of.

As for my garden, well...see for yourself. I've enclosed a photograph. The black-and-white won't do it justice, but just look, Rita! Look at how lush it is, with the sea peeking out from behind the tall sunflowers at the back. I've named those sunflowers. I call them Rita 1, 2, 3, 4, 5, 6, 7 and I say good-morning each day.

Sending you love and prayers for peace,
Glory

P.S. I just got another letter from Robert. His division will be moving from Sparta to New York. 1 should be happy, right? Because I'll surely see him, then. But I know that being stationed back near the coast will mean that he'll go overseas soon. I wish he could be with Toby or Sal. Maybe we can write to them and tell them to try to take care of one another? I know Toby and Sal are not fighting on the same fronts, but what if you petition them to be nearer? Can we do that?

There's so much I don't understand about this war. So much I wish I knew.

Oh, well. I suppose I just have to keep learning. And writing letters.

June 17, 1943

IOWA CITY, IOWA

Dearest Glory,

Thank you for accepting my letters with such grace. I've been in such a state these past few weeks, and your words act as a balm to my frayed nerves. Sometimes I wish the censors would attack domestic letters with the same ferocity they do those going overseas. I'm certain my ravings would merit a few slashes of black ink!

So, to address your most important question: my stockings look like they've been in a gunfight at the OK Corral. I will gladly accept any charitable donations to my lingerie wardrobe. I can repay you in heirloom seeds and advice.

I'll give you an advance on the advice—make sure your children know who their daddy is. We don't know how long this godforsaken war is going to last, but we do know that our guys are in it for the long haul. I don't mean to depress you, but that baby of yours could be walking about singing "The White Cliffs of Dover" by the time Robert returns. Levi should be Levi. Papas are Papas.

But then, I don't know if someone like me should be handing out advice like a regular Queen Bee. I've behaved shamefully, Glory. Remember my friend Irene? Well, Irene is a real plain Jane, if I'm being honest, and she's not one for mixing. In warmer weather, the university hosts a social outdoors near the Old Capitol Building. I convinced Irene to go, and promised I'd join her for moral support. Turns out I'm the one who needs help in the morality department.

As you could guess, the women outnumbered the men ten to one. We hens stood in clusters, some tittering about nothing in particular, others wondering why the men who did attend weren't in uniform. I caught Irene staring at one of them—a tall, cowboyish sort, with thick, straw-colored hair and an easy smile. I gave her a nudge, but like I said, she isn't the mixing type. Irene shook her head and started sucking down her ginger ale, like it suddenly required all of her effort and attention.

With a quick apology to Sal—I swear!—I sauntered over to that man, completely brazen, and asked him to join us. He did. We introduced ourselves. (He's probably only in his mid-thirties, but called himself "Mr. Clark," so we went by Miss Vincenzo and Miss Wachowski, like a couple of coeds.). Then darn if he didn't reach into the pocket of his suede sport coat and pull out a flask. Irene just about keeled over.

"Ladies first," he said, and poured a couple of thumbs into what was left of Irene's ginger ale.

He turned to me and I didn't have a glass. With one raised eyebrow he watched as I took hold of that flask and knocked back a shot! I haven't done that since before Mr. Roosevelt was in office. Irene's eyes grew big and her mouth pursed tight as a fisherman's knot.

Well, I talked for both of us, and the next thing I knew I'd invited him over for dinner next Wednesday (with Irene, of course). I'm not sure what I've gotten her into, but I'm calling it a date. Irene doesn't show it much, but she's excited. I swear, she's asked me six different times if she should roll her hair up or not.

I love my husband, Glory, but I can't tell you how nice it is that a man will be admiring my cooking and the way I keep my house. Your suffragette women would probably give me a good pounding if you told them I said that, but it's true. I suppose what I'm saying is I understand why you have Levi around, it's just you must understand there are lines we can't cross.

Warm regards,
Rita

P.S. I haven't seen Roylene since our trip to Ohio. I didn't embarrass her or Toby that morning, but I think she suspected I knew what went on. She stared out the window the entire return trip, and scurried off as soon as we arrived in Iowa City.

P.P.S. I haven't gotten any V-mail at all. Not one letter from Toby or Sal. I think the postman is afraid of me. Every afternoon I nearly tackle him as he approaches our mailbox!

———

July 4, 1943

ROCKPORT, MASSACHUSETTS

Dearest Rita,

I know it's been a while since I wrote back to you. So many things are happening right now and I don't quite know what to do with myself. The earth moves and I'm trying to find a foothold.

First things first. This letter is inside a box of all sorts of stockings. I hope you like them. I also included a jar of strawberry jam I put up. (If you knew me really well you'd know what a surprising thing that is!) But I wouldn't have any strawberries, or any garden for that matter, if it wasn't for you.

Thank you for that.

I'm purposely writing this letter today as it is the birthday of this great nation. The one we sacrifice for every day. One town over, in Gloucester, we have a parade and then bonfires on the beaches. And I took baby Corrine and Robbie. Corrine is getting so big now. She's a smiley baby with fat cheeks. She soothes me so. I put her in this fancy new pram Claire gave me (she's a good one for presents, that Claire…), and Robbie helped me push. We were a bit early so I strolled them over to the beaches that Levi, Robert and I made our magical paradise as kids. There were bonfires already starting even with the sun not quite set. And that's when I saw him. Levi, staring out over the ocean. I'd invited him to come with us…but he told me that the three of us (the children and I) should be spending more time as a family. That happened right after I asked him to stop encouraging Robbie to call him Papa. I've known him long enough to know I'd hurt his feelings.

"Papa!" Robbie shouted as he ran down the beach. Levi caught him and threw him up in the air. Two dark shadows against the setting sun, laughing as if they didn't have a care in the world.

As they walked toward me, I heard Levi talking to Robbie.

"I'm not Papa, I'm Uncle Levi. You have a daddy who is fighting for our nation. He's a hero, and we want to remember that every day, okay, pal?"

Robbie looked up and nodded.

"Want to come watch the parade with us, Levi?" I asked.

"You bet," he said, and put Robbie on his shoulders as he found a place for us in the crowds.

The parade itself was beautiful. As well as the celebrations afterward. And to be quite honest, I'm not usually a fan of parades.

It was the strangest thing. The celebration felt many layered. Like a quilt of sorts. See, some of the families are beginning to get notices more and more that their boys are gone. I don't know how you do it, with both your men out there. Everywhere I looked there were people waving their small paper flags and crying. And I know they were tears of joy and pride...but tears just the same. Tears don't belong at parades and bonfires.

No word from Robert about when he might be going overseas. It's the not knowing that kills me.

And because of that, I started to cry, too. Levi took Robbie down from his shoulders and pulled me into a hug. It shouldn't have been awkward...we've hugged lots of times. But his embrace felt different. Painful as well as safe. I can't really explain, except it scared me a little. When he released me, he tucked an errant wisp of hair behind my ear. Oh, Rita. In that moment I felt what you must have felt at that dance. Like a woman. A young, attractive woman. And it felt wonderful.

Anyway, I've missed your stories. So write back and tell me what is going on in your life. And maybe a new recipe? I'm getting darn tired of my own.

By the way, guess what I did? I went down to city hall and changed my affiliation. I am now a proud member of the Democratic party.

Father and Mother are turning in their graves!

With much affection,
Glory

July 8, 1943

V-mail from Marguerite Vincenzo
to Pfc. Salvatore Vincenzo

Sal,

I got your letter yesterday. You didn't ask for my opinion, but I'm going to give it anyway (surprise, surprise).

What happened on that battlefield might be your fault, and it might not. It's definitely Hitler's fault. He started it.

I'm not making light, but I don't think you should beat yourself up for decisions made on only a second's worth of thought. Mistakes will happen. Yes, I do realize we're talking about a boy's life, and I know what a slipup can mean, but if you hold yourself to the standard of God, you will forget what it's like to be a regular old human.

And what has prepared us for this? The Depression? We had our hard times, and we pulled through. Did we find out we were made of tougher stuff than we thought, or did circumstance breed heroism? I'm not sure. This war is certainly forcing out the best in everyone, so it follows that a little bit of the worst will squeeze out, too. Even from you and me.

I love you, and more important, I believe in you,
Rita

July 13, 1943

IOWA CITY, IOWA

Dear Glory,

I was so glad to get your letter, kiddo. For a minute I'd worried I'd lost you to the uncertainties of this damn war. And I need a friend more than ever. Iowa City clears out in the summer, our population dipping to half of what it is when the college students are here. The sun shines so mercilessly on these empty streets, I can't go barefoot on the cement for more than a second.

So, thank you for the stockings. I hope you don't mind, but I gave a pair to Irene. She was desperate, about to surrender to the last resort of swabbing her legs with tea bags and tracing the seam with a kohl pencil. I believe Irene is knitting a chic beret for the baby as a thank-you gesture. I'll send it along when she's done, which should be sometime in 1963.

I sincerely hope you've gotten more information about Robert's shipping out. Being kept in the dark is tough. Before this war I felt like if I needed to know something I could find a way to know it. But so much is unknowable now, completely beyond my grasp. Sal's letters make me question if I've ever truly understood anything about human nature.

Including what's been happening these past few weeks. I don't wish to distress you, hon, but this letter might do exactly that, so I apologize in advance. It's just that I've been keeping everything inside me, and not having anyone to talk to is starting to do some internal damage. Does it help to know I feel better confessing my sins to you instead of Father Denneny down at St. Mary's? At least I know you aren't going to make me say any rosaries.

So.

Remember the big dinner with Irene and the cowboy?

Irene came over early. The poor girl's hands shook so hard she couldn't hold a bobby pin to save her life. I rolled her hair and helped with her makeup. She looked very presentable. Maybe not pretty, but polished, put-together. A guy could do a lot worse.

The cowboy was on time, I'll give him that. Turns out his first name is Charlie, which surprised me. I thought it would be Tex or Hank or some other rodeo name. He brought a bottle of wine with him and that same easy smile. Irene kept her lips glued together so I yapped and yapped until I had to take care of the meat loaf. I poured them each a glass and disappeared into the kitchen.

I must have been gone a while because when I came back half the bottle was gone and Irene's face looked like the beets I've been pulling from my garden. Charlie sat in Sal's chair, his long legs splayed out so far the tips of his boots nearly touched Irene's ankles. Their laughter filled my house, every nook and cranny, leaving no room for the sadness I'd been cultivating.

I hated them, Glory. That's a strong word, *hate*, but it overtook me. Those two had nothing to worry about. The Germans weren't going to march into their living rooms, crushing their hearts to bits. The Japanese weren't dropping bombs in their backyards. *How dare they?* I wanted to kick at his stupid feet and shake Irene until her teeth rattled.

Instead, I walked back into the kitchen. I got what was left of Sal's bourbon and had a nip, then two. I drew a few breaths, brought the food to the dining room and called them in to dinner.

When they saw my cooking their faces just about melted with

gratitude. I used all my rations to buy beef, veal and pork, so I could make the meat loaf right. I boiled some carrots with the early potatoes, and you would have thought I was serving caviar.

The guilt crept up on me, but when I tried to make up for my terrible thoughts, I overdid it. I ate too much, laughed too hard, polished off Sal's bottle. Charlie was open and polite with Irene, but he kept an eye on me, wary almost, like I was the bomb about to go off and shatter the evening.

I don't think Irene noticed, so taken was she by this cowboy. When I saw the stars in her eyes I grew even more ashamed. This was my friend, and she deserved a little fun. I collected the plates and excused myself, retreating for the safety of the kitchen.

I took my time washing and drying. When I heard Irene's tinkly laugh I took the pan out back to add the grease to the Mason jar on the patio. (Mrs. K., who is only talking to me out of a sense of patriotic duty, is in charge of lard collection for our block.)

In Iowa, the summer nights are still as can be. I heard him walk through the kitchen. I heard the match strike and his first deep drag on the cigarette. When the screen door slammed it sounded like a gunshot.

"Everything hunky-dory?" he drawled.

"Where's Irene?" I said in place of a real answer.

"Powder room. She was feeling a little queasy." Everything he said was outlined in humor. I didn't know if it meant he was basically kind or inherently mean-spirited. It was impossible to tell.

He sat next to me on our patio and balanced his cigarette on the edge of the cement. Then he leaned back, reached into the pocket of his trousers and pulled out a pressed handkerchief.

"Give me that," he said, and caught my wrist with one large, rough hand. He wiped the grease from my fingers, one by one, slow and methodical.

Oh, Glory, I didn't stop him. After he'd cleaned my hand, he stuffed the kerchief back into his pocket like it was nobody's business, picked up his cigarette and went back in the house.

I sat on that patio until Irene came out to tell me Charlie was going to take her home. She slurred her words, and I should have talked her into staying the night. But I didn't.

After they left I sat on my bed, picking at the chenille with my fingernails. I yanked at the threads, over and over, talking to Sal in my head and blaming him for everything. He's forty-one years old, like me. At that age he could have waited out the lottery until the end of the war. There is no reason for him to be in a strange land, the grim reaper holding him close, saying, "Yes, today is the day," or "No, not yet."

We were having a fight right there in the bedroom, a fight we should have had a year ago, and he wasn't even around to defend himself.

I went to bed with my clothes on, on top of our ruined bedspread. Before I fell asleep I tried to think of what North Africa was like, to imagine it, Glory, but all I could think about was those rough hands pulling the grime from my fingers.

I woke up early the next morning feeling pretty low. Before putting the kettle on, I got pen and paper and wrote to my husband, telling him about my sunflowers and the broken shed lock and funny stories of Mrs. K., strengthening his tie to me and our life together. That is my job, right? To comfort him. To keep the portrait of what he left behind intact. Isn't that a woman's duty during wartime?

I've confessed all my guilty thoughts to you, but I'm going to devise my own penance, if that's all right. Toby's asked me to check up on Roylene, but I've been avoiding the tavern. I walk past the dingy windows with my head down, staying clear of that sad, skinny little girl. I need to make an effort. My Toby is fighting for the world's freedom and he asked me to do one simple thing. I might as well try to do it.

Love,
Rita

P.S. I used the last bit of corn syrup to make a War Cake. Do you know it? I've included the recipe. I figured it's the least I could do after unloading all my neuroses on you. Instead of butter I smeared your wonderful strawberry jam on it. Heavenly!

War Cake
1 cup molasses
1 cup corn syrup (light or dark can be used)
1 1/2 cups boiling water
2 cups raisins
2 tablespoons solid vegetable shortening
1 teaspoon salt
1 teaspoon ground cinnamon
1/2 teaspoon ground cloves
1/2 teaspoon ground nutmeg
3 cups flour
1 teaspoon baking soda
2 teaspoons baking powder

Directions:
In large pot, combine molasses, corn syrup, water, raisins, shortening, salt, cinnamon, cloves and nutmeg. Bring to a boil. Remove from heat and cool to room temperature.

Preheat oven to 350°F. Sift together flour, baking soda and baking
powder. Combine with molasses mixture and beat well.
Divide batter between two well-greased 9x5-inch loaf pans. Bake
45 minutes or until done. Cakes will be dense and will not rise much.
Recipe makes two loaf cakes.

=========

August 1, 1943

ROCKPORT, MASSACHUSETTS

Dearest Rita,

Reading your letter I could only think of one thing. Something
Mrs. Moldenhauer (she's asked me to call her Anna) said to me not
a week before I received it. (And what is the matter with the post
these days? I feel like it takes YEARS to get a letter, or to send
one. And I live for your letters, Rita. Almost as much as I live for
Robert's. Maybe that's because his don't come on a regular basis
and yours eventually do!)

Anyway, she said, "Make sure you remember that you are always
afraid, and that fear does strange things to people."

Now, it's obvious what she meant about the "strange things" over
here in my part of the world. She was talking about how I allow
Levi into my life more and more these days.

But we don't have to talk about that right now, let's talk about
what's going on in Iowa City. (Sometimes I feel like all I do is ramble
on and on about myself without asking about you.)

I guess you are afraid. More afraid than me, dear Rita. Because you have been married to Sal for so much longer than I've shared my life and bed with Robert. And your son? Please! Right now both of my children have little summer fevers (that's why I'm able to sit and craft this LONG letter…they are both sleeping the afternoon away, my angels) and I'm worried sick over nothing. But to have one of them in harm's way on a daily basis? I can't even imagine the fear.

So if fear makes us do strange things, then your whole experience that night was…well…warranted. In my opinion. I think you deserve the attention. And if it makes the time go by, if it makes the waiting easier? Well, then, my friend? Do what you need to do.

Once everyone here is well, I might take myself up on my own advice.

Before you judge me, let me explain.

I am so angry at this war for taking Robert away. I know it sounds unpatriotic, but sometimes I just can't help it. I am so damn angry that I'm here caring for our sick children, tending this garden all by myself. Levi and Marie can't take his place. It's a lonely, sick hole in my heart.

I stare at his picture and try to remember the way the back of his neck smelled. How much I loved his hands enclosing mine. The sweet and tender way he kissed.

And then there's the other thing. In the twilight of the garden a few evenings ago, I engaged in something far more devious than your flirtations.

We were just cleaning up after working in the garden.

"Long day," said Levi.

"Yes, it was," I replied. "Long but lovely."

"You are lovely," he said.

"I'm glad you think so…. Just look at me—I probably have dirt all over my face!"

Levi looked at me and I knew in a heartbeat I was in trouble.

He had that look on his face that he used to get when we were kids right before he'd do something silly.

"Well, you could be dirtier…" he said as he reached down, picked up a clump of soil and threw it at me.

"Oh, it's like that, is it?" I asked, laughing as I grabbed one to throw at him, but he was running so I had to chase him out into the yard. We ran and finally I got close enough for a direct hit. He fell dramatically to the ground as if he'd been shot. I fell in a heap next to him and we were laughing and out of breath. The sky grew quiet as our laughter and breath steadied. And then he took his finger and placed it on the side of my forehead, and let it trace my whole face as if he were blind and trying to recognize me. And I should have stopped him, but I swear my skin had a life of its own and arched right out to meet his.

When he brought his hand down we looked at each other for a second too long. We didn't speak again. We put our tools away side by side in the garden shed and shut the door. That's when Levi stole his kiss. He pressed me up against the shed. He didn't even need to ask, or woo. He pressed my shoulders back and kissed me so hard that I had to pull rough splinters of wood out of my hair for hours.

So different from Robert. So urgent.

Oh, I knew I shouldn't have, but it was exactly what I wanted right in that moment. Comfort. To be young and carefree again. To be taken out of this world for even a few seconds.

Or simply taken back in time. Levi was the first boy to ever kiss me. We were eleven years old and Robert was called back from the beaches early because he had to attend a party with his mother. My parents were going to that party, too, but they wanted me to stay home. My mother and father always loved a night out to dance under the summer stars. And I wasn't needed underfoot. Claire, on the other hand, wanted Robert with her all the time. Anyway, the sun was setting and Levi and I were skipping stones.

"You sure are good at this," he said.

"Thank you, sir," I said.

"Are you mad you aren't at the party?" he asked.

"Not even one little bit," I said.

"You could be dancing with Robert."

"Ew," I said.

"Hey, he ever kiss you?"

"Who?"

"Robert."

"Nope."

"Can I kiss you?" he asked, like he was asking if I wanted a soda water. I think I simply looked at him and pursed my lips together. And I know I wasn't expecting to feel anything…I mean, I was only eleven, and both he and Robert were my best friends in the whole world. But when he kissed me, stars lit up behind my eyes…and for the rest of that summer I thought I was in love. Robert said it was the most boring summer—watching me and Levi make googly eyes at each other. My mother put a quick end to that childhood romance as soon as his letters started arriving at Astor House from Rockport in the fall. "He's not one of us, and you are nothing but a child. If you write back to him I won't let you see him at ALL next summer, believe me." And I did believe her, so I never wrote him back. I believed my parents with my whole heart. And I believed that if I listened well enough, behaved enough, that they'd notice me a little more.

I've been looking at photographs of them (my parents) all afternoon. I'm tucking a picture of them in with this letter. That's me when I was a baby. I look just like Corrine. Or she resembles me. How does that work, anyway? They looked so serious for well-off people, didn't they? Sometimes I wish I'd known them better. Really known them. What they thought on the inside, behind all the gloss. I'm also including a recent picture of the kids and one of my wedding day. Isn't Robert handsome? Please send me your picture, Rita. Maybe one of you and Sal and Toby all together? I'd love to put faces to all these names. Especially yours.

I wonder what my mother would think about me now. Stockingless. Cleaning my own house and making my own food. (That recipe was divine, by the way. Send more!)

I wonder if they'd be angry with me. Or disappointed. So much to wonder about.

Oh, dear. There's the baby. See what happens when I think I'll get five minutes peace? Marie tries to soothe her, but this baby of mine wants me and only me. "Born into an insecure world," says Anna. Maybe my mother's ghost just pinched Corrine on her chubby thigh as a sign.

Also, I've copied a recipe for you out of our local newspaper. Anna started a column to help women use their rations better. She's an inspiration. Honestly. Enjoy!

With much love,
Glory

Vegetable Scrapple
(I don't like the way the word scrapple *sounds, do you, Rita? Doesn't change the fact that it's a satisfying dish, though.)*

Ingredients:
1/4 cup finely diced celery
1/3 cup diced onions

1/2 cup diced carrots
2 tablespoons diced green pepper (My fingers hurt from all the dicing!)
1 teaspoon salt
3 cups boiling water
1 cup wheat meal (Or corn meal. Even flour works as a thickening
agent.)

Preparation instructions:
Add vegetables and salt to boiling water and cook until vegetables are
tender (not too long or they'll get mushy!) Drain; measure liquid and
add water to make 3 cups. Combine liquid and vegetables and bring
back to a boil. Add wheat meal gradually and boil 3 minutes, stirring
constantly. Pour into greased 9x4x3-inch pan. When cold, slice and
sauté in small amount of fat until lightly browned.
If you want to, substitute 1 1/4 cups chopped leftover cooked vegeta-
bles for raw vegetables in above recipe. Or, if you prefer a little meat,
you can turn to a recipe which extends the meat. (Serves 4 to 6, but
keep it in the fridge and have lunch for a week!) I like it with gravy!

———————

August 2, 1943

V-mail from Gloria Whitehall
to Sgt. Robert Whitehall

Darling Robert,

How are you? I hope you are keeping yourself safe and warm.
Everything is good here, so I don't want you to worry about one

little thing. The kids and I are fighting a little summer cold. Sweet Corrine looks so cute with her red nose! The garden is beautiful. I'm so happy I struck up this friendship with Rita. You remember, the woman from Iowa? She's giving me such good advice about all sorts of things. Mostly it's nice to have another woman who's waiting and worrying to talk to. I know there are plenty of women in town, but there's something about Rita. I trust her. I'm enclosing a current picture of Corrine and Robbie. See how fat she is! She's such a delightful baby. We look at your picture every night. I'm trying to teach her to say, "Da Da."

Love and kisses,
Glory

August 8, 1943

IOWA CITY, IOWA

Dear Glory,

My sunflowers have grown taller than me. They guard the house, like good soldiers, blocking me from the assault of Mrs. K.'s disapproving glances, but also from the sun, the sound of street traffic, the children playing hopscotch down the block. I'm cowering behind them, Glory, but you are not. Obviously your sunflowers have not reached the same heights. Or maybe you took hedge clippers to them? Or made Levi do it?

I was surprised by the contents of your last letter, but not shocked.

I tried to muster a fair amount of outrage, but it seems I already know you too well for that. Did it feel like jumping off a cliff when he kissed you? I imagine it did.

I'm not one for cliff-jumping. You were right about the fear. It's getting into everything—my thoughts as I make the bed, the fibers of my dress, the dust settling on our dining room table, the lettuce on my sandwich. It whispers in my ear as I tend the garden, calling "Sal" or "Toby" or, sometimes, my own name. I'm afraid, Glory. Afraid of what I read in the papers. Of not knowing if Western Union will deliver a telegram from someone I've never met, telling me my husband or son died on soil my feet have never touched.

I'm also afraid of what I might do, that without my family I am unmoored and untethered, about to float into the horizon, never to be seen again.

Is this weakness? I don't know. The first time I read your letter I blamed Levi for catching *you* in a moment of weakness, the skips in the phonograph record where we forget who we are, no longer mothers or wives or citizens, but simply beings without a thought to the past or future, just the present. It sounds crazy, but I wanted to yell at him, to force him to give the moment back to you, so you could decide what to do with it. But then, you took it, didn't you? You didn't push him away.

Which makes me want to yell at you. Why aren't you hiding? Why aren't you sitting in your front parlor, the windows darkened by the flowers planted with your own hands? Why are you kissing men on sunny days, your hair wild, your conscience untroubled?

I'm sorry, Glory. My mind and heart are skipping beats. I'm looking at the photograph of your mother right now, holding her baby, and I can't help but wonder that if she knew—if any of us really understood the nature of things at the start—she'd have scooped you up and run like hell.

Rita

———

August 9, 1943

V-mail from Marguerite Vincenzo
to Pfc. Salvatore Vincenzo

Sal,

Big news on the Iowa front: Irene has a beau. His name is Charlie Clark. He's younger than our gal, but not by much, and probably 4-F, though he looks healthy as a horse. Flat feet, maybe?

Irene and I still meet for lunch every day, but our movie nights at the Englert have been replaced with romantic rendezvous about which she is curiously tight-lipped. I don't bug her for details. Instead, I've been spending my expanding free time at the American Legion helping Mrs. K. and her minions prepare for the massive canning campaign this fall. I hope some of it gets to you, hon. Should I slip a fiver in with the sweet corn? Maybe then you could get your hands on some cigs.

Well, take care. Please write soon if you can.

Miss you,
Rita

P.S. Now that you and Toby are ganging up on me, I'll go back to the tavern to see how she's doing. I did try once, but it was closed for inventory. Ha! I bet that Roy fellow can't even count.

———————

August 28, 1943

IOWA CITY, IOWA

Dear Glory,

After I sent that last letter to you I almost ran down to the post office to steal it back. But when I thought about digging through all those V-mails, burying myself under a mountain of hopes and fears and flop-sweat, well, I just couldn't. I let my words go.

And now I've offended you, haven't I?

I treasure Sal's and Toby's letters. When they come I breathe a little easier, and let myself think of the future.

But when I receive a letter from you I make a pot of tea, and sit down with it like an old, dear friend. My life would be darker without them, Glory.

Please write back.

Sincerely,
Rita

Sept. 1, 1943

Telegram from Mrs. Anna Moldenhauer
to Mrs. Marguerite Vincenzo

MESSAGE FROM GLORY. ALL FELL ILL WITH FLU.
IN HOSPITAL. CORRINE AND GLORY RECOVER-
ING WELL. ROBBIE CRITICAL. PRAYERS.

A. MOLDENHAUER

Sept. 2, 1943

Telegram from Mrs. Marguerite Vincenzo
to Mrs. Anna Moldenhauer

HEARTBROKEN. SENDING PRAYERS. HOW CAN
I HELP?

M. VINCENZO

September 5, 1943

ROCKPORT, MASSACHUSETTS

Dear Rita,

I have no adequate way to begin this letter. I must have started six times. Thank God we're timber-rich here in America and our paper isn't rationed. Not yet, anyway.

I suppose I must begin the way my heart wants me to begin. With an apology. I'm so sorry, Rita. I'm so sorry I asked Anna to send you that telegram. It was a selfish thing to do. In my defense, I was so sick. And Anna was kind enough to bring me my mail. When I read your letter I realized I was still too weak to pen a whole one back. But I was frantic to let you know that I was not, in any way, offended by the stern words in your previous correspondence. As a matter of fact, they were just the words I needed to hear. So my only thought was to send word as fast as I could and explain my tardy response.

It was only when I sent Anna off with my message that I realized what a telegram delivery would do to you. How your heart must have stopped. I can be a selfish, silly twit. I hope you will forgive me. I'm sending this letter off with extra postage for priority mail. I hope it gets to you quicker than the others.

How kind you were with your telegram back to me. And I didn't have to shoulder the same moment of horror you must have felt, because my Robert was right next to me when it was delivered. We'd only just returned home from the hospital with Corinne and we met the delivery boy on the road. Robert's gotten an emergency leave. He can stay with us up to thirty days. Can you imagine?

And I'm so sorry about my last letter and all that it held. I can't even recognize the woman who wrote it. I am almost convinced that my wantonness lured that horrible fever straight to us. I sound like Robert's mother...but with Robbie still so ill, I can't help but think it was all my fault, somehow. We were all diagnosed with scarlet fever, Rita. Evidently there was an outbreak in Boston that came here on some unlucky wind. Corrine was the least sick. Anna tells me it is one of the best reasons to nurse our children. They stay healthier that way. I believe her, and knowing I could do something for one of my children helps me stay sane. Robbie's fever was worse. And then he contracted rheumatic fever. The fact that he's alive is a blessing...but he's so pale. I can't really speak of it any more right now. He's had to stay at the hospital. I can't stand the thought of him there without me.

Corrine is almost completely recovered and we've been assured by the doctors that with her, at least, there will be no lasting damage. I'm still weak, but each day I grow stronger. It's better now that we've been at home. This house is connected to my soul, I swear it. It's breathed new life into me.

Right now I'm sitting on my side porch, Rita. Robert has tucked me (using too many blankets) into a wide wicker love seat and I'm watching him in the garden with the baby. She's bundled up, too, but he's carrying her like he's done it all along. He has an easy way with her already. I'm watching them through a curtain of grape leaves trimmed into a circle. A natural window onto the world. Their leaves are so broad and strong. I can see their veins pulsing with the autumn already. Having him home makes me whole, Rita. And it makes my skin itch to think of that day by the shed. I can't even look at it. I'd like to paint it red.

Levi came over, but was sullen. When he left, Robert turned to me. "What's the matter with him?" he asked

I wanted to tell him. To confess. And I opened my mouth fully prepared to tell the truth, but instead I used your words.

"Rita tells me that the boys left behind are broken, somehow. I suppose he feels like he's not doing his patriotic duty."

Robert scratched his head, and Corrine gave him kisses on his cheek. One kiss, laughter, another kiss, more laughter. How she loves her daddy.

"He IS doing an honorable thing, though. Don't you think, Glory?"

"What's that?"

"He's helping me fight with the peace of knowing you and the kids are in good hands."

Oh, Rita. What have I done? And why, when Levi left without a word to me, did I want to cry?

Soon Robert will ship out overseas. Soon the garden will be covered in frost. And soon I'll be strong enough to leave Corrine with Marie and spend my days at the hospital with Robbie. He's frightened of the dark and those nurses are always switching off the lights. It makes me want to clobber them. Knock their crisp white hats off their tidy pinned hair.

I've missed your stories. Write soon.

Love, and many thanks for sharing some sorely needed sense,
Glory

P.S. You know the best thing about Robert being home? The little things… Coffee in the morning, hearing him sing in the shower, the way his skin always smells like soap. I know this sounds treasonous, but I wish we could all run away to Switzerland.

September 12, 1943

Dearest Glory,

Please stop thinking your actions had anything to do with Robbie's illness.

There is nothing more unavoidable or more damaging as a mother's guilt. This I know perhaps better than most, though I was never meant to be a mother.

Back in grammar school, I fell from a tire swing and landed hard, fracturing some necessary bones in my small pelvis. I can barely remember the pain, but I can clearly recall the doctor telling my father, in hushed tones over my sickbed, that I was ruined.

I'd never heard my father cry before, but he did, either for me or the grandsons he surely thought would someday come. My mother soothed him, saying, "Wait and see. Wait and see," over and over until even I was able to sleep, to dream, to heal.

For months I walked with crutches and drank half a cup of wine before bed to thin my blood. I rested when I could and ate so much cheese I got a little plump. Eventually the bones fused back together and I tossed my crutches into the fire.

We never talked about it. When I first saw spots of blood on my underthings Mother hugged me tight and said it was God's sign I could have a baby. Even at thirteen I knew she was simply wishing for it to be true. Still, I decided I would take her word.

I never told Sal. It shames me to write this. We married, moved into his parents' building on Chicago's west side and tried for a baby. Nothing happened. After a year Sal cupped my chin and said, "Maybe it'll be just you and me, kiddo. And that's fine in my book." I cried through the night with Sal holding my face, kissing away each tear.

When I skipped my time, I figured I was coming down with something. A few weeks later Mama Vincenzo caught my eye at Sunday dinner, smiling her cryptic Mona Lisa smile. She pulled me aside after dessert and asked when the bambino was coming.

The realization sent a tremor through my body, head to toe. Mama V held my hand and told me not to worry, assuming my distress came from fear. But it was joy, Glory. Pure delight.

I couldn't wait for the baby to come. Toward the end I showed up at the hospital where Sal worked every time I got a twinge. The nurses started teasing Sal about it, calling him "Mr. False Alarm," which is why I waited so long when I finally did go into labor.

Mrs. Vincenzo delivered Toby on our kitchen table. "It will be quick," she said. "Ten minutes." And it was. By most standards I had an easy birth. But my pelvic bones—the ones my mother lovingly guided to health so many years before—cracked along those old fault lines.

The pain…it was like a couple of wild dogs tearing at each hip. Mrs. Vincenzo put the baby to my bosom, but I could only stare at a crack in the wall, a fixed point to hypnotize myself into oblivion. Sal whispered loving words in my ear, telling me how beautiful I was and how perfect the baby looked, but I could barely breathe, let alone talk.

Mrs. Vincenzo said I just needed rest, and Sal agreed with her until three days passed and I still could not get out of bed.

He sent word to a doctor friend at Cook County, who showed up after his shift. I blacked out during the exam. When I came to, Sal knelt at my bed, saying over and over, "What's wrong with us that we didn't notice?" He never once said, "What's wrong with you that you didn't say anything?"

I withdrew from everyone, even Toby. Mrs. Vincenzo said all women had "the darkness" after childbirth, to varying degrees, and since I'd broken my bones I needed extra time. But my darkness came from guilt—I felt like all the things I'd kept from Sal had weakened my insides, each lie causing a small fracture. All my goodness came out with the baby, and my body, with nothing to stabilize it, shattered.

Sal brought Toby to me for feedings, carefully drawing my breast to the baby's small mouth. He changed him and cleaned his pink body. He sang operettas and patted his tushy with powder. Sal mothered.

Eventually Sal had to return to the hospital, and Toby failed to thrive. His skin took on a yellow hue and he lost interest in nursing.

On the day he refused my breast entirely, Mrs. Vincenzo came into my room with a bottle of sugar water and a pair of crutches. She pushed me to sitting, grabbed one foot and planted it on the floor, then the other, and shoved the bottle in my hand.

"I can't," I said.

"He's dying," she said.

Then she brought her round face right up to mine, looked me in the eye and whispered, "Whatever it is, he'll understand. Don't you know that?"

I did. Sal would understand. Why didn't I trust his love for me? I was punishing my child for my own stubbornness, my despicable insecurity.

I stared into Mrs. Vincenzo's deep brown eyes for a few seconds. And then I shoved those crutches under my arms and started mothering my son.

But I continued to let fear guide my actions. I never told Sal.

One day, while he was eating breakfast, I blurted, "I'm sorry I failed you and Toby."

He left his oatmeal on the table and came to my side. "You've never failed us," he assured me. "And you never will."

He was wrong.

When Toby was seven he ran around with a pack of boys from the block. They were a little mean and a lot rough, and Toby was neither. I always watched from the back porch, pretending to knit while I kept an eye on their shenanigans.

One evening the *Mirro Cooking Class* came on the radio, and I got caught up listening to a recipe for roast duck. I didn't hear Toby scream. I didn't hear anything until little Giuseppe from across the hall came running into the kitchen shouting, "Signora! Vieni! Vieni!"

They'd been playing cowboys and Indians. Chief Toby was tied to a tree, the rope snaking around his neck pulled over a high branch. His feet swung a few inches above the ground and the blood had already drained from his lips. My negligence had brought him to death's door again.

I lifted him and yanked on the rope until the knot loosened. I gave him my breath and rubbed his limbs. He came to.

After church the following Sunday, Mrs. Vincenzo said she wanted to take Toby and me out. I assumed for lunch, but instead she walked us over to her sister's apartment.

Zia Gialina was the neighborhood medium, or quack, depending on how you looked at life. Zia led me and a wide-eyed Toby into her back bedroom, where a bloodred velvet coverlet lay across the largest bed I'd ever seen. She sat on a mountain of embroidered pillows and motioned for us to join her.

"My sister says there's been trouble," she said.

I nodded.

"Give me your hand."

I held it out to her, palm up.

She studied my lines, seemed unimpressed with what she saw and gave me back my hand. "Now the boy," she demanded.

I didn't want her to scrutinize Toby's palm. But he straightened his skinny back and stretched out his arm.

She ran her sausage-thick fingers over his smooth palm for a very long time. "I see what it is," she finally said. "His soul is crowded."

"You can't be serious," I said.

Zia must have been used to resistance. Instead of addressing my lack of respect she called Mrs. Vincenzo in for a conference in Italian. When they finished, Mrs. Vincenzo said, "He needs open spaces or the black cloud will come back. You need to move."

I was forming a smart retort when I saw the tears in her eyes. Toby was one of her greatest loves. She must have really believed Zia if she was considering sending us away.

And since she believed it so strongly, I believed it.

"We need to convince Sal to take that job," she said.

Sal had been offered a position at the University of Iowa by an old college friend. It was a standard research/teaching position, nothing special, so Sal planned on keeping his lab job at Cook County.

I told Sal what his aunt said, and about my worries. He didn't laugh at Zia Gialina's reading. "Do you want to move?" he asked. I nodded. He went to bed to sleep on it.

The next day Sal called his friend and accepted the position. We took a house on a quiet street in Iowa City, not far from the Pharmacy Building.

Sal flourished. His lab work satisfied him and his classes were popular, filling up before the terms began.

Mostly I was happy, but a small part of me—the mothering part—failed to thrive properly. I grew so worried for Toby's safety I kept him too close. He did the normal childhood things, but always with the veil of my protectiveness thrown over his head. Zia Gialina worried our crowded Chicago block was impinging on Toby's soul, but it was me. My fears kept him fenced in.

But push hard and your kid will push back harder. At first Toby ran toward the open spaces in his head, gobbling up books about the solar system, New York skyscrapers, the mountains of Africa.

Later he ran toward the wide-open Pacific Ocean.

But I fear Toby's made a mistake. He's on a ship, packed close as a sardine. I worry his soul is being smothered....

Oh, Glory, I'm sorry. Here I am rambling like a drunk. I've turned this into a letter about me. It's not right to attach my shame and regret to you. It's horrid to assume that my response will be your response, that Robbie's illness will cause you to—

[Letter never sent—stuffed in a drawer.]

September 13, 1943

IOWA CITY, IOWA

Dearest Glory,

I've been thinking of little Robbie every morning, and of you and Corrine and your husband. I don't know what use my thoughts are, but each one carries with it a wish for healing, and for happiness.

I also asked Father Denneny to call your name with the weekly intentions. I'm not sure what kind of pull he has, but there are a hundred tea-stained elderly ladies on their knees come Sunday, every one of them desperate for more reasons to beat their breasts and cry out to Our Lord. You'd think they'd have enough reasons these days....

I wish there was something more I could do for you. I suppose the only thing I can offer is more advice: don't blame yourself, hon. There are some people who believe everything happens by chance, and others who think every outcome was set into motion long ago. I think it's a little bit of both. The fever befalling your family swept like a tornado through your corner of the world and caught the Whitehalls on a whim. The changes happening to you before it came through? Well, I believe those took up residence years ago, and were only just making themselves known. They're not likely to leave anytime soon, either. They might go into hiding, but they're there, and you'll need to face them straight on.

But I didn't write this letter to upset you. If I was really a good friend, I'd be offering a distraction, so here goes.

News on the Iowa front: Sal's and Toby's letters aren't coming regularly, but they are coming. Sal hasn't said where he is, but I have a feeling he was with the surge of troops into Italy. How strange that must have been for him. His parents were born there, and a good chunk of his family still lives in the Tuscan hills. It would be his first trip to the country where his parents met and married, where his grandparents and their parents farmed the land he is now overtaking. Would he look into a pair of enemy eyes and see a resemblance? On second thought, I hope he's not close enough to see a flicker of anything!

Toby's letters are poetic and gentle, though I can read between the lines enough to know his soul is taking a rubbing. It's the unwritten words which tell of his true feelings. How many years of war will it take to undo the eighteen years of a (relatively) peaceful childhood? I wonder. I worry more for him than his father, who's had a lifetime of observing the sometimes destructive nature of human beings. My Toby is going to need some careful handling when he gets home.

He also hasn't mentioned Roylene lately, probably—knowing Toby—out of respect for me. He doesn't like to point out anyone's faults, and my avoidance of that girl is a shining one.

In my next V-mail, however, I can report a Roylene sighting. I didn't initiate it, so I can't brag, but I did speak to her, and she did respond.

I was sitting on the greens eating lunch with Irene and Charlie the Cowboy (Irene's been seeing him since that crazy dinner at my house). Turns out old Charlie's got a perforated eardrum on the left side, so he won't ever be in uniform. I think he hears just fine, and I sit on the left side and talk really low sometimes and he answers well enough, so I don't know. But that's Irene's business, I suppose.

Anyway, we were enjoying the Indian summer heat, stretching our legs out over the grass and tilting our heads toward the sun, when I heard a squeaky noise, like the kind a mouse makes when caught in a trap.

Roylene was pushing a loaded cart up the hill, its shelves piled high with sandwiches and sacks of potato chips. One of the wheels must have been off, because it made a racket. Our eyes met, and I left Irene and Charlie and walked over to Roylene. She had her colorless hair tied up in a knot and a layer of sweat covered her body like the skin on vanilla pudding.

"Can I help you?" I asked, bringing out my best smile.

"No," she said, and kept pushing that darn cart.

No question mark at the end. Roylene had made a declaration.

The exchange distressed me, so I made my excuses to Irene and Charlie and walked home. I went to bed early that night consumed with remorse. I should have helped her anyway, right?

But I made a decision to step back and let things play out. Maybe some part of me knows that's the way it's got to be.

I know you'll take good care of your boy, and I hope you'll take good care of yourself. Sounds like Robert is doing a fine job of that, as well. As far as the other stuff, maybe it makes sense to take a step back temporarily. I don't think you can walk away, but maybe it will give some necessary perspective.

Sending love over the miles,
Rita

———————

September 24, 1943

ROCKPORT, MASSACHUSETTS

Dear Rita,

How relieved I was to get your letter! I felt a whole world of trouble run off my back and for the first time in nearly two months I can exhale properly.

Oh, the pictures you paint with your words. I can see those women on their knees (thank you for the prayers by the way...my little man is weak, but alive, thank God).

And Roylene? Is it me or the words you've woven that create an unease in my spirit? She seems like a loon. Perhaps you should stick to your guns and steer clear of her? Has Toby written to you about her? Or then again, maybe you just make her nervous. Fear and nerves drive people into strange ways.

That's what I've been doing lately. Pushing that lazy summer "before" in the back of my mind and rationalizing my behavior with preposterous statements in my diary, like: "I was nervous. And my own fear led me straight into a crazy, spinning time when I did things so out of character I'm still trying to grasp it all." Silly—but still, the early summer here feels like a hazy, watercolor dream. A dream that I want to forget, but bubbles of it pop up in my mind every now and then. They make me smile. Then the guilt washes over me again.

Robert is due to ship out overseas soon. I stare at him as he sleeps. We keep Corrine in our bed and the two of them curl around and cling to each other like vine to flower. I want to memorize him more than ever. His jawline, his smell, his grace. For so long I thought his wiry frame weaker than rugged Levi. And now? Now I can't imagine being held by anything less gentle.

Levi seems to have gotten over his pouting spell. He and Robert are going about doing all the things they love to do together. Fishing, taking drives into Brimfield to see antiques shows. Getting boiled lobsters straight off the dock and sitting on the benches with hammers, cracking open the goodness. Sometimes I wish I was a man. Men have so much fun together.

The two of them are gone right now, gone to collect my pale boy from the hospital and bring him home. Robert's even asked me to encourage MORE of a relationship between Levi and Robbie while he's gone.

You see…Robbie has a weak heart now. Like Levi. And Robert thinks having Levi as an influence would be appropriate. Even when I want to get away, life lines up the obstacles. I can't help it…I feel like this is a test of some sort. A test of biblical proportion. It makes me want to growl. Growl, growl, growl.

But really, all I am is scared.

What happens when Robert leaves? Will my fickle ways spread around again? I don't trust myself. Not one bit. I wish I did.

I worry about your boy, too. Both our sons. Both changed from who they were before. One from war, one from illness. Who will they be when it's all over?

Looking forward to your next letter.

Humbled and with love,
Glory

October 1, 1943

V-mail from Marguerite Vincenzo
to Pfc. Salvatore Vincenzo

Happy birthday, honey!

In my mind we're getting ready to paint the town. Vito's got our table waiting, and he's covered it in oysters, chopped salad and a steaming double portion of osso buco. You've got tickets to the Englert in the back pocket of your gray suit, the one with the piping. I'm wearing my gold dress in case we want to go dancing after the show. Va-va-voom! We'll stay out past midnight and not care. We'll dance so close they'll need to pry us apart with a crowbar.

I love you, Sal. More than ever. You keep your handsome self safe.

Rita

October 3, 1943

IOWA CITY, IOWA

Dear Glory,

Robert reminds me so much of my Sal. Your last letter poked and prodded at my memories of our first years together. (It seems the only things keeping me company lately are your letters and the past.)

I'm going to tell you a story about my husband. It's about time you got introduced to him, isn't it?

I was working as a waitress at the Mondlicht Café, a German restaurant, when I met Sal. He showed up at the lunch hour one day, and quickly became one of my regulars. After a few weeks, he asked me to go to the movies after my shift and I said yes.

I liked him. Sal isn't a big man, but he is big on talking. That first date I don't think either of us shut up until the movie started. He took my hand in the darkened theater, and it was cool and soft, not like the sweaty, calloused boys I was used to. At the end of the night he didn't get the least bit fresh, only asked if he could take me on the town again.

We started seeing each other frequently. Sal took me to the Art Institute and the Oriental Theater, to Maxwell Street for ices and to the tailor shop on Western Avenue where his entire family worked. I was young, but my parents had both passed, and Sal's mother and father welcomed me like a gift.

When Mama Vincenzo pulled me into the kitchen and said she wanted to teach me to make Sal's favorite minestrone, I didn't exactly need to be a genius to know what my beau had in mind. I begged off, saying I cooked enough in the restaurant. She smiled, a cryptic Mona Lisa smile, and I wondered just how much she understood about me.

A few nights later, a man sauntered into the restaurant and requested a table in my section. He didn't have Sal's thick, shiny hair or kind eyes, but his face had a quality I admired. I could tell he was sharp, not book-smart like Sal, but the kind of knowing that comes from looking at people, really looking at them, and seeing who they are and what they need and how far they'd go to get it. Another waitress mouthed the word *gangster* as she passed with her pot of coffee, but that didn't bother me. Everyone was a criminal back then, to different degrees.

I approached with my order book and he waved it away. "Just a lemonade," he said, staring at my name tag. "Marguerite, huh? I would have pegged you for a Madeline or Colette."

I'm sure I blushed. I *know* I blushed.

I brought his drink and he nursed it, watching me as I moved around the room. At first it made me self-conscious, but then a whispery thrill traveled up my arms and legs, giving me goose bumps. I'd catch him looking, and by the end of the night I'd give it right back, staring at him as bold as a streetwalker.

We ended up behind the restaurant, kissing against the rough brick wall. He moved with the slow assurance of someone who always got what he wanted, but never took it for granted. I was hooked.

He returned the next night. And the next. I made excuses to Sal, lied to him without batting an eye.

After a week the man stopped coming in the restaurant. He waited for me in the shadows, smoking in the alley until the last customer paid his bill. My shifts passed so quickly, knowing he was out there, and knowing what we were going to do.

One night I told the manager I was sick and walked out the front door, away from the dark alley. I kept moving, not stopping until I got to Western Avenue. I went to the tailor shop and made up some story to excuse my disappearance. They welcomed me back. They'd worried about me.

I quit my waitressing job.

I learned to make the minestrone.

It wasn't until many years later—after Toby was born, after the doctor told me I couldn't have any more children, after all the many things a married couple suffer together, the things that bind more than a ring or a slip of paper, that Sal told me. He'd watched me leave with the man one night, watched us steal to the recesses of the alley, watched me walk out twenty minutes later with my hair a mess and stockings askew. And he took it as a test. He said he trusted me enough to make the right decision for myself. And he said that it was such a rare thing to find someone he trusted so completely, that he felt, crouching behind a Dumpster watching his girlfriend giving herself to a gangster, that if I chose him he would marry me.

He had faith, and thought enough of me to expect I'd walk away from this man. He also knew he would never really get close to me if he forced my hand.

Since that one time, I've never been unfaithful to Sal. I worry, though, that he was wrong about me, and my fidelity has more to do with his proximity than some kind of inner moral compass. To this day I don't know why I walked away from that man, only that I did. Maybe, as I said before, I'm not much of a cliff-jumper.

It's funny. Bombs drop from the sky every day, chaos and mayhem spread over the globe, but we're more afraid of the mines buried deep in our hearts, the ones we hope to never give cause to explode.

Love,
Rita

P.S. Give Robbie a kiss for me, or better yet, I'm sending some extra meat rations. A little iron will get some strong blood flowing through him in no time!

———

October 7, 1943

IOWA CITY, IOWA

Glory,

I completely forgot to send this recipe with my last letter. A couple of days ago, I picked up a bottle of Lysol at the co-op grocery and it came with a free rationing cookbook. Aren't I the lucky duck?

So I was flipping through and, lo and behold, found this dish called Eggs Marguerite. Irene and Charlie thought it delicious when I had them over last night.

Those two continue to confound me. I've hosted them for dinner a few times, and on the surface they seem quite the young (-ish) couple. Charlie is very solicitous of Irene. He holds her chair when she sits, and outstretches a gentlemanly hand when she rises. He makes her laugh, and teases her in the manner of someone who knows enough of her personality to do so. Irene smiles at him in response, and I caught her staring at his angular face when he was preoccupied with dessert.

Something is off, though. I can't quite put my finger on it. Whenever I broach the subject of romance with Irene, she finds a polite way to steer the conversation in another direction. Could it be Charlie has something to hide, therefore Irene does? He did show up at my house with a full box of cherry chocolates. How in the world does a vitamin salesman get his hands on that?

The more difficult explanation almost pains me to write. Do you think there are some people who are meant to be alone? Or possibly, has Irene, at thirty-eight, kept the door closed on love for far too long and now finds it's sticking?

Then again, I suppose people can take a while to find each other, even when the person is standing right in front of them.

Anyway, enjoy the recipe. I brought some over to Mrs. K. to try after Charlie and Irene left. She chided me for using common cheddar, but gobbled it up before I walked out the door. If you have the rations, it accompanies a meat dish quite nicely. The two together would make a very nutritious meal for your Robbie. Here goes:

Eggs Marguerite
6 baked Idaho potatoes
3 cups creamed vegetables (Melt 1 1/2 tablespoons butter, add 1 1/2 tablespoons flour to form almost a paste, then 1 1/2 cups hot milk. Stir over heat until boiling. Turn off the burner and add some nutmeg, salt and pepper. Keep mixing as it thickens. When it does, add a whole mess of lightly cooked vegetables from your garden. De-lish!)
6 poached eggs
1/2 cup grated American cheddar cheese

Scoop all pulp from potatoes; mash; season. Fill shells with creamed vegetables. Make a border of mashed potato; place poached egg on top of creamed vegetables. Sprinkle egg with cheese. Place in a moderate oven (350°F) until cheese melts and browns.
This makes six portions—enough to feed all of you.

Well, I've got to run—we're rolling bandages today at the American Legion and if I miss it Mrs. Kleinschmidt will force me to join her for lard collection duties.

Take care, hon,
Rita

P.S. I passed the tavern on my way to the co-op. Roylene was standing out front, sweeping the sidewalk in her tattered men's overcoat and galoshes. Her eyes grew round when she spotted me, and she stepped back to let me by without saying a word. This time I didn't keep walking. I invited her to tea, Glory. Oh, yes, I did! And after a moment of looking completely panic-stricken, she agreed to come. I know it's unseemly, but I'm feeling ridiculously proud of myself.

October 20, 1943

ROCKPORT, MASSACHUSETTS

Dear Rita,

I love it when I get two letters in one day. It's like Christmas. Anna brought them. (Our road is private and all the mailboxes are gathered at the front road entrance. Because I have to stay so close to Robbie, Anna's been taking that long, twisty walk for me. I miss it so. The freedom of it.) The postmaster had them tied together with a blue ribbon! He's a strange little man, that Sam. Anna tells me he has a strong inclination toward a fondness for other men. I find this information hilarious *and* fitting. I hope you don't take offense.

Truth be told, I think Anna and her friend Marie are more lovers than friends. I see lovers everywhere these days. My mind's been mooning over all sorts of love lately, no matter the persuasion.

I miss Robert. I know he's overseas now. Our goodbye was much worse this time than it was the first. Maybe because I know we'll be an ocean apart. Maybe because I know what I'm capable of once my heart begins to feel lonesome. Levi carried Robbie down to the small whistle stop station where we all said goodbye, and then later that day we talked about "us." It was nice to have it out in the open. He told me he'd always loved me. And he loved the children, but that he respected Robert and didn't want to dishonor him. I knew I was in trouble already because I got a little mad. I still can't tell if it's because he's deemed our "romance" no longer acceptable, or because he beat me to the punch. Either way, the gray smoke that rose out of my head can NOT be a good sign. Sometimes I wish we'd never met. I'd give up our entire childhood together if I could have a moment's peace to still my heart. We have so much history behind us—Robert, Levi and myself. Too many tragic twists and turns. Levi and I have always been on the edge of something I could never understand. It worries me, Rita. How much can I take?

Thank you, thank you for sharing your love story with me. Hearing about another love story did my heart good. I sat under a tree with Robbie getting some fresh air while Corrine crawled around trying to eat the leaves that are collecting. (I can use them in my compost, right? There are so many leaves and usually we burn them....) I read the letter that held your story. Then thought on it for a while looking up through the red maple leaves to the blue, blue sky. Then read it again. Smiling each time. What a gift! When I smile, Robbie smiles. They're weak smiles, but smiles nonetheless.

So I suppose I owe you a story of my own. And sadly, I have much more time to pen letters these days. What with Corrine not walking yet (soon though…) and Robbie a shadow of himself. Like I said in my last letter, the fever weakened his heart. (Thank you for the delicious recipe and the extra rations, too. So, so appreciated.) He doesn't run. He doesn't play. He laughs in a whispery way that frightens me. Sometimes I wake in the night and watch him sleep and the tears, they just come. Where is my beautiful boy? Where is he? It's like garden fairies came, took my rambunctious child and left this quiet version in his place. I am so ashamed I ever complained about the boy's energy. I'd give my own life to watch him make mischief. My world is, suddenly, so, so quiet.

Anyway…I've told you a bit about Robert, Levi and myself as children. But I suppose you might be wondering how I settled on Robert. It was simple, really. The three of us decided that our friendship had no room for romance (after that summer when we were kids and my heart belonged to Levi). And we stayed true to our pact all through our early teens. It was so much fun, I have to admit…going to the summer dances with a boy from Connecticut and then being swept up by Levi and Robert…their dates glaring at me from the punch bowl. How we'd dance! All three of us. I think we always knew that somehow we would end up all together…. But I suppose we couldn't have imagined this war and how it divides us now more than class or time could have. It drives a wedge between us like a million autumns. When my mother died I was lost. I don't remember much, except brushing her hair. I was taken to the hospital to recover, and when I woke up, there he was.

Robert.

He was the one who came. And in that moment, when he looked into my eyes, I didn't see anyone but him. It was like a clearing in a dark forest. You get there and it was like you always knew it…an internal map…. He was always mine. We were born to be together.

"I'll never leave you," he said, speaking softly against my brow. And I knew he wouldn't. Even this war can't rob me of his heart.

Of course, there were obstacles, but we were so in love we swept right through it all. I may be paying for that sin right now. Levi took it hard, and we callously pretended not to notice. And now, just look at the mess I'm in.

Claire Whitehall didn't approve, either. But she wouldn't have approved of Princess Elizabeth.

Levi was Robert's best man at our wedding. He smiled through the whole thing, but I could tell he was in pain. I avoided his eyes for the whole day. And later, when he got me alone near the tall willow at the back of our yard, he said, "You made a wise choice, Glory. Don't ever doubt it," and he kissed me on the cheek.

"Hey! What's all this?" asked Robert with a good-natured laugh in his voice.

"I suppose we are saying goodbye to childhood romances," I said lightly. Too lightly, because Levi cleared his throat and made some excuse about having to leave early.

"He'll get over it," said Robert.

And I thought we'd all get over it. But the past is a curious thing, dear Rita. It keeps our feet all muddled up when we yearn to run free.

My mother and father had a better story than my own. I was seventeen when I fell in love, newly orphaned with a boatload of money and three houses to choose from. I'm not hard to look at and neither is Robert. It's a small world and we just…well…he saved me. He saves me still.

Now my parents, on the other hand, had a grand love affair. My father knew all there was to know about money, property and investing. He saw the crash a mile away and kept all of our assets safe. He was rich his whole life. Steeped in money. I think it was opium—way, way back. Scandalous, isn't it? He wasn't as handsome as he was rough-looking. Kind of like Levi but with colder eyes. Father used to say, "Feelings make you weak, which is fine if you want to be a weakling," and then shake his newspaper. I sent you a picture. I'm sure you can see what I'm talking about.

My mother, Corrine, was another story. She didn't have anything but her stunning face. Born into poverty. No one will tell me how they met, so it leaves me to believe she might have been his "lady friend" before he married her. My mother did everything for him. The sun rose and set by his desires. I think I was an accident or afterthought. Don't get me wrong, I think they loved me (I know they loved me) but Franny (I wrote about my Portuguese nanny, right?) was the one who filtered down that information. And Father demonstrated his love by leaving me all the money and property. Legally binding me to it. I couldn't sign it over to Robert or any other husband even if I wanted to. That was kind of him. Women rarely get the opportunity to have such responsibility over their own finances. I didn't even *know* that until Anna told me.

This house I live in was our summer home. It was always my favorite place because it's where we were all together. It's smaller than the other two (one in Cambridge and one in Old Lyme, Connecticut) and I was at boarding schools from the time I was six. Father said it was better to raise me like an "English boy." Said he thought America was due for a "shake-up" and we'd all be better off European.

For someone so right about so many things, he was wrong on that account, don't you think?

I think they met out West somewhere. California or Oregon.

They always kept their past between themselves. Like some sparkly secret hidden behind their eyes. I like to imagine that my mother was working somewhere wild and romantic (even unseemly!) and my father found her and swept her off her feet. Carried her away and brought her into a life of wealth and leisure.

I imagine he looked at her and said, "You magnificent woman, I do believe you were meant for better things. Come live with me and be my love...."

And she replied, "I've been waiting for you my whole life."

I'd like to think he took her to dress shops and let her buy whatever she wanted and then brought her home like she was a treasure found deep at the bottom of a roaring river.

Robert says I'm a "hopeless romantic." I suppose he's right.

Anyway, those are my stories. I hope they've amused you! I'm sorry to ramble on like this but besides Anna you have become a divine source of comfort.

Love,
Glory

—————————

October 27, 1943

IOWA CITY, IOWA

Dear Glory,

I got such an itch to see a Fred and Ginger picture after your last letter. That's how I imagine your parents, dressed to the nines and gliding across the dance floor like figure skaters over ice. My father only danced with my mother once a year, at Oktoberfest, and he counted the box step the entire time.

There is nothing wrong with being a romantic, Glory. It just means you see the world through a softer lens. The mind will go to great lengths to protect the heart. It sounds like yours prefers to wash memories with a little saltwater to smudge the harsh lines. I wish mine would do the same.

I never know quite what to say to a wife when her husband ships out. I suppose I'll settle for two wishes—safety for Robert and a peaceful heart for you.

Well, I need to run out to the grocery—Roylene is finally coming to tea. I'll finish this letter after she leaves so I can give you the whole scoop.

Later...

Please excuse my penmanship. I've gotten into Sal's secret bottle of rye, found wedged between his tackle box and an ancient Christmas tree stand. I have no idea how long it's been there. Whiskey doesn't go bad, though, unlike everything else.

Roylene showed up on time. I asked to take her overcoat, but she refused. "Come now," I insisted. "You'll broil in my kitchen."

But the stubborn thing wouldn't give. She walked past me and settled in at the table, toying with the silverware. "What's that cooking?" she asked, wariness framing her question.

I went through the trouble of making stuffed beef heart. Anyone looking at her can tell Roylene's diet is deficient in most nutrients. When I told her the luncheon menu, she paled and crinkled her nose. "I thought we were having tea."

I wanted to show her the door, but instead, for Toby's sake, I poured her a cup and one for myself. We sat across from each other, the silence stretching out like taffy.

"Well..." I finally said.

Roylene drew the teacup to her lips, and proceeded to dribble its contents down the front of that damned wool coat. "Too hot," she complained, fanning her mouth.

"Off it goes!" My voice sounded shrill even to my ears. "I'll spot clean it while lunch finishes cooking."

Roylene hugged herself, clawing at the nubby wool. "I'm leaving this on or I'm leaving!" She stood and I was next to her in a flash, my fingers moving nimbly over the cracked wood buttons. "Take it off," I cried. I knew what was underneath. Oh, Glory, I knew.

We tugged and pulled, but my words weakened her resolve, and her grip loosened ever so slightly. I gave a final yank and pulled her arms free. Sure enough her tummy was round as a robin's breast, straining the seams on the front of her cotton dress.

Roylene was breathing hard, her hands protectively over her middle. "It's Toby's. Don't you say it's not."

I don't know what force kept my heart beating. I stood there, breathing in and out, wishing a dust storm would swoop in and take Roylene and Roy and that damn tavern back to the hell they came from. I pressed my wedding ring into the palm of my hand to keep from slapping her cheek.

She'd stolen my son's future, just as if she'd shown up with a telegram from the War Department.

"You…thief."

Defiance twisted her sharp features. "I didn't steal nothing. I don't want nothing from you and I don't want nothing from Toby he doesn't want to give."

"Have you written to tell him?"

Roylene straightened her shoulders and put her hands on her still-slim hips. "Not yet."

Toby hadn't kept it from me. That was something to hold on to. "When are you going to inform him?"

A slight shrug. "I dunno."

"I will, then."

She took a step forward, those dull hazel eyes catching fire. "No. It's mine to tell. I want your promise you won't."

I didn't want to make any promises to Roylene. In the back of my mind I heard Sal's gentle voice telling me it was not my place. At least, not yet. "All right," I agreed, "but don't wait too long or I will."

She lunged for the coat in my arms, but I held on tightly. Roylene was going to sit down and eat a healthy meal, so help me God. I steered her to the table and she choked down every bit of the overcooked beef heart. A couple of times it nearly came back up. I didn't care.

"I'm surprised your father hasn't shown up at my door with a shotgun," I said while she chewed and swallowed.

"He doesn't know. I've been wearing this coat everywhere. He hasn't turned the heat on yet so I tell him I'm too cold to take it off."

I poured her a glass of milk, and then sat across from her while she drank. "You can't fool people for long. One day soon you're going to wake up looking like you swallowed a bowling ball. It's important to decide whether you want to tell people on your own terms or if you want them to discover your secret by accident. If I were you, I'd want to control the situation."

She reached across the table and wrapped her bony fingers over mine. It felt odd, touching this woman—this stranger—who would give birth to my and Sal's first grandchild. "Please give me some time, Mrs. Vincenzo," she said softly.

So I'm giving her time. Someday she's got to pay me back, though. I can't write any more. My head is a mess.

More soon,
Rita

P.S. Scratch what I said earlier. Give your eyes a good rub to clear all your romantic visions. There's no place for it during wartime. I think I can understand your father's way of thinking. Feelings do make us weak sometimes, but other times they make us invincible. I don't know which one is worse, to tell you the truth.

P.P.S. I am too young to be a grandmother. I AM.

===

October 31, 1943

V-mail from Marguerite Vincenzo
to Seaman Tobias Vincenzo

Toby,

Happy birthday. Do you know what your present is? A child. Roylene is carrying it. How's that for a surprise?

Here I am, worrying myself to death that this war is going to take you away, when the assassin was right here in Iowa City, biting her fingernails and peeling potatoes. Is this the life you had planned? Is she what you want? I can't see it. And I thought I knew you better than anyone.

I should have known enough to save you from your mistakes. I should have banged that motel door down. I should have kicked it in.

But...what's done is done. That baby is on its way into the world without you here to greet it. Do you trust me to do your job until you get home? I'm not sure I would, given my track record.

Your birthday gift is a promise to try. That's all I'm capable of at this point.

I love you.
Your ma

[Letter never sent—slipped into the lining of Rita's sewing kit.]

November 1, 1943

IOWA CITY, IOWA

Dearest Glory,

I skipped All Souls mass. I just could not go, not with Roylene's news, not with this war escalating. It made me crazy to think about the thousands of new souls crushed together, huddled in a universe too small to contain them. And those kneeling women, begging for their time to come? So selfish. I couldn't stand it. Not today.

Instead, I hung our family's Blue Star flag in our front window. Please don't think me morbid for my decision, or unpatriotic for waiting so long. I know it should have gone up the minute Sal reported for duty, or when Toby went off to Maryland. I always found an excuse not to. It wasn't denial, so much as superstition, I think. Am I growing into a silly old hag?

I cut the stars myself from one of my navy blue winter blouses, one for Sal and one for Toby. Identical. If it comes time to replace them with gold, I won't do it. Tragedy should not shine like a Christmas ornament. Neither should sacrifice. If the worst does happen I will cut new stars from my black mourning dress, and I will wear it, holes and all.

About an hour ago I caught Mrs. Kleinschmidt standing at my gate, staring hard at the flag. She had the strangest look on her face. I walked out onto our porch and she didn't say a word. But then, she of all people should understand how little it sometimes takes to knock someone into the abyss.

She's a sliver in my big toe, that woman. At the YMCA on

Friday there was talk of a German POW camp being planned for Algona, a small town to the north of us. Mrs. K. went white, and I feared she was going to keel over right into the pile of scrap metal the children had collected. You'd have thought she spotted an M.P. coming her way, ready to haul her off. Glory, Algona is over two hundred miles away!

That evening we had a blackout drill. I turned off all the lights but didn't close the side curtains, figuring that even though they're fading, my sunflowers would do a fine enough job shielding my windows. After the siren stopped I heard a sharp rap on my door. It was Mrs. K. with a black armband snug on her fleshy arm, and a flashlight at her hip. Our new air-raid warden.

She threatened to place me under a citizen's arrest for defying the government's order. I told her where she could stick those orders. Her face turned purple and she started shouting *"Dummkopf! Dummkopf!"* so loudly I'll bet the Führer heard her in the Bavarian hills.

I leaned over and said, very clearly, *"Nazi-liebhaber!"*

She unsheathed her flashlight and hit me smack across the thigh. It hurt! I ran out the front door with her chasing me, brandishing that heavy stick, and I kept yelling, "Nazi-lover! Nazi-lover!" like an overgrown schoolyard bully. Oh, Glory, I couldn't help myself.

There is a welt on my leg the length of an ear of corn. I guess I deserve it. I suppose the strain of the past week made me lose control. Maybe I need to keep busier to take my mind off my worries? A bunch of the ladies from our USO club work at the canning plants on a temporary basis. I think it's time I considered taking a job. Soon enough there'll be another mouth to feed.

Speaking of which, I left a note at the tavern for Roylene to stop by so I could take her measurements. She came yesterday. That girl is about ready to bust out of her clothes, but Roy hasn't noticed. I don't think he'd look up from the till if she was giving birth right on the bar.

She chose some red wool from my fabric stash for a nice shirtwaist. (I can put in a drawstring instead of elastic.) I can't have her fainting dead away in that ugly overcoat, can I?

I'm trying, Glory. Really I am.

Hope all is well with the Whitehalls.

Love,
Rita

P.S. Is Robbie getting bored during his convalescence? Can he hold a pencil yet? I would like him to draw something for me. I'll post his work in my *other* front window.

P.P.S. Roylene still has not written to Toby. I have a letter ready to go that'll get the job done. She's got until Thanksgiving.

———

November 5, 1943

V-mail from Gloria Whitehall
to Sgt. Robert Whitehall

Darling Robert,

Oh, I have such news. Corrine is walking! I'm watching her right now, taking tentative steps, finding her footing. Her laughter nearly drowns out the bell tolling for the dead in this town. So full of life.

In other news—and don't call me a gossip hound, this is important—my friend Rita is going to be a grandmother! You know…my pen pal? Well, get this. Her son, Toby, must have fallen in love with the town misfit, this young skinny thing by the name of Roylene. Toby's back overseas, and Roylene is four months gone! A baby! Rita's having a hard time with this news, as can be expected. But I can't help but be excited for her. I'm looking at Corrine play and all I can see is the happiness she brings our family. Make sure you stay safe, my Robert. Don't be a hero. Be good to yourself, and don't worry about us. We are fine. I promise.

All my love,
Ladygirl

November 6, 1943

ROCKPORT, MASSACHUSETTS

Dear Rita,

I am so glad you are making clothes for Roylene. Really. It might be because I have this chubby, perfect baby on my knee…or maybe because I realize how precious every little moment is because of Robbie's illness. Nevertheless, I am excited about your new addition. Babies are babies. And they are darn cute. You are coping with this whole thing with a gracefulness that I admire. And I'm sure Toby and Sal will be over the moon. There's nothing like a baby to keep our boys alive out there. I was hoping I might be pregnant again after Robert's visit, but I was so sick. Your grandchild is a blessing in disguise. I promise you.

And you will make a wonderful (YOUNG) grandmother! Just look at what your gift did for my boy. Robbie made you a picture! He doesn't hold a pencil well but I went out and bought some nice watercolor paints at the artist colony here on Rocky Neck. He made you a rainbow. It's in my little care package. I've also sent more stockings, a book of holiday recipes I found at Toad Hall bookstore (I bought two, one for each of us) and a jar of my famous (first) rosehip jam. Can you tell I'm trying to keep busy?

Rita, would you consider coming for a visit? Maybe for the holidays? Is it too strange for me to ask? I have plenty of room here. Too much room.

Oh, Rita, I had a hearty laugh when I read your letter. I know that's serious business, but my goodness. I adore your stories about Mrs. K. I know she's a thorn in your side, but she amuses me to no end.

On another note, I've been going back to services with Anna. And meetings, too. We are doing all sorts of things to help the war effort. Tinfoil collection, newspaper, book drives, helping connect women who need money with jobs left empty by servicemen. I'm thrilled! I really like working next to her. I can see so much hope in the faces of the people who come down to that little meeting house.

And I believe in Hope, Rita. I hope so hard all day long. Hope for the war to end. Hope for Sal, Toby and my dear, dear Robert to come home safe and sound. Hope for Hitler to be strung up by his you-know-whats. I hope for Robbie to be Robbie again. And I hope you'll come to visit me someday.

I've your room picked out already. Upstairs, it faces the sea. I've taken one wall and commissioned one of those artists to come and paint sunflowers. It's where I'll go to read your letters.

What will you do for Thanksgiving? I invited Robert's mother and for once she's accepted. So I'll be having Claire, Anna and

Marie and Levi. I'm going to do all the cooking and decorating myself. Who needs hired help? Not me!

With love,
Glory

P.S. Robbie asked who he was painting the picture for and, I hope it's all right, I told him, "Auntie Rita."

———————

November 12, 1943

IOWA CITY, IOWA

Dear Glory,

Your last letter sounded so cheerful. I'm glad. Does this mean Robbie is getting some color back in his cheeks? I certainly hope so. Please tell him Auntie Rita posted his gorgeous watercolor in her front window because she wanted the entire neighborhood to appreciate its artistry. Irene said it's better than some of the abstract pieces in the university collection. I completely agree.

Well, you've piqued my imagination, my dear. I can see the sunflower room vividly in my mind's eye. Someday I will come for a visit, but right now I'm stuck in Iowa City because—get this—I have a job! It's temporary and part-time, but it is an official job and I do have a number of responsibilities. I'll be acting as secretary to the dean of the English department. Irene put in a good word, and when I proved I could type he hired me. (Pray he doesn't ask me to take shorthand—I don't know anything about all those squiggly lines.) The current secretary, a sweet-faced girl by the name of Florence, will leave for California directly after the Thanksgiving holiday. She's going to San Diego for welder's training, and will likely work in the shipbuilder's yard until the war is over. So until then I am an employee of the esteemed University of Iowa, just like my Sal. Happy for me?

Speaking of Thanksgiving—I went a little off my rocker and invited Mrs. K. She knocked on my door again, this time holding a snow shovel. I asked her if she meant to bump me off this time, and she cracked the tiniest of smiles, like when a baby passes gas, I kid you not.

Then she asked me to clear her walkway, though we only got a dusting. I think she was trying to apologize, in her way. I agreed, which was me apologizing in mine. After I finished I returned the shovel and invited her. She promised to come by after she hands out turkey dinners at the USO. I bet she's stingy with the gravy, don't you?

Thank heavens there are plenty of birds this year, but it seems everything else is rationed. I used eight points to buy a can of cranberries at the grocery. I wasn't going to make it, but Sal loves my sauce, so it felt wrong to leave it off the table. Maybe I'm superstitious, but changing my menu seems like an invitation to the gods of chance to start up some trouble. With that in mind, I'm making Toby's favorite cornbread stuffing as well, with extra raisins and celery.

While I was picking up items at the grocery, I ran into Irene and Charlie shopping for their dinner. They didn't notice me at first, so I spied on them from behind a towering RC Cola display. I'm not proud of myself, but there's a lot to learn when people don't know you're looking, and there's a lot about those two I want to know. Charlie's behavior didn't set off any alarm bells, quite the opposite, in fact. He orbits Irene, walking close but not too close, holding his hand under her elbow but not quite cradling it—it's almost as if he fears she's made of fine blown glass, and one false move could end in disaster. Irene does nothing to dispel this notion. It puts a barrier between them, thin and transparent like a photographer's scrim, but there all the same. Was it made of fear? If yes, then my duty as Irene's friend was to help push it aside. I stepped around the cola display, all smiles, feigning surprise. I invited them over for Thanksgiving dinner, as a couple. They accepted graciously. I told Charlie to bring some wine, which I intend to pour generously into both their glasses. Hopefully it'll loosen them up some.

On my way home, I stopped over at the tavern and left a note on the alley door inviting Roylene. I asked her to come a few hours early. It's about time I teach her to make a Vincenzo Thanksgiving feast. Maybe the two of us can figure out a way to get a container of stuffing to the South Pacific.

I also—drumroll—invited Roy. I know I should have extended the olive branch in person, but I have no idea if Roylene finally took off that overcoat.

Well, I need to head over to St. Mary's to help with the linens for the memorial mass honoring the five Sullivan brothers of Waterloo. I can't believe it's been a year since they were killed. I think of their mother, traveling around speaking for the war effort with the weight of all that grief on her shoulders. She's a better woman than I.

Difficult as it is, I am trying to believe hope has a place in this war, just like you suggested. Thanks for the reminder, hon. I should be thankful for what I do have at this time of year, and my blessings are many.

Have a lovely Thanksgiving dinner,
Rita

November 25, 1943,
Thanksgiving Day

ROCKPORT, MASSACHUSETTS

Dear Rita,

It's late here. The children are asleep. The dishes are washed, the floor is swept. The leftovers covered and tucked topsy-turvy on top of themselves in the icebox. I'm afraid to open the thing! I made way too much. Seeing as I used most of my rations, I suppose leftovers are a good thing.

Oh, darling Rita. A job? I'm so, so happy for you. And so proud. How wonderful it will be to work at a university. You'll be great. You'll pick it up in no time. Shorthand is nothing after you've battled and won over the terrifying Mrs. K.

Robbie is doing well. But he's still a different boy. Lately I've become absolutely obsessed with the ease at which we humans adapt to things. Three years ago I was a young bride in a Free World. Now I'm the mother of two children and an army wife. And the world is on the verge of chaos and tyranny. (I sound just like Anna giving one of her talks. I'm happy to even hold those words in my mouth, to let them come out of my pen is divine. I want to write speeches, too. What do you think? Would it be too horrible for Robert to come home to an activist wife?)

Here's what I've adapted to in terms of my son. He will never be a soldier. He will never be an athlete. He will be at risk of death every time he gets ill…and he will be prone to such illness. To put it bluntly, he could die. Any moment. But so could Robert and Sal and Toby. At least I am here with him. He's not alone. Our other boys? They are alone out there without us.

Levi kissed me again tonight. There was wine with dinner. Anna and Marie had gone. My mother-in-law never made it here. There was a little snow on the ground and it scared her away. He put the children to sleep. He's been here more and more lately, so I'm sure I should have expected this. We've been exchanging glances, and every once in a while his hand brushes mine. I've been writing to Robert almost every night to assuage my guilt. And I miss him, Rita. I don't want you to think I don't. I miss him so much. But he's not here. And the attention and friendship I get from Levi… the little everyday things like putting the children to bed. That sort of normalcy has lulled me into a false sense of what is real and what is not.

I washed the dishes and listened to the radio. I was missing Robert. Missing the way he used to dance with me in the kitchen.

I felt Levi behind me before he even touched me. When I turned around, his face was right in front of mine. "Gloria," he said. I closed my eyes and it was as if my name echoed across a thousand million years. His mouth. I still feel the burn where his stubble scraped my skin. God help me, Rita, I wasn't the one to pull away. He was. I was leaning, almost in a backbend over the sink. I could feel him pressing against me and I wanted him to just do it already. To make me the woman my mother must have been.

Then a dish hit a glass and he ran out of the kitchen, out the back door and into the night. I followed him as far as the porch. He was standing in the dark yard staring at the sky. He didn't turn around.

"I can't do this, Glory. I can't pretend to live this life with you." He ran his fingers through his hair but never turned around. He just walked into the night. Thank God Marie left a package of cigs. I'm smoking right now. Sitting here in your sunflower room and smoking. Thinking about writing activist speeches and becoming an adulteress. See? Look what we can adapt to. All sorts of things.

On November 11 (Armistice Day), I received my first "romantic" letter from Robert. Mostly he fills his letters with domestic things. But not this one. He misses me, Rita. He aches for me and this is how I treat him? Is it possible to be in love with two men at the same time? Or is this feeling I have for Levi a memory? The memory of love.

Living inside of all this anxiety is difficult. I don't know if I should grab at life or wait for it to grab me.

Please don't be angry. I'm young and reckless.

Love,
Glory

P.S. Robbie sent another picture. This one is of a turkey. See his handprint?
P.P.S. It's morning now and I am posting this letter. I thought about ripping it up and giving you a rundown of my menu instead, but I want you to know everything. Levi was sitting on the front porch this morning drinking coffee. He'd come in and made a pot. "Never again," he said. "Whatever you say," I told him. So I guess that is THAT.

November 30, 1943

IOWA CITY, IOWA

Dear Glory,

Tell Robbie this Garden Witch can read palms. I look at his adorable handprint and see only the brightest of futures. He has a long lifeline, with lots of finely etched paths all leading to a heartline of equally impressive length. He will be special, that one.

As for his mother…

Oh, Glory. I want to lecture you, but I'm sure your confusion is punishment enough. Maybe Levi should go away for a while? It seems your closeness only breeds temptation. Will Robbie miss him too much? Maybe. Will your focus shift entirely to Robert without Levi skulking about? I'd bet on it. Give it a shot.

And, yes, I do think it is possible to be in love with two people at the same time. The funny thing is, it can never be the same kind of love. People are different, so the way you love them has to be. Doesn't that sound logical?

I'm sorry your mother-in-law didn't make it to Thanksgiving dinner. If it makes you feel better, Mrs. K. got stuck working, and Irene had to take a bus to Omaha to take care of her mother, who'd fallen ill. Roylene never showed—more on that later.

I had no one at my table, so I boxed everything up and brought it to the USO. There were some boys there about to leave for training, and it gave me a thrill to know they'd get such a meal before they left. Something to remember America by, you know?

Anyway, when I got back, Charlie stood on my doorstep, holding a bottle of Chianti. Turns out he didn't know what to do with himself after waiting with Irene at the bus terminal. I wondered why Irene hadn't just brought him with her.

I felt odd about the two of us being alone in the house, so I suggested we sit outside to take in the brisk evening air. I ran in for some glasses and when I returned Charlie had stretched out on the porch swing, his long legs nearly tripping me up. I poured us each a healthy glass and we sat quietly for a while, letting the pleasant warmth of the alcohol play against the wind biting at our fingertips and noses.

When I finished my drink, I asked, "Why didn't you go with Irene to Omaha?"

Charlie refilled my glass, then his own. "I wasn't asked."

"Do you love her?" A little wine always makes me impolite, Glory. You should know this about me.

"I like being around her," he answered. "She's better than me. Better than I deserve."

Probably, I thought. But I said, "Nobody's better than anyone else."

He looked at me, and I saw a hardness in his eyes, and a weariness in the faint lines surrounding them. "Now, darlin', you know that's not true."

I had nothing to say to that.

Desperate to change the topic, I blabbered on about Mrs. K.'s oddities, Sal's latest letter and Toby and Roylene's situation.

Charlie polished off the last of the wine as I talked. When I finally shut my trap, he said, "You haven't heard from Toby?"

"I don't even know if that crazy girl has written to tell him. I'm going to do it if she doesn't."

"You've got to give her every chance." Charlie stood and grasped my hands, pulling me to standing. "Come on. There ain't too many places she could be."

We found ourselves downtown, and next thing you know I was walking a little unsteadily through the door to Roy's Tavern. The place was empty—even the rummies were down at the American Legion enjoying a free meal. Roy wasn't behind the bar, but Roylene was, pushing an old rag over and over the dull wood. She wore the red shirtwaist—no men's overcoat. A splotch of crimson marred her cheek. On closer inspection it took the shape of a man's hand. My arm twitched. I didn't know if I wanted to hug her frail body or slap the nonsense out of Roy. She noticed the look in my eye and backed up a step, skittish.

Charlie and I planted ourselves on some stools and I ordered two straight whiskeys before he could open his mouth. Roylene's hands shook as she placed the short glasses on the bar.

"Your old man likes an open hand, huh?" Charlie drawled. He casually dropped a ten spot next to the bottle. "Pour one for yourself while you're at it."

She did, and sipped the liquor like an aristocrat, pinky up.

"Is your daddy around?" I asked after she finished her whiskey.

"No, ma'am," she said. Her face was as red and mottled as my cranberry sauce. "He ran off to Des Moines for the night. Said he didn't want to look at me."

I smiled at her. "You took the coat off."

"It was starting to smell like wet dog," she said, laughing. It was contagious, and the three of us were roaring like mountain lions. It felt good to laugh with her, Glory.

When it was time to leave, I asked if she'd like to bunk with me for a few days, until Roy simmered down. She declined. "And Toby," I said, slipping into my coat. "You've written to him?"

She hadn't. "I can't get the words right, Mrs. Vincenzo."

Well, I wiggled out of my coat again and found pen and paper by the till. I curled Roylene's small hand over the pen and guided her to a stool. "It's not a math test," I said. "Whatever you write will do just fine." She sat there, mouthing the words as she etched them into the paper, pausing occasionally, as if transcribing a conversation only she could hear.

Charlie poured us another drink. We waited, silently sipping, the whiskey keeping me sedated enough to stay in place, to not poke my head over that poor girl's shoulder.

When she was done, Roylene placed the unfolded paper on the bar in front of me, for approval. She has a girlish scrawl, all loops and fat letters. I folded it into thirds and slipped it in my purse. It took everything I had not to read it, and more than that to stop myself from adding a postscript. I sent it off the next morning, unread. Promise.

In a few days I'll write my own letter to Toby. It's a fragile method of communication, isn't it? The South Pacific is such an impossibly long journey for those light slips of paper. I hope he gets it.

Love,
Rita

P.S. I started my job yesterday. It's going well so far. I typed three letters, filed some grade forms and went grocery shopping for the dean's wife. Easy peasy!

P.P.S. Watch the smoking, hon. It'll give you wrinkles.

December 2, 1943

IOWA CITY, IOWA

Glory,

I'm writing to you because if I do not put pen to paper I will use my hands to pull my hair out. I've been so damn distracted. I haven't been listening to the radio, and this morning, when I picked up the newspapers for the first time in days, the headlines are screaming about Tarawa. Heavy casualties, the general said. The American people must prepare themselves, he said.

I don't know if anyone can prepare me. Tarawa, Tarawa, Tarawa. I keep repeating it in my head, a prayer to the gods of chance. Over a thousand dead. They said marines in the paper. Toby is USN. So it can't be him lying dead on that beach. It can't. Right? Oh, I want to crawl out of my skin.

I should imagine my relief when I find out it's not him. I should picture my smile, feel the heaviness rise from my chest. It isn't Toby. He is not among the dead.

Is it unforgivable to do this when Western Union is already busy readying telegrams? What universal force has deemed my family worthy of dispensation?

I'm disgusted with myself. But I want my Toby. It can't be him. It can't.

Pray for him, please, please,
Rita

December 4, 1943

IOWA CITY, IOWA

Dear Glory,

Two days later and no telegram. When I'm not working I sit in the cold on the front porch, watching for that smooth-cheeked, towheaded delivery boy, the angel of death.

Mrs. Hansen down the road says by Christmas I should be in the clear. Or, maybe the V-mail will come and I'll get a letter from Toby. Or maybe Roylene will. She stopped by yesterday, cheerfully anticipatory, so I didn't say a word. That girl has more worries than most, and a baby inside her who should live in peace until it's forced into this troubled world. At the end of our visit my mouth started to hurt, I was smiling so hard.

After she left, I tried to hold on to that optimism—pretend as it was—but my thoughts wouldn't let me. Something I haven't told you, hon, is that Sal's letters often contain stories from the front. I didn't want to upset you, or give you nightmares, so I haven't passed along any. I guess I'm in a selfish state, but I want to share one so you understand where my mind's at.

North Africa was gruesome. Sal is trained, but some of the other medics are no more than boys with strong stomachs and first aid kits. One such boy clung to Sal, who was happy to have him along. They'd nearly run out of litters, and he'd needed the extra set of hands to carry a wounded soldier back to the medical unit. Once in the field, the screams came from all directions. Sal decided just to stop, pick one spot and try to help as best he could. He motioned for the younger boy to head off to the right and he took the left.

Time stopped. Sal didn't know if he was coming or going when he went to search for the boy. When he found him, the medic stood next to a G.I. who'd obviously passed. Still, the boy pressed himself against where the soldier's arm once was, using his body as a large bandage. There had been no place for a tourniquet, no hope, but still the boy tried, sweat rolling down his face, blood seeping onto his uniform.

The young medic stared at the red stain blooming over his chest and started to mumble the Lord's Prayer. You see, in his confused state, he thought it was his own blood, that it was him about to die.

Sal gently pulled the young medic away from the dead man. He brought him back to the unit, gave him a shot of whatever rocket fuel they could scrounge and took his own turn at praying.

He prayed for God to turn back time, so he could send that poor boy in the other direction. He asked our Lord to promise that the rivers of blood spilled that day meant less would be shed the next day, and less the day after.

Then he realized he wasn't sure if he believed in God at all. What he did know was that the blood on that young medic's shirt could have been his own. Sal felt certain that even through his horror this boy would have given his very lifeblood to save that poor G.I. And if there was a God, that's where He resided, in the determination of one soul desperate to save another.

I was thinking about Sal's story while standing over the sink this morning. I'd left the dinner dishes sitting last night and while I scrubbed at the frying pan I wondered what I would give. I picked up the paring knife and ran it over my thumb, then I held my hand in the murky water until the blood tinged it the color of rust. I would let it all flow out, an offering to the gods, if it guaranteed Toby would return.

I'm not going crazy. I wish I was, then it would excuse my self-indulgence. I just can't handle the waiting. Three weeks. An eternity, really.

Rita

December 10, 1943

ROCKPORT, MASSACHUSETTS

Darling Garden Witch,

It isn't Toby. I am praying and praying and praying. Robbie is, too. We kneel at bedtime and we pray. For Toby and for Sal and Robert. Robbie asked who Toby and Sal were—he's so smart. Just turned three and speaking in full sentences. I guess the universe makes up for lost things, right? He's lost his ability for making mischief with his body so he makes it with his mind. Anyway, he asks me, "Who are Sal and Toby?" and I say, "Auntie Rita's husband and son." And he says, "Don't worry, Mama. Daddy will protect them." It's so odd. Sometimes I clean forget that Robert doesn't know much more than your name. It's strange how certain parts of lives intertwine while others stay so solitary.

Don't worry, Rita. (As if just saying the words makes it true.) You can't lose your boy because I didn't lose mine. That's the way it goes, right? Two strangers connect and there has to be a reason for it. I've often felt that perhaps we are creating some sort of shield around each other. A magic cloak to protect us. I believe it. I really do. So try—try not to worry too much.

My heart aches for you as I know how you must feel. When Robbie was sick in the hospital I'd watch over him and think, *Where did he go? Where is he now?* But mostly the thing I thought and still want to scream is, "I want my boy back!" You want your boy back. You're his mother. It's what we do.

My mother, when she was sick, told me she thought I'd take to mothering more than she ever could. She didn't apologize for being distant or for sending me away. I didn't expect her to. But she did say that I was different and she thought I'd make a good mama. And when Robert was there, next to me at her funeral, I saw my children in his eyes.

Then, when I found out I was pregnant I was thrilled. And I do love being a mother, but I can almost understand my own mother's reservations. When you put your whole heart in something you risk just that. Your whole heart. It's a high roller's type of gamble. I can tell by your letters that you love with your whole heart. As I love with mine. Too much lately, but I'll save that for another letter.

It's coming on Christmastime and my Christmas wish for you is a letter from Toby telling you he's just fine and that he'd like nothing more than to curl his grown body up in your lap in front of your tree. I've already put mine up. Levi cut it down from the back of some property we own up the road. I'm full of Christmas this year, I don't know why—but the whole town is. Festive, festive, festive. I've bought an ornament, a ceramic sunflower and I had the jeweler etch *Rita* across the base. It hangs at the front and dangles in the firelight. I do wish you were here.

Do something for me if no word has come from him by the time you get this letter. Try to think of Toby as a ball of light. A ball of shimmering light bounding across the ocean and running through forests, over mountains and into the fields next to your sweet home. Anna calls this "Creative Visualization." I use it. It works.

Love,
Glory

P.S. OH! I almost forgot. I made my first speech at the Women to Work forum. I was so scared, Rita. I could HEAR my heartbeat in my ears. I thought I might pass out or even toss my lunch. But Anne told me something that helped. She said, "Just picture thirty Robert Whitehalls out there. Tell him your speech as you would have practiced it in your own living room in your own sweet, white house. Oh. And speak slowly, Glory. You talk much too fast."
And you know what? Those words just came right out of me. And before I knew it there was applause. APPLAUSE! (Can you believe it?)
But Anna said I talked too fast anyway.

December 14, 1943

ROCKPORT, MASSACHUSETTS

Dear Rita,

I wasn't expecting your second letter. I was Christmas shopping with Corrine and Marie in town. Levi was watching Robbie—the wind is too cold for him and sets him coughing. Yes, I haven't sent him away altogether. We just go on as if nothing happened…but there's something in the air between us. I wish I could forget all of it.

Marie took Corrine to play in the toy store (They have a miniature carousel, it's grand!) and I was looking at the bustling people all around me, with ruddy cheeks and shining eyes. Christmas is everywhere in Rockport. A garland on every light pole. A wreath on every door. But what captured my attention was the color of the sunset. Do you see the same sunset as me, Rita? In the winter our sunsets are like red fiery jewels lighting up the sky in a tapestry of color. I hadn't realized that I'd stopped to stare at the way the colors played against the tall, white steeple of Christ Church. People had to walk around me, but no one mumbled or bumped me. I suppose they all surmised I'd lost someone.

Then the postman, Sam, came flying out of the post office with your letter. "Here! This came on the last train, Glory!" At first I thought it must be V-mail…but the envelope was wrong. When I saw it was from you I sat on a bench in front of the church and I read it and I cried.

How I wish I could be there with you or you with me. How unfair that the war keeps us apart from those we love the most, both overseas and here at home. And then I thought of our letters traveling toward each other, out of rhythm, like a fast and necessary conversation. They may have mingled in the same postal bag!

And this war. How skillfully you sum up what we have danced all these months around. I'm glad we feel the same way.

What can I say about this war that you don't know in an even greater way than myself? That it is necessary? It is. There is an evil out there, Rita. An evil that must be taken care of or we are at risk of the same pathogen. Sometimes I wish I could go over there, too. That I could wear that uniform and spread the Good News that freedom and Eden do exist and open their arms to all who would like to partake in it.

I suppose I need to copy those words down as they may be the beginnings of my first speech at Anna's ministry. Impassioned, yes. But from my heart, Rita. From my heart to your heart. Our boys are dying all around us. Every day. But they are dying for a reason. If there is such a thing. If there was *ever* a time to put our lives on the line, it is now. Don't you feel it, Rita? The being one with history?

Please let me know when you get news. I'm sending love and joy.

Merry Christmas, Rita,
Glory

═══════════

December 24, 1943 (very, very late at night...)

IOWA CITY, IOWA

Oh, Glory!

The postman delivered a letter this morning—from Toby! It's dated the third of December, days after that horrible battle, so he is alive!

I danced in my front yard until Mrs. K. came out, cross as the dickens, wondering why I'd gone stark-raving mad. When I told her the good news she ran into the house and came out with two small glasses of kirshwasser and we drank to Toby's health at ten o'clock in the morning!

I think Mrs. K. holds a sweet spot for him. She always yelled at Toby when his ball bounced into her yard, but then, on Christmas, we always found a new ball on the front porch with a very formally written card from "Your next-door neighbor." Before he left for training, Toby did pay his respects to the woman, and I know she worries about him, even when she is making voodoo dolls of me.

Speaking of dolls, I hope the children received my package. I've been in such a daze I didn't mail it until last week. Corrine's doll is wearing a dress I made myself, and Robbie's ball was once Toby's. I hope he can chuck it into the neighbor's yard very soon. I also hope my Lebkuchen traveled well. I included the recipe in the box as it doesn't require sugar, just honey.

Oh, it's been a good, good day, Glory.

Roylene stopped by for lunch. Her gift to me was the sublime pleasure of feeling my grandchild kick a Morse code greeting against my open palm.

Later, Charlie and I talked Irene into skipping midnight mass and heading out on the town instead. A few miles from my house there's this real juke joint—Sal and I used to go when we first moved here. Back then there'd be folksy singers holding court and communists meeting in the beer garden, yelling about the evils of capitalism to the stares of wide-eyed students. Like everything else, though, it's changed.

The place was done up in red, white and blue tinsel, and the folk singers were gone, replaced by some real swingers, a five-piece band made up of guys serving stateside who'd gotten leave. They were in uniform, and it was a sight to see. The holiday had everyone full of cheer, and the drinks were flowing, lighting faces up like the Christmas tree suspended from the rafters! Yes, it was hanging there like a children's piñata! The barman said they didn't have room for it anywhere else. We laughed like crazy!

At the end of the night, when everyone got red-faced and sentimental, the band started playing "When the Lights Go on

Again, All Over the World." They had no singer, so we all took over, every person in that tavern, holding on to one another's shoulders. I had Irene on one side and Charlie on the other, belting away, and I could feel the heat of their bodies through their clothes and the sweet smell of liquor on everyone's breath and the hope in that room lifted me up, up, up till I felt like that Christmas tree, hanging over the world, twinkling like the stars.

I'm drunk, though more with happiness than whiskey.

Toby's alive, Glory. And my Sal. And Robert and Robbie. Corrine and Levi and Mrs. M. and Mrs. K. Irene and Charlie. Roylene and the baby she is carrying. Us. We're alive!

The Merriest of Christmases to you and yours, my beloved East Coast friend, and may 1944 treat you well. It will bring Victory, and our heroes will come home. I just know it.

Love,
Rita

January 1, 1944

ROCKPORT, MASSACHUSETTS

Dear Rita,

Happy New Year! And it is a happy new year. Especially with your letter and the good news it contained. Relief flooded through me as if he were my own son. Oh, Rita, we are so fortunate, aren't we? In so many ways.

It's my birthday today. I'm a New Year's baby. Twenty-four years old. I feel much older than that. Levi helped Robbie make me a beautiful candlelight meal—we combined New Year's Eve and my birthday. The children were so well behaved. Corrine is such a happy, sweet baby. She sat smiling and eating her macaroni in her high chair. They made me Pasta Puttanesca. Do you know it? Quite fancy and something I ate frequently when my parents returned from Italy. (Mother used to have our cooks experiment with dishes she liked when she returned from exotic places.) I think its meaning has to do with women of the night.

Which could have something to do with what happened after the children were asleep. Can I blame it on the dinner, on the wine, on the name of the meal...? Can I blame it on the war? Or should we blame Robert? Robert who wrote to Levi (not me) about the horrors of the war. About fearing he would not return. About Levi taking his place in my home and my heart if the worst should happen. Imagine.

On my wedding night I was ready for the moment. The giving in to pent-up passions. Robert is a quiet lover. Gentle and graceful. A comfortable breeze of a man.

Tonight started innocently enough. Most terrible things do, right? We were cleaning up together, and dancing around the living room to "The Pennsylvania Polka." I just love the Andrews Sisters! But then, as luck would have it, an older song came on the radio, "Someone to Watch Over Me." It never fails to make me cry. So I started to sing along to it...and teared up a bit while I did.

"You okay?" Levi said from behind me, putting his hands on my hips and meeting their sway. And I should have pulled away, but the music...that song... A weaker moment there never was. A weaker woman there never was. I turned around and we were in an immediate embrace. We danced a lovers' dance, his head buried in my neck, mine taking in all of the familiarity of years and years of wondering what it would have been like if I'd chosen Levi and not Robert. The curiosity overwhelmed me.

"I love you, I love you, I love you," he crooned into my hair.

And that was all it took. I closed my mind to the world. To propriety. To everything.

Levi was a storm. We stumbled together across the living room like clouds in the sky full of rain. Falling half on the couch and the floor. Buttons flying, fabric tearing. I think I was crying. I don't remember. Clapping thunder and lightning all around. Fierce and frightening. Not like the love that Robert and I make. This was the sort of thing that even in the act felt doomed, but like flying off a cliff...exhilarating.

I doubt I'll recover soon. My heart flutters in my throat and a shiver goes up my back just thinking about the placement of his hands. That, above all else, is what made me toss up my entire birthday meal after Levi left. The Guilt. Shame. Oh, Rita. What have I done?

"I am a wretched wife," I said to myself after I scrubbed my body raw in a scalding hot tub. I might be able to wash the sin from my body, but how do I purge it from my mind?

Please don't hate me.

So, so much love,
Glory

P.S. I've been thinking so much about your Roylene lately. Maybe because she had a fall from grace, too? I don't know. But, please let her know that if she needs anything, I'm here to help. Okay?

January 6, 1944

IOWA CITY, IOWA

Glory,

Today we celebrate the day the magi brought gifts to our Lord. We Catholics call it the Epiphany. And yes, I do realize I'm not being subtle.

You must stop. Levi must stop.

There are complexities to this situation to which you are not giving sufficient thought. I don't know if it is because you are young or a blithe spirit or simply a girl caught in a rough spot. The reason doesn't matter as much as the actions you take from here on in.

Think about it this way—our actions speak truths our words cannot. So whatever you decide to do next is telling the world what you think of your husband. It doesn't matter that Robert's not there to see it. You'll know, and Levi will know where you stand.

So you need to figure out exactly how you really feel.

It is clear to me that your husband loves you very much. If he is discussing the possibility of another man taking his place, then he is a man who feels death is imminent. There could be no other reason. It must be very, very bad overseas, possibly worse than we are led to believe, or worse than our imaginations will let us construct.

So you must honor Robert's sacrifice by making one of your own. Levi will accept this, as your friend, as Robert's friend.

Glory, if you intend to speak before sensible women and expect to give power to your words, you must be as free of moral ambiguity as you can. I'm not a big believer in fire and brimstone, but I do think a certain purity of heart and intention is necessary when we expect to be heard. We often realize too late that passion only lasts when it is married to truth.

Now before you say I should go find a ladder to climb onto my high horse, let me state this—I do understand. I haven't been intimate with anyone but Sal since our wedding, but that's not to say there haven't been offers, and I'd be lying if I said I hadn't considered those offers. Sal spent the past ten years of his life standing in front of coeds, and he is still an attractive man. I'm certain he's been tempted as well. But for a marriage to work you both need the ability to see all the possible outcomes of a moment's weakness. Most of them are less than satisfying. And none of them end with "happily ever after."

I'm certain Mrs. Moldenhauer would say the same should you ask her. Have you spoken to her about this? To Marie? There are times in a woman's life where she requires a veritable Greek chorus of women's voices to keep her on track. Even if one of them is shouting from Iowa City.

Which brings me to my next topic—Roylene. I believe your postscript sprang from both your generous spirit and a need to connect with a gal at a similar stage in life. You can help Roylene. Be her friend. Write to her, hon. Even if she doesn't respond, it'll do your heart good.

Rita

January 11, 1944

V-mail from Marguerite Vincenzo
to Pfc. Salvatore Vincenzo

Sal,

Damn you for being so good at reading between the lines. You're right. I am shamed. Every time Mrs. K. clucks her tongue at Roylene's growing belly, or that Hansen woman asks me when the wedding is, I want to shut the door and never come out.

But then I'm ashamed of my shame. He's our son. And this situation might not change much after all, right? Toby can still go to college. He can still meet his goals. Did he mention signing up for classes after the war?

Did he mention marriage? He hasn't with me. I know what you're thinking—I won't jump all over the two of them once this war's over. A few months after…maybe.

I secretly love a big wedding. And we clean up pretty good, the two of us. I should start pressing your gray suit now. You do love a sharp crease.

Love,
Rita

January 12, 1944

V-mail from Marguerite Vincenzo
to Seaman Tobias Vincenzo

Son,

You're right, but sometimes being right doesn't amount to much. No, it isn't an ideal world to bring a child into, but if we all waited for that this planet would only house dandelions and cockroaches.

And...I am quite often a hypocrite, but not in this situation. I *was* mad—spitting mad—but that was just my initial reaction. An understandable one at that. I don't dislike her. To tell you the truth Roylene's growing on me, maybe not as quickly as the baby growing inside her, but steadily, incrementally. It began when I noticed the brightness in her smile. She shines like a new penny if you catch her at the right moment.

Her daddy is another story. I haven't seen much of Roy, but I know he's around, crawling on his belly, a cobra ready to strike. Irene's boyfriend, Charlie, had a talk with him. I didn't ask for specifics, but whatever transpired has kept things status quo.

When you get home you'll take Mama Vincenzo's ring to the jeweler, and then we'll work out the living situation. And yes, you are coming home. Stop that kind of talk—you don't want to give the universe any ideas.

I love you, Toby.

Your ma

P.S. I'd like to be called "Nana" instead of "Grandma." It's more elegant.

January 20, 1944

ROCKPORT, MASSACHUSETTS

Dearest Rita,

Please forgive me if you hear a bit of nervous laughter in my letter today. I mean no disrespect, at ALL. But I have to say I could fairly feel the spit of your rage and worry in that last letter. I imagined you in my own kitchen banging around pots and pans, only stopping to point at me, throw your hands up in disgust and bang around some more.

I tend to laugh when I'm in trouble. It isn't one of my best qualities. One night when Robbie was in the hospital a nurse found me laughing on the bench outside of his room. I mean, laughing with tears streaming out of my eyes. There was a horror in her gaze that I won't forget, ever. Please don't be horrified with me. I'd be lost without you.

Know that I hear you. And I *am* doing my best to keep things under control. Once again Levi and I talked in the early-morning hours on the porch, only this time our breath came out like smoke, as the days are like ice here now. I know we both agree that it can't happen again, but no matter how I try, I can't ignore him. He's been a part of my life forever, and the days drag on endlessly without him. Little by little he creeps back into my mind, heart and house. I'm praying for the strength to keep away from him. Yes, me. Praying. Because even though I'm strong—and even though my love for Robert is the realest thing I know...the other day Levi did the darnedest thing. I was on a chair trying to trim the grape arbor and couldn't reach the top. Just then Levi walked up the path and I almost fell over. He grabbed me about the waist and helped me down, but his hands stayed put on my hips.

"You okay?" he asked

"Yes. Fine. Please let go," I said, but I whispered...so he didn't let go right away.

"Make me," he said, and leaned his head in like he would kiss me again.

I turned my head.

"Never again, Levi. Never again," I said.

It was only then that he let go and walked away. How my heart ached for him.

So to say I'm confused would be an understatement. I'll leave it at that and say thank you for your advice. Your caring means more to me than you will ever know. And you made some valid points that I had not thought on. Food for thought is always a wonderful thing.

Speaking of which, did you see the article in *Reader's Digest* by Ayn Rand? About active vs passive people? Here's what it says in a nutshell. That we are American because we are individuals, but we can only be productive in society if we *act* as individuals. If we are passive, the world goes by, and those that act can act in terrible ways without any of us interceding. So, we must all act! Fascinating.

I'm using her analogies in my mind almost every day. It is the best thing to do in terms of helping Robert. I will actively support him here at home by helping to make his community, his country, a better place through my speaking engagements. And I need to keep my heart open to Levi. Not open the way it wants to be. Not romantically. But friends, like it should be. Like it always was. It would do no good to stay here and turn my heart and my body to stone. You have to try and trust me. The only thing I'm risking here is a broken heart. And to be quite honest, it's already broken. It broke those days in the hospital while I watched my boy go from alive, to half-dead, to half-alive. I am steeled against sorrow now. At least I think I am.

I'm planning a letter to Roylene.

I love that you care.

With deepest respect,
Glory

P.S. As a peace offering, and in hopes that my madness hasn't changed our friendship (and a bit of me eating a "Humble" portion of it myself...) here is a wonderful pie recipe I found. I hope you enjoy it, Rita.

Mock Apple Pie (This one feels like a magic trick!)
Prepare a 2-layer pie crust
14 saltine (soda) crackers broken into pieces
Cook and cool the following:
1 1/2 cups water
1/2 cup sugar (or corn syrup)
1 teaspoon cinnamon
1 1/2 teaspoons cream of tartar
3 tablespoons lemon juice
1/8 teaspoon nutmeg
Place crackers into the unbaked pie shell. Pour the cooled mixture over

the crackers. Cover with the second layer of the pie crust. Bake at 325 degrees until crust is light brown.

(One would never know there were no apples in it!)

=====

January 29, 1944

IOWA CITY, IOWA

Dear Glory,

There's this boy, Ted, who comes down to the USO club to pass the time until he figures out what to do with himself. He lost an eye in Salerno, and wears a patch just like a pirate. His family owned a farm but sold it in the '30s, and now his father manages our local hardware store. I'm sure Ted will work there once his mind recovers, but for now he's content to count cans of sweet corn and roll bandages with us housewives.

At first we avoided all war talk around him, figuring it was impolite, but then it became clear he wanted to discuss his experiences. I can't say it's enjoyable to speak with this young man, but it is an education.

One particular comment he made sticks with me, and I want to share it with you. Mrs. Hansen's youngest, Vaughn, asked Ted how many Germans he killed. Ted's remaining eye watered up, and Mrs. Hansen moved to console him, saying that fascism must be stopped, and he had every right to kill the enemy—it was his duty as a U.S. soldier.

I'll never forget what he said to her: "It might be my duty to my government, my brothers and my God, but it still don't make it right."

Now you may think I'm being purposefully obtuse, but you know I like telling stories, and it might be worth your while to pay attention to that boy's sentiments. What he'd done offended his personal morality, the one deep within his heart. When you feel weak in spirit, think about the agreements you made with yourself about how to live an honorable life. We all have them, but unfortunately the contracts are often written in invisible ink when they should be signed in blood.

Okeydokey. Enough said about your situation. I will return to it, though, so I'm giving you fair warning. (Toby says when I've got a discussion I feel is unsettled, I bury it like a squirrel does a nut in autumn. It will certainly see the light of day again.)

Now go kiss those sweet babies for me. And tell Robbie to send another drawing—I need something sweetheart-y for Valentine's Day!

Love, your bossy friend,
Rita

===

February 10, 1944

ROCKPORT, MASSACHUSETTS

Dear Rita,

It's been a year plus, dear friend, since we began our letters. Did you notice? What a year. What a crazy mixed-up year. God knows what He's doing. He knew I would need someone...and there you were, at the bottom of a hat.

Thank you for your honest opinion of my situation. In all fairness I do know that what I feel for Levi isn't right. But somehow, and I don't know why this is, my love for Robert grows as my love for Levi grows.

But, if it makes you rest easy...there's been nothing more between Levi and me since New Year's Eve. And we've had plenty of moments that tried both our constitutions, let me tell you.

Every night Corrine and Robbie pray for their dear daddy, clutching his photograph to their hearts. It's a beautiful if not odd sight. Levi, big and strong...his arms encircling two small tots. Praying to a picture of my soldier husband. All of them honest with their love. I wish you could see it. I wish Robert could see it, or maybe I don't. It's all so confusing.

Sometimes it just takes my breath away and I turn the corner and lean against the wall, the sobs catching silently in my throat. How I long for the way it used to be. How I miss those days before the war when Robert and I were newlyweds. I can still remember bringing him to this house and sheepishly asking if we could make our home here. "I thought you'd never ask," he said. Everything from those days seems bathed in golden summer sun. Even the winters.

Damn. It makes the sorrow take off on winged horses.

So enough of it. You will be my moral compass, but I can't promise you I'll fly a steady course.

And don't stop reminding me of all the things I need to be reminded of.... I don't have anyone else. Anna tells me to embrace my feelings for Levi so that I can let them go. But what does *she* know of men? Really.

If you see that boy again (Ted, from the USO), you kiss him smack on the lips for me. You kiss him and tell him that our bodies do things that our minds don't need to take notice of. No notice at all.

Now…I've enclosed a letter to Roylene. Please give it to her. Thank you for suggesting it.

Love,
Glory

P.S. Have you purchased your seeds yet? I found this magazine article that boasts it can sell all the seeds you need in one shipment. Should I trust it?

February 10, 1944

ROCKPORT, MASSACHUSETTS

Dear Roylene,

I hope you don't mind me writing to you. Rita (Mrs. Vincenzo) has apprised me of your situation. May I take a moment to commend you? It takes a brave woman to face this kind of thing head-on.

I suppose I just want you to know you are not alone. I, too, have found myself in a preposterously difficult situation. But unlike me, you get to face your fear, walk into it. Be active inside the new life that waits for you. It's like a storm, isn't it? A storm with sun shining on the other side. And there you are, braving it like a hero.

Well, I'm here. If you need anything. And I don't judge. And I don't cast stones. I'm just a Ladygirl who likes to listen.

Gloria Whitehall

February 14, 1944

ROCKPORT, MASSACHUSETTS

Dear Rita,

I forgot to enclose Robbie's sweetheart in the last letter. He padded into the kitchen this morning and found it tucked into a stack of papers on the kitchen table (my new desk).

"You didn't send Auntie Rita my valentine?" he said, his innocent eyes brimming with tears.

"Oh, love! Mama forgot!"

And do you know what Robbie said to me? Out of the mouths of babes, that's what they say, isn't it, Rita? I almost dropped the teacup I was holding. And that would have been a shame, because it has a sunflower on it. I bought it last week in honor of you. So here's what he says to me, that little smarty-pants: "Like you forgot about Daddy?"

Oh, Rita. When you are right, you are right. Three and a half years old and he's a font of truth. What have I done?

This war. It's stolen our peace. It's stolen our tomorrows as well as our yesterdays.

Here is your valentine, Rita. A red heart on a paper doily. My

Robbie loves you and he doesn't even know you. Maybe he can just feel how much *I* love you.

Children are wise.

Love,
Glory

―――――――――

February 19, 1944

IOWA CITY, IOWA

Dear Glory,

Thanks for whatever you said to Roylene in that letter. It didn't feel right to read it (it wasn't addressed to me) so I folded the paper in half and slipped it to her in the alley behind the bar. When I explained who it was from she held it like I'd just handed her the Shroud of Turin.

She wanted me to include some lines from her in this letter, but I refused. If she wants to say something to you, then she needs to write a letter herself, even if she'll soon be cradling a newborn with one arm. I'm going to hold firm on that for messages to Toby, as well. I know there's a possibility writing is difficult for her, but isn't now as good a time as any to tackle that problem? Is that the active me talking? If she gives me something before I mail this, I'll include it. If not, don't take offense, as she is about ready to burst.

And, please write to her again if you have the time and inclination. A baby's birth does usher in a busy time in a woman's life, but it is a lonely time, too. The more people filling in those dark spaces, the better.

So…news on the Iowa front: I got a letter from Sal. In it, he drew a caricature of himself smoking a cigar, the proud grandpapa. Sal thinks Roylene, Toby and the baby should move in with us permanently when this war is over and done with. That man wants a full house, like the crowded apartment on Western Avenue. I haven't decided if I like this idea. Don't young people value privacy these days? Would you want me breathing down your neck?

Sal filled the rest of his V-mail with passionate declarations of his love for…the olive. Yessiree. Over the past few weeks my husband has gotten a tutorial on harvesting olives. This must mean he's still in Italy. I'm surprised the army didn't black out the entire message. Maybe the censors were too embarrassed for him to read the whole thing. You would have thought the olives looked like Betty Grable from the way he was going on.

In all seriousness, the letter cheered me. If Sal has time to pluck olives from a tree, then there must be a lull in his corner of the war.

I wrote back and told him I would plant an olive tree in our backyard if it would always put him in such an excited state!

I also told him about my new job. It's going remarkably well, given the deeply neurotic personality of my boss, Dr. Aloysius Martin. I think he applied for an academic deferment when the war started and regrets it every day since. He's obsessed with the war, and probably knows more about it than General MacArthur himself. "You can always volunteer," I told him. He didn't say a word to that.

He's posted a map of the world next to my file cabinet and one of my duties is to mark battles and what troop movements we do know about with pushpins. No wonder Florence blew out for California when she had the chance! I told Dr. Martin we had to be sure to lock the inner door because, with all the POWs coming into Iowa, what if one escaped and broke into his office? That map would be pure gold to a German spy.

Of course I was kidding, but the next day Dr. Martin handed me a black cloth to cover the map with before I left for the evening. It knocks out all the pushpins and I have to follow all the holes in the map with squinty eyes to put them back. So I guess the joke's on me!

So…about the one the subject I promised to avoid…

I've been hard on you, kiddo, but I think both you and Levi are making the right choice. Your family will be whole again soon enough, and these experiences will retreat to the place where we keep all those things that make up who we are…but we don't want to think about all that much.

Love,
Rita

P.S. When it comes to procuring garden seeds, I believe in sticking close to home. Try a local farmer—I'm certain he's got more than enough.

P.P.S. Has it only been a year since we started writing? I feel like I've known you a lot longer than that! I'm grateful you chose me, hon. I really am.

P.P.P.S. I'll let you know as soon as my grandchild makes its way into this crazy world.

February 19, 1944

IOWA CITY, IOWA

Dear Master Robbie Whitehall,

Thank you for the sweetheart, sweetheart. At first I posted it on the cabinet but it is so sweet it ate up all my sugar! Now it's on the icebox.

Be sure to send me more, Michelangelo (ask your mother). Spring is coming soon, will you draw me some flowers?

Love,
Auntie Rita

February 21, 1944

IOWA CITY, IOWA
(MORE SPECIFICALLY—*the maternity ward!*)

Glory,

It's a boy! Salvatore Whitman Vincenzo. Quite a mouthful, huh? Toby came up with the poetic middle name, but Roylene insisted on naming the baby after Sal. Funny, isn't it? I don't believe she's ever set eyes on him. I do appreciate the gesture and I told her so. The baby looks like his grandpa—thick dark hair and azure eyes as deep and fathomless as the celestial heavens. Grandpa Sal is going to be over the moon.

The poor girl had a rough time. We were sipping tea on the front porch when her pains started. That baby was in such a hurry, tearing at Roylene in its haste, until he realized the chaotic world he was dropping into. Then smart Little Sal dug his feet in, refusing to come. Of course, all I saw were the nurses scurrying in and out of her room, features strained with worry. I paced the ward like a nervous father-to-be, alone, until Roy showed up looking for trouble. "You're gonna wear a hole in that rug," he said, and I reluctantly settled next to him on a hard-backed bench. We sat, fidgety and silent, until he said, "I guess I lost my best worker for a few weeks. War or not, your boy is responsible for that."

I felt every muscle in my body tighten. "This is hardly the time."

"Soon enough," he muttered, extracting a pack of cigs from his cuffed sleeve. He didn't offer me one, and left to smoke without another glance my way. Which was fine by me. I spent the next ten minutes devising methods to strangle him without getting caught.

It's getting dark now, but Roy hasn't come back. Roylene is spread across the bed like a wet dishrag, but there's a lovesick smile on her face, even in sleep. My grandson dozes next to her, his tiny chest rising and falling, the bit of peace he brought with him casting the room in a silver glow, the color of hope.

It's beautiful, Glory. It really is.

Rita

February 23, 1944

IOWA CITY, IOWA

Dear Mrs. Whitehall,

Thank you for sending me a letter. You didn't have to do that, but I'm glad you did. I keep reading it over and over while I'm sitting here in the hospital. They say I have to lie in this bed a week. I don't see why, but I don't have it in me to walk out.

Mrs. Vincenzo visits when she's not working. Roy, my daddy, only came once, but it was enough. He did say I could stay in the house with my baby, only he called Little Sal another B word. I'm telling myself he will learn to love him, but he's still learning to love me, so it might take a while.

I don't like owing anybody anything, especially someone I don't know, but you said you like to listen, so I figure maybe you got some time you'd like to fill. Would you mind listening to me? I got some things I want to get off my chest, and no one to tell them to. I've been talking to Little Sal, but I shouldn't place such burdens on him, even if he doesn't know up from down. The morning before Little Sal was born, I got a V-mail from Toby. It made me cry, but I didn't know why. I waddled over to Mrs. Vincenzo's to show her, but then the pain started. Maybe that was nature's way of telling me to keep my mouth shut. I haven't shown anyone else, but I'm going to write it out so you can read it, and tell me what you think it means. I didn't shine in school, so I don't trust my own understanding.

Toby's Poem
In the days of boyhood, summer came late

and the fan hummed low
and I couldn't see past the sunflowers
Sometimes, here, in the damp heat
I wake and think I'm there.
But the hum doesn't drone
it grows
Airplanes, not out of boyhood dreams,
a nightmare sort of use
Clearing rows of passage
by massacring tall flowers
Spreading seeds of hate
for violent gardens
The enemy, my shadow,
Looked at me
loomed in me
and though my gun won
I lost
I will wake soon
in my summer room
And all this blood
Won't ever have happened.

Something's not right, Mrs. Whitehall. At first I thought he'd
written a poem for the baby, but no one would read this to a child.
I'd like to get your take on things. It doesn't seem right to ask Mrs.
Vincenzo.

Thank you kindly.

Regards,
Roylene Dawson

March 6, 1944

ROCKPORT, MASSACHUSETTS

Dear Rita,

My letter is a bit late because Robbie was ill. He's fine now, don't worry. But watching him fight, pale again. Gasping for air again. It tore another piece out of me. Soon I'll be a Frankenstein of worry. All patches and zigzag stitches of the girl I used to be. Like I said, he's fine now. But his recovery is slow. I hold my breath when he coughs. I'll be so, so happy to usher in the spring.

Now, about your news… Congratulations! A boy. I'm so happy for you. Please send my regards to Roylene and let her know I've sent a layette separately. I ordered it from the Spiegel Catalog. Did you get yours yet? I sent one in the package just in case you haven't gotten one. Their spring collection is just lovely. I hope you are getting a lot of time with that new baby. Corrine is a running terror now, just like Robbie used to be. I miss those quiet infant days. I remember being able to stare at my babies for hours on end, never knowing where the time went. Would you mind sending me a picture?

And, thank you for sharing your stories about Sal! An olive tree…oh, I'm getting one, too. Tell Sal that your silly, Able Grable of an East Coast pen pal is going to grow olives for him, as well. What a wonderful letter to get. I wonder about that so, so often. Those other memories the boys are making. Robert fills his with domestic things or life at camp. The food, the care packages, the nights when they all sit out and stare at the moon aching for home, smoking. But he doesn't tell me about battle, and he doesn't tell me about the culture. I wish he would. I'll write to him after I finish this letter and ask him some leading questions. Perhaps he'll take the bait and talk to me about where he is stationed. I'd love to know.

Things are getting awkward again in my home. How long did I think it would last? This ridiculous arrangement between Levi and I? Did I really think that we could be around each other every minute of every day without something happening?

Here's what happened. It was the first warm day. About a week ago. I asked Marie if she'd help me wash my hair outside. It's a habit I cling to from when I was a little girl. My mother used to wash my hair with a mixture of baking soda, rose water and apple cider vinegar out in the sun. I know it sounds smelly, but the vinegar dries free of any odor. And the hair is simply silky afterward. Anyway, I was sitting out in the middle of the yard on a kitchen chair waiting for Marie to come and rinse out the vinegar with warm water. I had the basin next to me and the cider had been sitting in my hair for a little too long. I called to her. I don't know what happened. Either she is unaware of what's gone on in this house, or she was simply too busy with the kids…but when the warm water began to run down my hair, rinsing out the acrid smell of the vinegar, it was Levi's hands, not Marie's, that began massaging in the rose water.

My first instinct was to jump. Or at least speak. But I couldn't. His hands felt so good in my hair. From the roots, up to my scalp. His strong hands. Those hands I held and trusted when I was still a little girl. Those hands that rinsed my hair before…before we ever touched each other in inappropriate ways. Only now—now they stirred my soul.

"All I want to do is kiss you, Glory," he said. "Just one more time." His voice seemed to move as he poured more water from the basin onto my hair. Some splashed on my face and he ran his hands over my closed eyes, over my nose and lips.

It took everything I had not to answer him. Not to open my eyes. Because I knew that even if my intention was to scold him, my mouth would open to his mouth instead. So I stayed there. Quiet. Mute, even. And when he was done, he wrapped my hair in a towel and walked away.

I cried a river, Rita, but at least I kept my word.

It's hard. But it feels like a sacrifice that focuses my attention on the war more than any ration book ever could.

God grant me strength.

In other news: my speech went well at the Women to Work rally! I'm not so nervous anymore. Not like that first time near Christmas. I don't know why or how, but when I stand at that podium a surge of energy goes through me and I feel as if I could talk for hours and hours. I wish you could see me, I really do.

As for the garden, I did follow your advice and purchased my seeds from a local farmer. My entire dining room is covered in little greenhouses and every day the children and I watch for the first green sprouts to push up through the dirt. Mother is rolling in her grave seeing our fancy dining room covered in little buckets and glass slabs. Not to mention the smidgens of dirt always on the floor. But this is a garden house now. A garden house where people are waiting between what was and what is going to be.

All my love,
Glory

P.S. Give that baby a kiss for me. Tell him Auntie Glory sent it.

March 6, 1944

ROCKPORT, MASSACHUSETTS

Dear Roylene,

I am so pleased that you feel you can entrust me with such a task. You are being very brave and your actions are commendable. I wish you were closer because I'd have you come and speak to the women in our group. You are quite an inspiration. And I know it isn't something you feel you have a complete grasp on, but keep on pushing through. For Toby…and for you. Okay?

Now, about Toby's poem. First: I am so honored that you would share it with me. Really. I cried when I read it. What an amazing young man.

If I were to break it down for you I'd say this: Toby's longing for home. He wishes he was back in Iowa with you and with his Mom and Dad. And something's happened to him that makes him worry that even if…when…he does come home he won't be the same person he was before. Does that make sense? I think he's telling you he's changed. That something violent has happened.

If you write back to him, I suppose it might be good to let him know that there isn't any change that would keep you from caring for him. He's still Toby no matter what happens over there.

Please don't hesitate to contact me about anything else you may need. I'm here. Waiting like the rest of us. And these letters make the time go by.

All the best,
Glory

March 11, 1944

IOWA CITY, IOWA

Dear Glory,

Make sure to let those seedlings get accustomed to the outdoors incrementally. Plants resist change just as much as people do. Are your hearty perennials poking their sleepy heads through the soil yet? When your lemon balm comes back, pluck some leaves and make a tea for Robbie. This Garden Witch says it's good for promoting healthy breathing. Use dried chamomile for yourself. It calms the mind.

Don't worry about the timing of your letters. (Though your last one nearly had me reaching for the smelling salts. Maybe you should stick to washing your hair in the bath?) Difficult as it is, you obviously have your priorities straight, my dear. Time and devotion will heal Robbie, and it appears you are giving him ample amounts of both.

Roylene has taken to motherhood like a duck to water. She's back in that kitchen, peeling potatoes with Little Sal watching from a basket on the floor. I'm helping when I can, but you know how much a baby needs his mother at the start.

The gorgeous layette arrived yesterday. Thank you, hon, for your kindness. I walked the package over to the tavern and Roylene nearly passed out in the tomato soup when she touched the fine lace. I expect you'll hear from her soon.

Overall, Iowa City has been pretty calm. My job for Dr. Aloysius Martin (He's such a formal man I always feel the need to use his entire name!) has fallen into a steady, predictable rhythm. I know my duties, and I know what's expected of me, and when I shut the light off and lock the door I know when I return in the morning I will find the office exactly as I left it. I can't say the same for the other aspects of my life.

Besides a quick telegram responding to Little Sal's birth, Toby hasn't written. I also haven't heard from Sal since the "olive tree" letter. I like to think he's moved on to tomatoes.

On the homefront, Mrs. K. is causing trouble again. Only this time it's...complicated.

Last weekend we had a burst of unseasonably warm weather. I invited Irene and Charlie over to meet Little Sal, and for some iced tea and cheese rarebit (recipe to follow). The sun shone so brightly it seemed a shame to stay inside, so the three of us settled onto the front porch, leaving Roylene inside to nap with the baby.

Mrs. K. decided, at just that moment, it was extremely vital that she sweep her already immaculate front steps. I took the hint and called her over. She'd met Irene before, but not Charlie, at least not formally. I made the introduction and she offered him a limp hand. That should have been my first red flag. I quickly settled her in with a glass of iced tea and a heaping plate.

Then the interrogation began.

"How do you earn your living, Mr. Clark?" was her opening shot.

Charlie sells vitamins door-to-door. He was explaining this to Mrs. K. when she interrupted with, "Why aren't you serving in the armed forces?"

He told her about his perforated eardrum. Her eyes narrowed to slits and she fell into a ponderous silence.

Later, Mrs. K. volunteered to check on Roylene and Little Sal. When she returned she squeezed her generous hips between Irene and Charlie, so she could sit on his left side. She rejoined the conversation, but you would have thought Mrs. K. was a radio with a broken tuner, her voice kept dipping and rising so. But I knew what she was doing. It was my old trick to gauge Charlie's hearing abilities.

The sun finally set and we stood to say our goodbyes. Charlie stuck out his hand to Mrs. K., who wouldn't take it. "I'm not sure whether it's the scent of the past or a whiff of the future, but, sir, you stink of the jailhouse," she pronounced.

I wanted to die. Charlie still bowed his head to the old hag, but then hightailed it off my property with a confused Irene in tow.

I was furious with the old woman and I told her so.

"His eardrum is perfectly fine," she insisted.

I couldn't argue with that. I'd suspected the same.

Mrs. K. sensed her victory and stepped closer. "And did you see his shoes? How shiny they were? Who in this town has new shoes?"

I didn't have an explanation for that, either. Mrs. K. accused him of profiteering and said I shouldn't ever ask him back. If he is involved in the black market I *would* never allow him on my property again. I don't like "ifs," though. I should talk to Charlie, right? Talk to him without making it feel like a confrontation? But I guess that's what it will be, regardless of how I frame it.

Well, take care and write when you can, not before.

Love,
Rita

P.S. I heartily enjoy picturing you preach to the masses. In my imagination you have a clear, musical voice, and everyone listens intently, not even daring to cough. Don't tell me if it's not true— it's what I want to believe. So there.

Hearty Cheese Rarebit
1 pound grated American cheddar cheese (or, as Mrs. K. insists, Swiss)
1 tablespoon butter
1 cup beer
2 egg yolks, slightly beaten
Hot buttered toast or crackers
Paprika

Melt cheese and butter over hot water, slowly. When about 1/4 of the cheese has melted, add half the beer slowly. Continue to cook until cheese is all melted, stirring constantly. Stir in remaining beer into egg yolks; add slowly to cheese mixture. Stir constantly until thick and smooth. Serve immediately on toast or crackers, garnished with paprika.

———

March 21, 1944

ROCKPORT, MASSACHUSETTS

Dearest Rita,

Spring! Oh, beautiful (cold, dreary, icy) New England spring! My plants are growing and I just can't wait to put them in the ground. It's not safe to plant most things until Mother's Day…and that seems a world away.

Rita, how I enjoy your stories of Mrs. K. I've begun reading them to Levi…I hope that's okay. Not your entire letters—those belong to me. But your stories! My goodness. You should pen a novel while you're sitting at that desk. I love to think of you there at work.

Making all the women in your life, in your town, realize that it's possible to leave their kitchens and be active members of society.

Here in Rockport things are waking up after the long, icy winter. The church bell tolls almost every day. I've stopped being able to attend most memorial services. Too many boys are dying. It seems like a lie. Like an impossibility. And the war itself seems stuck in the mud of a European spring. Robert says it feels like "two steps forward, three steps back" all the time.

I've been a wizard in the kitchen. I love to cook. I think it's so *odd* that every week now I make speeches trying to liberate women from the shackles of wifely serfdom…at the same point in my life where I'm learning just how good I can be at homemaking. I've learned to sew, knit and crochet. (Truthfully I used to do these things with my nanny, but I haven't revisited the skills as a grown woman.) I know you probably do all these things better than I do, but I've made you something. I hope you like them.

Overalls. Yes! I've taken men's overalls and pulled in the midsection and shortened the length. I've completely guessed at your size. (If you need them bigger or smaller just send me your measurements. Look at me, assuming you will like them.)

I've taken the liberty to embroider some vines and flowers on the legs and bib. I've made them for the women in town, and they are quite popular. Who would have thought such things were possible. Such joy coming from overalls.

I love wearing them with Robert's old flannel shirts. And I never wear my hair up anymore (only when I'm cooking). And I don't even try to have it cut or tame the curls. They just fall all around me. Levi tells me Robert won't recognize me. I don't know if that's good or bad. That situation is still holding…but it's so, so complicated, Rita. I can't even tell you.

Anna is getting older by the day. It's a sad thing, watching someone so vital begin to age rapidly. Marie has taken over the Sunday masses, but I'm in charge of almost all the organizing now.

And did you hear? They've begun allowing students at Radcliffe to attend classes at Harvard! When I heard the news I immediately thought of a good use to that abandoned house of mine in Cambridge. I've decided to turn it into a boardinghouse for women who want to go to school but can't afford it. I've gone so far as to speak with some architects about possible renovations, and I've applied for the necessary permits.

Someday, mark my words, women will be allowed into elite colleges. Harvard was my father's alma mater. And I would have loved to go. But no matter how much money or power you have in society, women are always excluded. Is the university where you work coeducational? I sure hope so. Someday I'd like to set up scholarships. In my mother's name.

All my best,
Glory

P.S. As soon as the lemon balm revives I'm going to make your tea for Robbie. I'm certain it will put pink right into my son's cheeks. Thank you so much for being my darling Garden Witch

—————————

March 25, 1944

IOWA CITY, IOWA

Dear Glory,

Oh, your package came today and I had to write immediately. I adore your gift. Thank you ever so much. Good, strong fabric is hard to come by, and my pair of dungarees has just about disintegrated. You got the height right, but I'm going to take the waist in an inch or two. Turns out rationing is good for one thing besides feeding our troops—trimming my figure! I'm about the same size I was before I had Toby—imagine that! I can't wait for Sal to see the newly svelte me.

I was delighted to hear about your philanthropy. The University of Iowa—I'm proud to say—has always allowed women to attend. In the first group of students, one-quarter were women. That was a century ago—do you feel the turmoil of the past few decades has made folks less open-minded? That's certainly something to think about, and definitely something to fight against if the answer is yes.

Providing young women with opportunities is as wise an invest-ment as putting your money in oil or automobiles. We don't know what the world will be like after the effects of this war settle. Will Hitler have his New World Order? I don't like to think so. However, the world will be a new place, with all the shifts and realignments that come with change. We best prepare *all* of our citizens for that.

I was fifteen when the first war ended. I don't remember much about Armistice Day—my mother would not let me attend parades because she worried I'd catch the Spanish flu. I do have memories of my father saying he was glad he'd left Germany when he did, mostly because he understood the suffering that would befall the losers. ("To the victors goes the future," he said, or something like that.) My pop was a conservative man, fairly risk-adverse. We lived in a neighborhood we could afford surrounded by people who'd set up a small island of no-nonsense Germans in the middle of wild, lawless Chicago.

He called my mother his "Mäuschen" (little mouse). She did have a tiny frame and retiring demeanor, but also a tubercular cough, a sure hand in the kitchen and the kindest blue eyes I'd ever seen.

Occasionally she'd shave enough off the household budget to take me down to Marshall Fields & Co. for window-shopping and lunch at the Walnut Room. One day, a few months after the war ended, she told me to put on my best dress—we were headed downtown.

It was winter, but late in the season, when the sharpness in the air is replaced by the promise of spring. We strolled down State Street, arm in arm, and I remember thinking I was going to order the chicken pot pie, even though I always did.

But then we walked right past the department store. I tugged on my mother's arm but she was surprisingly strong, pulling me over to where a policeman stood absentmindedly tapping his baton against his open palm.

"Sir, could you please tell me where I can find the Prison Special tour?" she asked in halting, overpolite English.

He leaned over her, I thought, because her voice barely rose above a whisper. Then I recognized the curl of his lip and the cruel gleam in his eye. It was the expression of a boy I knew at school who liked to push me in the mud.

"Go home, lady," he said in a rough Irish brogue, poking at her shoulder with one thick finger. "Don't be bringing your daughter to see those harlots."

My mother turned seven different shades of red. "Come, Marguerite," she said to me, and we wandered the streets of Chicago until we spotted a large, agitated crowd. Many had signs shouting "Votes for Women!" and "Suffrage Not Torture!"

A group of stern-faced women stood on a dais with a Prison Special banner flapping high above their heads. My mother fell into contemplative silence, so it was up to me to piece together what I was looking at. I stood very still and pitched forward, trying to hear every word.

After a while the circumstance became clear. These women had spent time in prison for exercising their first amendment rights. They'd been abused and humiliated. A few wore prison costumes— horribly rough calico dresses with rags pinned to the waist.

They exhibited more energy and passion than any women I'd ever met.

We listened, my mother and I, until the chilled earth seeped into our shoes and our cheeks stung with cold. When the speeches were done and the rally began to disperse, my mother placed one gloved hand on my arm, squeezing until I looked her in the eye.

"Sie sind nicht eine Maus," she said.

You are not a mouse.

My mother would be so proud of what you are doing, Glory, as would your mother.

As am I.

Love,
Rita

———————

March 30, 1944

ROCKPORT, MASSACHUSETTS

Dear Rita,

My hands shake as I write this letter. The most horrible thing has happened. Well, not the most horrible thing. No one (close to me) has died.

But I went to a memorial for another boy I knew growing up. A neighbor of Levi's. I felt I needed to go and support him. Levi cried silently through the service, his body steeled against the internal shaking. The grief and the shame radiated off him like August sunlight. I left the children with Marie, and as it turned out, that was a VERY good decision.

After the mass I held Levi close. Closer than I've allowed him in ages. We sat in the pews after everyone went down to our local coffee shop for the reception. He placed his head against my chest and I murmured empty words of solace. Right there in God's house, I comforted him. All he could say was, "Why can't I go? Why can't I go?" and I cried, too. For him…and for the boy who died…and for Robbie. May he never be kept from doing anything he feels he must do.

Afterward, we went to a local coffee shop. (The proprietor closed it for the family whose house is too small. It was really so gracious. If there is one thing this war is doing it's helping us be more human to one another….) I approached the boy's mother to pay my respects.

And she slapped my face.

"I'd spit at you if I could, you tramp! Who do you think you are? Who do you think you are with your house high on your hill and your deeded ocean rights? Making speeches telling our daughters to go to work instead of staying home—which is their godly duty? JUST WHO DO YOU THINK YOU ARE fooling with a man who is not your husband while that husband is at war? We know you! We ALL know you!"

The room went dead silent. She shook with sobs. Her husband looked at me, and there was apology in his eyes which—I think—hurt me most of all. And then he ushered her out of the shop.

I began to walk…and then I ran. I ran, Rita. All the way home. Down Main Street. Through the rotaries, I ran where only cars should go. And then I ran up my private road to my house on the hill.

And she's right.

Who do I think I am?

Glory

P.S. And, I've only just realized something that I hadn't before. If this town knows, then Robert will find out. Oh, Rita. I'm in a big, fat mess. One of my own making, but a mess just the same.

—————

April 3, 1944

IOWA CITY, IOWA

Dear Glory,

When I got your letter I truly hoped you'd found mine waiting for you when you returned from your walk. Consider it an embrace from across these many miles.

I can't condemn someone for talking through grief. That woman felt her sacrifice gave her the right to speak to you in that manner, but it doesn't mean her opinion is a correct one.

Even so, being slapped with someone else's reality is still a slap. What did it awaken in you? An awareness of the harsh nature of cause and effect? In some ways you've allowed this woman to construct her opinion, and though it may be as flimsy and unstable as a house of cards, the deck was comprised of your actions.

So act differently. Those three teenagers dancing under an indulgent moon? They're gone. Let them go. The fairy tales spun by the past have no bearing on our present. History is telling us to. Your current life demands it. That woman says she knows you? Impossible. You don't know yourself yet. But you will.

You are capable of so much, hon. I don't always agree with your choices, but it's a sign of your growing spirit that you continue to make them…and cheer the outcome or suffer the consequences. Unfortunately, you are doing the latter right now, but in no way should that stop you from figuring out where you fit in this changing world.

And poor Levi. He needs to find his place, as well. This war has so many casualties, including his self-respect. It truly is the touchiest of topics, the boys who stayed home. I thought you were absolutely right in your observation, however ironic, that war gives so many opportunities for kindness. Can you find a way to be a good friend to Levi without wrecking your marriage? You must.

As for Robert, I believe honesty is ultimately the best route. That said, I haven't always lived by that belief. Secrets are strange, volatile things, often bursting into the public sphere at the most inopportune times.

I'm seeing this play out before my eyes with Charlie and Irene. They've grown uncomfortable around each other since that ill-fated meeting with Mrs. Kleinschmidt. Charlie's secret—whatever it is—is a knife scraping at the slender rope tying them together. I know Irene wants to ask him questions, but I fear she already believes the worst scenario her feverish brain can envision. For her, it's more tolerable to suffer through this strange purgatory between a healthy and broken relationship than risk an actual confrontation.

Charlie's got the itch to run. I can see it in the way he sits—back stiff, legs folded, feet on the ground, palms down and ready to push off. The thing is, it's taken me a while to figure out what's in his heart, but I honestly think there is good in there. Or at least the good far outweighs the bad. It's only in the telling of his secret that the burden will release, for both of them. It's up to you to decide whether or not releasing yours will do the same, for Robert, Levi and yourself.

So my advice for the day is this: brush your hair, put on lipstick and go into town for a walk. Hold your head high and your spirit higher. Remember the words of our venerable First Lady: "It takes courage to love, but pain through love is the purifying fire which those who love generously know." (I snipped this quotation from her newspaper column years ago and keep it along with a bunch of others by my bedside. Sal teases me about it, but I've caught him reading them. I think he's got a crush on old Eleanor. But then again, who wouldn't?)

Take care, dear.

With love,
Rita

———————

April 5, 1944

IOWA CITY, IOWA

Dear Mrs. Whitehall,

I'm writing to thank you. I have never seen something so beautiful as the baby clothes you sent. I'll wrap Little Sal in the blanket on his christening day, which should be soon. I wanted to wait until Toby got back, but Mrs. Vincenzo said a new soul can't go too long without the Lord's blessing.

Everything is going all right, I suppose. I'm back at work in the kitchen with Little Sal to keep me company. Funny, I thought everything would change after he came along, but not much has. My daddy doesn't pay me one lick of attention unless I have to take a break to feed the baby, then he hollers until I come back. It's a miracle my milk hasn't dried up. For the most part, the days go by the same way. I make the same old food. The same customers come and go. Some tickle Little Sal's chin, but most act like he's not even there.

Toby says I am an important person because I'm keeping the world even—he's destroying God's green earth in this war, and I'm adding new life to it. I felt good thinking about that until I got your letter telling me about Toby's poem. It got me thinking that I haven't done enough. I worry this new life is too far away from Toby to do him any good. Hiding away in the tavern isn't helping him any, either.

Mrs. Vincenzo told me about your preaching. She says you're finding your way through helping others. She said you have more love in your heart than you have people to give it to. I think that's a good way to be.

Regards,
Roylene Dawson

April 11, 1944

Telegram to Marguerite Vincenzo
from the Department of War, U.S. Government

THE ARMY DEPARTMENT DEEPLY REGRETS TO INFORM YOU THAT YOUR HUSBAND SALVATORE ANTHONY VINCENZO COMBAT MEDIC FIRST CLASS WAS KILLED IN ACTION IN THE PERFORMANCE OF HIS DUTY AND IN THE SERVICE OF HIS COUNTRY. THE DEPARTMENT EXTENDS TO YOU ITS SINCEREST SYMPATHY FOR YOUR LOSS. ON ACCOUNT OF EXISTING CONDITIONS THE BODY IF RECOVERED CANNOT BE RETURNED AT THE PRESENT. IF FURTHER DETAILS ARE RECEIVED YOU WILL BE INFORMED. TO PREVENT POSSIBLE AID TO OUR ENEMIES PLEASE DO NOT DIVULGE THE LOCATION OF HIS BATTALION.

JOHN MCGOVERN, ACTING ADJUTANT
GENERAL OF THE ARMY

April 12, 1944

IOWA CITY, IOWA (VIA EXPRESS MAIL)

Dear Mrs. Gloria Whitehall,

My name is Irene Wachowski and I am a friend of Marguerite Vincenzo, as I believe you know. I'm sorry to bring such bad news in this impersonal manner. The enclosed telegram was copied in the office of Dr. Aloysius Martin. He owns a photostat machine.

On Tuesday afternoon, Marguerite did not show up for lunch. When I went to Dr. Martin's office to investigate, he said she did not come to work, which is unlike her. Concerned, my friend Charlie and I walked to her home.

She was in a very bad state, as you can imagine. Apparently, the death notice came as she was having her morning tea. I found shards of the cup all over the front yard, a tea stain on the sidewalk and Margie locked inside the house with the curtains drawn. Charlie coaxed her into opening the door a crack, but she would not come out and would not let anyone in.

I offered to send a telegram to the Vincenzo family in Chicago, and to you, as I know you've grown close. She went hysterical at the idea of you getting a telegram, and made me promise not to send it.

After a while Charlie and I were able to get into the house. He sat with Margie while I slipped away, running back to the university with the telegram in hand. I went directly to Dr. Martin's office and informed him of the tragedy. He immediately granted her a leave of absence. While in his office, I asked to use the photostat to make a copy of the telegram for Sal's family in Chicago. I made an extra for you. I found one of your letters on Margie's dressing table and copied down the address.

I asked to stay with her last night and she refused, quite violently, and pushed us from the house. She doesn't want to speak with or see anyone. She said she was going to stay put and let the sunflowers grow over the house, blocking the doors and windows and light.

I fear for her mind, Mrs. Whitehall, and I'm not quite sure what to do. Mrs. Kleinschmidt is sitting watch on Margie's front porch today. I'll head over there after work with Roylene and the baby. Charlie will take the night shift. If she won't let us in the house, though, we can't help her much.

Marguerite had such love for him, and I can't imagine the pain she is experiencing. Please write to her. One thing I can do is slip a letter under her door. At this point, I'll try anything.

Sincerely,
Irene Wachowski

═══════════

April 16, 1944

ROCKPORT, MASSACHUSETTS
(VIA EXPRESS MAIL)

Dear Irene,

I hope you don't mind the informality of using your first name, but I feel as if I know you. All of the people in Rita's life feel that way to me. Like close, close friends. So thank you. Thank you for letting me know about Sal. I did my grieving before I wrote these letters. Enclosed you will find one for Roylene. Will you give it to her? I'd appreciate it. And then a whole stack for Rita, too. I think your idea of slipping a letter under her door is a good one. I've expanded that idea (outlined below). Also, I've sent this package of letters via Express Mail. I hope they get to you swiftly.

Now, I've become quite the organizer of late, and I feel my skills kicking into high gear. I've concocted a plan of sorts.

* The first letter to Rita has a tiny "1" on the back of the envelope. Slip that under her door the first day. There are four more. Slip one under the door at the same time (I think morning is best) each day consecutively, okay? I hope this isn't too much to ask.

* I need to write a letter to Toby. Can you provide me with his V-mail address? There is a part of the plan I need his help with.

* Can you and Charlie begin to work Rita's garden? Work loud and joyfully so that she can see and hear you.

I think...pray...hope that my little plan works. She needs to survive this. She needs to survive it for Toby and for you and, well, for me.

I love her, Irene. I love her like she's my own dear mother, or older sister. I don't know when or how it happened but I don't think I could go on if she wasn't going on as well. My own friend Anna (an older woman who's taken me under her wing) told me that Rita might be a "Soul Sister," someone I've known through many lives. I believe it. Truly.

My first reaction is to come there. To get on a train, or in my car and just GO. Run to her. (I tend to run when I'm upset...) But I can't. I don't know how much Rita's told you about my boy Robbie. But whatever she's told you it isn't the whole story. I've been shielding her a bit from the whole truth. She's grown fond of him through my letters, and there's no need to spread sorrow around during these tearstained years, right? Well, he had a cold in late February which aggravated his heart condition. He spent most of March in the hospital under an oxygen tent. He's recovering very slowly. But he is a pale boy who spends his time wrapped in blankets and staring out windows. He stares at the yard he used to run through with wild abandon. He presses his tiny hands against the glass.

I cannot leave him. And I cannot bring him. So I cannot come.

This said, I do believe we might have some luck with this plan of mine. (Started by a grand idea from you!)

I've enclosed money so that you can send any correspondence back via Express Mail, as well. Please don't be offended by it. If you don't need it you can just send it back...but I felt like this particular situation called for skipping a bit of etiquette.

Yours in peace,
And with heartfelt thanks,
Glory

April 16, 1944

ROCKPORT, MASSACHUSETTS

Dear Roylene,

Please write Toby another letter. He's going to need you. His childhood is gone with his father dead. He needs a good reminder of who he is. I know you spent time with him before he left for training. Maybe you can help him recall a funny moment the two of you shared? A story he told you while keeping you company in that kitchen? Maybe something about the baby?

As for a response to the last, wonderful letter you wrote to me: Roylene, you have no idea how much I needed you to share with me that little bit of Rita's thoughts. It's like I've seen her through glass and you threw open the window and let me reach through and touch her. And if there were ever a time I needed a clear view, it's now.

I'm so glad you liked the layette and I am honored he will be christened in it. Thank you. I am here for whatever you need in the future. I am far away, and you don't know me, but in some ways I feel Rita's family is my own. Please don't ever hesitate to contact me with questions or requests. And please call me Glory.

Love,
Glory

April 18, 1944

V-mail from Gloria Whitehall
to Sgt. Robert Whitehall

Dearest Robert,

My heart is so heavy today. I received news that my friend Rita has lost her husband to the war. For some reason, this news brought the reality of what is at stake for all of us right into my kitchen. Please come home safe, Robert. You have two young children that need to know you, need to grow up with you by their sides. They need to learn to ride their bikes and dive off tall cliffs with their father. Not me. Not Levi. You.

How on earth will Rita recover? Why does her new grandson have to grow up in a world where that wonderful man is a memory, instead of a real, live grandfather?

I know I've said it before, but I'll say it again. Don't go out of your way to find danger. Stay safe. You became a hero the moment you enlisted. You have nothing more to prove.

And know that I am here and waiting for you. If I didn't understand what waiting meant, I do now. It's an active thing. Full of worry and solid, heavyhearted memories. I remember you, Robert. I remember your hair and your eyes and your beautiful smile. I won't forget again.

All of my love and prayers for peace,
Ladygirl

LETTER 1

Dear Rita,

I'm not going to pretend that I don't know about Sal. Irene sent me a letter notifying me. There are no words I can give you to comfort you over these many miles. I know that the place you need to be is deep inside your heart where Sal still lives.

You can dance with him there. And that's what you are doing, right? My darling Garden Witch, you are dancing in your heart with your husband and he is home with you in that house. I know a thing or two about ghosts.

Here is my only request, dear friend.

You close those curtains. You dance with Sal. Make your peace and let him know how much you love him. Don't let anyone tempt you out into the world until you are ready to be there. Okay?

When my father died I saw him in the garden the next day. In our house in Connecticut. He liked it best there. It's the biggest and the finest.

I saw him clear as day smoking a cigar and reading the newspaper.

I told my mother and her eyes got wide. She didn't reprimand me or even tell me she didn't believe me. You know what she did? She ran straight through the servants' kitchen into the back gardens calling his name. She called him by our last name. "Mr. Astor! Mr. Astor!" she shouted.

She needed to spend more time with him. Their love was untouchable. It never let me in. But it was glorious to watch.

You stay with Sal.

I'll write soon. And I'm here. You know I'm here.

Love,
Glory

━━━━━━━

April 20, 1944

V-mail from Roylene Dawson
to Seaman Tobias Vincenzo

Dear Toby,

I'm very sorry about your father.

I saw his picture in the paper with the notice. I knew his face. When I was about twelve I started working at the tavern, doing the sweeping and cleaning. Your dad came in once in a while for a sandwich. He liked to do a trick where he would find a nickel behind my ear. Do you know it? He always let me keep the coin. I had eight or nine of them before he stopped coming. I don't think he liked my pop.

Well, I took those nickels and bought a scrap of fine lace, cut it in two and sewed the pieces around the tops of my socks. I wanted to make a dickey but I figured my pop would notice, and anyway, the socks made my shoes look better.

I hope your ma can find some peace remembering the good things about your dad. I don't know if I'm supposed to tell you this but she's not doing so good. She doesn't leave the house. We're trying to help. Everyone is. I even held Little Sal up to the front window, but she won't come out.

I'll write again soon.

Your Roylene

———

LETTER 2

Dear Rita,

When I got home from that terrible moment at the coffee shop your letter wasn't waiting for me as you hoped it might have been. It came a few days later and you know what? I needed it more by then. I'd had a few days to grow more and more unhappy about all the decisions I'd made so far in this adult world. I felt, for the first time, that I'd taken on too much too soon. Who was I to think I could be this grown-up woman? It's a burden I (naively) wasn't expecting.

When I was little my parents threw glamorous parties. The summer parties here were my favorite. All the help would put tables outside and string up paper planters. I liked to run around and watch them. All the hustle and bustle of the big event. And I adore the idea of making the outside work like inside rooms. I wish I could live outside. I truly do.

Anyway, after Franny put me to bed I'd sneak back out and climb into the willow next to our yard. I watched and listened to those magnificent affairs.

And one night...one night my father looked right into the tree and caught my eye. He knew I was there. And you know what he did? He *winked!* Really. I never felt so close to him. He gave me his approval right then and there to buck the rules and the trends of society.

When I got home that day (The day the mourning mother slapped me across the face? Yes, that day), the first thing I did was climb that tree. You see…I'm trying to remember who I am.

And when I got your letter I thought long and hard about what you said about the lipstick. I looked at myself. Stared for a good two minutes at this strange woman I've become. And then I consulted Anna.

This is what she said: "Sometimes the parts of us that we don't like are useful."

So I started to think about my shameless behavior. My disrespect for both Levi and Robert. How much I hate to admit my own wrongdoing. Burying it under mountains of other things…I do that well, bury things. I am able to turn a blind eye to what bothers me the most. I get it from my mother. And truly, I dislike that ability.

But…it sure is useful.

And—if I am to "be a lady" it's only logical that I look like one when I'm in public. She also told me this: "Many times the world isn't ready for change. It has to be eased in or else it will be resisted. Change takes patience." Just like with the plants. I introduced them to the sun and wind, little by little. And they're doing fine.

So your life is changed now, Rita. And you need to ease into it. But just don't get stuck. We all need you.

OH! And guess what happened? Silly Glory…I did make a mistake…I planted sunflower seeds in my makeshift greenhouse. (Did I tell you? Levi is building me one in the yard. Says my fine mother should have her fine dining room kept nice for posterity.) Anyway…those seedlings grew too fast and got all leggy! I didn't know you just have to wait and put them in the real ground—the terra firma—so that they can root and grow up properly. Hide in the dark soil until they are good and ready for the sun. Oh, those wonderful sunflowers. So wise.

Love,
Glory

April 26, 1944

IOWA CITY, IOWA

Dear Mrs. Whitehall,

I've delivered two of the letters. Margie still won't come out of the house, but she is taking what the milkman brings, which is a good sign. The curtains haven't moved an inch, so Charlie and I talk very loudly when we are working in the garden. (Charlie speaks rather loudly already—his hearing is damaged.) Mrs. Kleinschmidt told us to stop making a racket, but I'll bring a brass band down the street if it'll get Margie to step onto the front porch. Roylene brings the baby daily, and watching her press his little hands against the front window would thaw even Stalin's wintry heart.

This is so unlike Margie. She is not prone to dramatics, which makes this worse to see. Charlie thinks we should just break in and drag her out into the sun, but I said no. She needs time. However, there are limits. After I finish your deliveries, if Margie still has not come out I will take Charlie up on his offer. It's not healthy to stay inside like that. Also, her canned food must be running out. I will stop by the USO to pick some up for her, to leave on the steps. I don't feel bad about taking it. She's just as much part of this war as the next person.

Thank you for being such a good friend. I know you would come to Iowa if you were able. I'm very sorry about your boy's illness, and pray he makes a complete recovery.

Best regards,
Irene Wachowski

P.S. I've enclosed Toby's V-mail address. Hopefully it won't take too long to get to his ship, though I've heard it could take weeks. I don't know if Margie has gotten anything besides Toby's telegram acknowledging his father's passing. It came early in the morning and Charlie intercepted it before the delivery boy could ring the bell. He wrote "not bad news" across the front before sliding it under her door. I suppose that was not necessarily true, but it was what he thought to do at the time.

LETTER 3
Dear Rita,

Boy! Do I have a story for you! Guess what I did? Well, remember when I went to the farmer to buy the seeds for my garden? He offered to sell me chickens. I said no that day. But thought on it... and realized that collecting eggs is one thing I could let Robbie

do. Also, feeding them won't take much effort. So Levi and me...
we built a coop and then went to pick up some chickens. A rooster,
too! But I have to keep them separate. You know all about this
stuff, I'm sure.

When you are feeling a bit better, will you give me some advice
on chickens? I trust you so, so much about these things. Well...
everything, really.

Robbie is getting better with pencils and he wanted to add
something to my letter so he drew a rendition of the chicken coop.
I've tucked it inside. Do me a favor? Just smell that paper! Don't
you remember the way that pencil lead smells on paper? I bet Toby
brought you home all sorts of essays and poems when he was small.
This smells just like the inside of my desk when I was a schoolgirl.

Okay, so the chickens were here and then I SWEAR I put them
in the coop and locked the gate. But a few minutes later Corrine
began laughing and pointing from the porch. Low and behold there
were chickens EVERYWHERE.

So there I was, running all over my yard like a loon, trying to get
those damn chickens back into that coop. I wish you'd been there.
It must have been quite a sight. And it reminded me, quite abruptly,
of a moment with Claire Whitehall, mother-in-law extraordinaire.

When Robert and I were first married I fired my entire household
staff. And when I found out I was pregnant I refused to hire a nanny.

One night when we were visiting with my mother-in-law in
Beverly, she had a little talk with Robert. I was tired and lying down
on her sofa. I suppose they thought I was asleep, but I heard every
single hushed word from the kitchen.

"You must have her reconsider, Robert! What does that girl know
about housekeeping? About mothering? That woman, Corrine
Astor? She was a reformed harlot who barely knew she even had
a child!"

"I don't order Glory around, Mother," said my sweet Robert.

"But you will have to do the work, too, son. And you married well. I may not approve of the girl herself, but I DO approve of her finances. I'm sorry to sound crass, but that's how I feel. If you are going to marry money, why not spend it?"

Robert was silent for a moment, but his next words came out fierce and between his teeth.

"My Glory is not her money. There's never been a girl less aware of what she is worth. She's wild and free. THAT is why I married her. THAT is why I love her. I will never, ever try to pen her in. I will never cage her capacity for greatness. AND we will NEVER speak about this again."

I've tried so hard to live up to those words he said. Because at that moment I didn't see that girl he was describing. It wasn't until I met you that I began to feel like he might have seen something besides a honeymoon kind of love.

So, returning to the question of "JUST WHO DO I THINK I AM?" I am Gloria Astor Whitehall. That's who I am. And I chase chickens and grow my own food. And I am a philanthropist. And I can be very odd. My son is sick all the time. I'm deeply in love with my husband as well as my good friend Levi.

My best friend in the whole world is Marguerite Vincenzo. And she recently lost her husband in this great and horrible war. She's mourning now. But soon, very soon, she will realize that her world is too big to ignore. There are sunrises that bring days of gardens and pins on maps. There are friends who are being harassed by Mrs. K. because it's Marguerite's job to annoy Mrs. K.—no one else can do that.

Mostly though, I miss her.

Love,
Glory

LETTER 4

Dear Rita,

Have you peeked out your window yet? I wonder what kind of mess
Irene is making out there. I don't know a lot about your day-to-
day life in Iowa, but I do know that YOU are the Garden Witch.
So you must have the nicest garden. Without you...I bet the rows
aren't straight.

Have I ever told you about my mother's hair? It wasn't curly like
mine. It was long and straight and thick. Black silk.

She used to let me brush it for her. Before she went to parties.
She had this beautiful, enormous dressing table full of perfumes
and pots and jars of powders and rouge. I'd stand behind her and
want to linger in those moments forever.

At the end of her life, when she was nothing but skin and bones
(the cancer made her so sick; her pain was so bad that no pain
reliever could touch it) she still had magnificent hair. I was brushing
it when she died. I knew the moment the air left her chest. But
you know what? I kept brushing her hair. I didn't stop for I don't
know how long. Someone came...and then a doctor gave me some
medicine that made me sleep for a long time. The next thing I
remember clearly is waking up and seeing Robert. There was this
mist in my eyes. Made everything foggy. Surreal. And then...I
looked at his shining face (it was literally shining, in the sunlight
from a high window) and the mist sort of...evaporated.

Is there mist stuck in the corners of your eyes, Rita? It will go
away. You can let it go. The mist doesn't hold Sal there. It keeps

him locked up. And it's time for him to fly into the heavens so you can see him as he is supposed to be seen.

Have you ever seen the autumn leaves up close? They are pretty... but spotted and imperfect. And you can't ever find ALL the colors together. Only the bright red, or yellow, or orange.

But if you look from far away at a hillside or mountain...there it is! In all its majesty. The full impact of autumn flora.

Let him go and you will see him clearly. I promise.

On another note...my chickens are not laying eggs. I need you.

Love,
Glory

May 1, 1944

V-mail from Gloria Whitehall
to Seaman Tobias Vincenzo

Dear Toby,

Please let me introduce myself. My name is Gloria Whitehall. I am a friend of your mother's. We met writing letters to each other.

This is a bit awkward as I feel I know so much about you, and I'm sure you know next to nothing about me. Suffice it to say that my husband is fighting this war, as well. And your mother and I have developed a strong bond because of the absence of our beloved heroes.

I'm sure by now you know about your father. I am so sorry for this tremendous loss. Please accept my deepest sympathy.

But this is not the reason I'm writing to you.

Your mother needs you, Toby. She's taken this news in an unexpected way. We all expect Rita (she likes me to call her Rita) to be tall and wise and strong. Stoic, even…but she's fairly crumpled under the weight of this enormous sadness. I've tried, through flimsy pen and paper, to draw her back into life. But she still struggles with your father's ghost.

I think (and I am by no means right about most things…) but I DO think that a note from you…something from your childhood? This might just do the trick.

Well, that's it, I guess.

Be safe, Toby. She needs you to come home safe. Don't look for more trouble than necessary. Okay?

With love and prayers for peace,
Glory

LETTER 5

Dear Rita,

The first thing I wanted to do when Irene contacted me was to come to you. Run to you. But I can't do that no matter how much I ached for you. And it makes me feel awful.

But I know that YOU of all people can understand my reason. It's Robbie. I can't leave him, Rita. He needs me. He is my son and he needs me.

I probably shouldn't share this with you…but Roylene sent me a poem that Toby wrote to her. She didn't understand the words… what he was trying to say. So she asked me to "translate" it for her.

I wish I had the right to share his poem in its entirety, but I don't. I can, however, share with a clear conscience my own interpretation.

Toby is homesick. And he remembers his boyhood with a fondness you might not be able to fully grasp. What a life you made for him! And he's afraid that he's changed. Something must have happened to change him. His fear is that everything will be different, that there won't be a home to come home to.

How will your boy find his way home without a talisman? And who better to be that talisman than his mother?

Rita. If you are still locked up in that house…throw open those windows and dust your boy's bedroom. Wash his sheets and let them dry in the spring breeze. Do it all the time so when he comes home they are fresh. Make his favorite meals. Prepare for his homecoming.

Because Toby will come home. God won't take them both. And when he comes home you damn well better be ready for him.

Get OUT of there, Rita Vincenzo! You are not dishonoring Sal by going on with life. You honor him by taking care of Toby.

Sal needs you to be prepared to take care of your son. His mind, his body. His soul. And you can't take care of someone's soul if yours is lost.

Write to me, Rita.

Write to me while you wash his things. Tell me how to care for my chickens. Yell at me about Robbie. Ask me for one of my speeches. Scold me about my wild hair. Tell me about the night you gave birth to Toby. Or day?

All of my love,
Glory

P.S. Robbie painted you a dove. Irene has it. If you want it, you better ask her for it.

———

May 5, 1944

ROCKPORT, MASSACHUSETTS

Dear Irene,

Please call me Glory. I suppose there's a whole lot of differences between Massachusetts and Iowa, but I feel so close to you. Don't ask me why. I don't really know why....

So by now my plan has hatched. I hope it worked. And if it didn't...yes. Have Charlie bust down that door. She has a son to take care of. And a grandson, too.

And I know a thing or two about taking care of sons. I can't tell you how much I appreciate your update. I am so grateful.

And thank you. Thank you for taking the time to work Rita's garden. It would be such a shame if it went sour. It's as alive as she is.

Well, I guess that's that.

Let me know what happens.

Yours in peace,
Glory

P.S. I've been aching to tell you this. It's my fault. All of her hysterics about the telegram. When Robbie was sick in the hospital I sent her a telegram without thinking. I won't ever forgive myself. Especially now.

May 6, 1944

IOWA CITY, IOWA

Glory,

Thank you.

The sun feels good.

Sing to your hens. Talk to them softly. Chickens scare easy, but they'll lay eggs if you don't give up.

And you don't give up, do you? Those birds are lucky.

This bird is lucky.

Love,
Rita

May 9, 1944

IOWA CITY, IOWA

Dear Glory,

The boy who delivered the telegram was beautiful. I watched him come up the road, my eyes following his path as he passed each house and rejected the address with a quick flick of his head before moving to the next, like a hummingbird in search of the flower which holds enough nectar.

His skin shone with health and the hair peeking out from under his cap was dark gold, a shade deeper than Toby's. I spent a moment worrying Toby's hair had darkened in the year since I'd seen him last. I decided it would still suit him, took a sip of my tea and studied my nails, disappointed in what typing had done to them. My mind visited the two colors of nail varnish in my bathroom cabinet, and I tried to decide which I liked better.

The boy approached the gate and I smiled and gave a little wave. His response was a twitch of the shoulder. His hand would not come up and his eyes would not meet mine.

And I knew.

The first part of my brain to respond chanted a quick prayer: *Not Toby, not Toby, not Toby*. It didn't occur to me that if God listened to my plea, then Sal's name would be on that telegram.

I felt the slip of paper in my hand. I must have signed the book. I don't remember. I read, mouthing the words like a young child.

Then I screamed. I know I kept screaming because the boy backed into the closed gate, wincing with fear. I yelled for him to go, shrieked, but he wouldn't budge. Later, I remembered they aren't supposed to leave a recipient alone after bad news. He was simply following guidelines. But I couldn't reason, Glory. I thought he might have another in his bag for me, the final one that said no one would come back, that the war had taken them both.

I threw my cup down and ran. With the door closed behind me I could breathe again. This was Sal's house. Our first house together.

He would come back if I willed it. If I shut everything else out and filled the room with memories, the past could become the present, and I could live there, with him. I would never leave.

What I was really doing was building a tomb. I have no body to bury. Sal could be anywhere. I needed him to rest. I had to draw his soul to me.

When I got your first letter I knew I was doing the right thing. And I did dance with him.

When I got the second, I thought about the things I did not like about myself. They were the very things that made Sal trust me enough to marry me. I had to do right by my husband.

When I got the third, I thought about a sweet, pale little boy drawing a chicken. I thought about a baby's palm pressed against my window, a boy named for his grandfather.

When I got the fourth, I did take a peek through the curtains to watch Charlie and Irene. They were digging holes for two tomato plants much too close together. The roots would intertwine. If one died and I had to tear it from the ground, the other would only survive if it could burrow into the soil with the roots that remained.

When I got the fifth, I found my mourning dress and buried it under a heap of junk in the front closet. Then I found my gold lamé dancing dress and cut a star from it. I sewed it over the blue one. Tragedy might not shine, but my husband did. More than anyone else. I rehung the flag in the window.

And then I walked out into the sunlight.

Thank you for bringing me there.

Love,
Rita

May 15, 1944

V-mail from Seaman Tobias Vincenzo
to Marguerite Vincenzo

I see the moon
and the moon sees me
and the moon sees someone
that I want to see
God bless the moon
and God bless me
and God bless the somebody I want to see.
I miss you, Ma.

—Toby

May 15, 1944

V-mail from Seaman Tobias Vincenzo
to Roylene Dawson

Dear Roylene,

Thank you for your letters.

I'm sorry for what I said in mine. You're right—a boy should know his father. It's just, I can't stand the thought of being introduced to him through a photograph, or a letter, or one of my ma's crazy stories.

I want him to touch flesh and blood. I want glorious recognition when I look into his eyes. I know what it's like to reach out for my father's solid hand and only get a fistful of memories. And Little Sal would get secondhand ones, at that.

Oh, baby, grief has made mush of my brain.

I can't help my mother. Writing words on a piece of paper isn't enough. I tried, but my hands shake, and everything I put down seems weak and lacking. I did send something, but I want you to do me a favor. Go over to the house and squeeze her, hard. Say it's from me. I know this might embarrass you, but the thought of you doing it will help me sleep at night.

Please send my regards to Miss Wachowski and tell that Charlie fella I appreciate his helping out. And thanks for the story about my dad. Do you still have the socks? I'd like to think you'd kept them.

I think about you day and night.

Toby

———

May 15, 1944

*V-mail from Seaman Tobias Vincenzo
to Gloria Whitehall*

Dear Mrs. Whitehall,

Thank you for writing.

Your name was not new to me when I got your letter. My mother has been writing about you for a year now. The first time she did, she called you "Mrs. Gloria Whitehall of Rockport, Massachusetts." I must admit I disliked you immediately because 1. You had obviously captured the attention of my ma, and 2. You had a definite place in the world. I do not. I am on a ship. I'm no longer Toby Vincenzo of Iowa City, Iowa. I'm not allowed to tell you where I am. I probably couldn't do that anyway.

And now my father has no place on the map. The only one of us who does is my ma. I need her letters to remind me. I need her.

It's my understanding that you helped keep her standing on solid ground when she found out about my dad. That you somehow held her in place.

I can't thank you enough.

Sincerely,
Toby Vincenzo

────────────

May 16, 1944

ROCKPORT, MASSACHUSETTS

Dear Rita,

I'm so glad you emerged from your house and turned your face toward the sun. I was worried, to say the least. But then, I worry all the time. It's some sort of low hum in the back of my mind. Do we all have it? A nation—a world—of constant worry?

I worry all the time about receiving my own telegram. Thank you for extending me the courtesy that I so rashly did not extend to you last year. I feel even more foolish now, if that's possible.

I worry about the boy who delivered your telegram. All those boys delivering all that bad news. What memories will they bring with them into their lives? Too much worry all around.

So…I suppose the best thing for both of us to do is to just try and move ahead. We can't move on…that's impossible. But we can go onward.

And so it's the middle of a beautiful spring here in Rockport. I don't know how to explain the beauty of my garden. The amazing growth. How things can be so healthy when the world is so in trouble I will never understand. Things have slowed down quite a bit here. Fewer people show up for the Women to Work meetings. Everyone is so busy with their own housework and end of the school year preparations. Also, after that hard winter, I think people are busy being outside. It makes me wonder if I should start to hold outdoor rallies. Maybe even move some of them to Boston as I believe people are becoming tired of me here. What do you think? Should I spend more time there? It's about three-quarters of an hour by train. An hour if I drive.

Did I ever tell you that I drive? I love to drive. My father taught me how when I was thirteen. He was drunk and annoyed with some people during one of mother's "Grand Rose" events. He took me out to the back fields and let me tear up the turf in his Model T. He called me a "Speed Demon."

Mother wasn't even mad when he told her. He said, "Mother, our girl is a mighty Speed Demon!" And I remember my mother looked at him—not at me—and said, "It's good of you to teach the child. A woman needs to be as independent as she can be or else the world will use her skirts as handkerchiefs and then toss her in the garbage."

I was mesmerized by the story of your mother and the suffragettes. I know my mother was part of movements like that, probably because she was so unorthodox. But your mother was just a proud citizen who wanted her own daughter to know her own worth. This is important for me to understand.

I'm learning balance.

The days are long now, so long. Robbie is well recovered from his latest recurrence of the fever, and Levi found a specialist in New Haven (Connecticut) at the medical school. There is a trial of a sort of medicine that will hopefully stop the progression of the disease. We leave next week. Say a prayer.

The other day I was watching the two of them eat lunch on a red-and-white checkered tablecloth out in the yard by the garden. The sunflowers are as tall as Robbie now (he calls them Rita 1, 2, 3, 4, 5, 6, 7…too!) and Levi held Robbie's hand to his heart and put his own strong hand on Robbie's wispy chest. "My heart doesn't want to work sometimes, either. But see? I'm strong. I can do a lot of things," I heard him say.

But the truth is, they are very different conditions. Levi has a murmur. It doesn't even really affect him. And that is why he's so ashamed not to be able to fight.

Oh, well. Life does go on. And as the weather turns warm, my taste buds ache for the flavors of summer! I can barely wait for a plump tomato. I look every day hoping for an early yellow blossom that will promise a big, ripe fruit!

But until then…more beans.

All of my love,
Glory

Baked Beans
Ingredients:
2 cups navy beans (or your favorite dried bean—not lentils or peas, though, they cook too fast)
2 teaspoons salt

3 tablespoons brown sugar
1/4 cup molasses
1 bay leaf
1/2 teaspoon dry mustard
1/4 cup chopped white onion
1 cup boiling water
1/2 pound salt pork

How to make it:
Wash beans, then cover with water and soak overnight and drain well.
Cover with large amount of boiling salted water.
Boil slowly for 1 hour, then drain well.
Combine salt, sugar, molasses, bay leaf, mustard, onion and water, then add to beans.
Pour into bean pot.
Score rind of pork and press into beans leaving rind exposed.
Cover beans with more boiling water and bake at 300°F for 4 hours.
Remove cover for last hour of baking.

———

May 23, 1944

IOWA CITY, IOWA

Dear Glory,

I'm sleeping, breathing, washing my face, putting on clothes. I'm also back at work for Dr. Aloysius Martin. Is this living? I don't know. It's an approximation, and I guess that's good enough for now.

When I read about the medicine for Robbie, I immediately thought, *Sal, honey, investigate it when you get home.* I'm talking to him all the time, Glory. Don't call the white jackets yet, though. I know he's gone, but like I said, I drew his soul to me to rest, and he came. I haven't been leaving him alone much, but then Sal was always big on talking. And anyway, that's what I would be doing if I was going to church, right? Speaking with spirits?

I must say it's helping. So is Dr. Aloysius Martin. When I first returned he treated me like a porcelain vase with a small crack— one false move and I would shatter to pieces. He also took the map down. First thing I did was put it back up. I want to watch us win this war on the wall in front of me. It's heating up, but the result will be in our favor. I just know it. My Sal contributed to that. Dr. Aloysius Martin was enthusiastic, to say the least, and even bought be a new set of pushpins. He's also stopped being so nervous around me.

I like occupying my brain with talk of longitude and latitude, and I like the way a flat map allows one to take in the entire world at a glance. I haven't been outside this country. When we had a little time and money, we usually visited Sal's family in Chicago, or my cousin in Atlanta. Once, we took Toby to the Black Hills and watched workers carve away at Mount Rushmore. But that's pretty much it.

It shames me to admit this, but one of the reasons I was furious with Sal for enlisting was that he would see the world without me. When he'd write about North Africa or Italy I would grow jealous. I'm not proud of my pettiness. I've reread those letters over the past few weeks, and now I see he was trying to help me see those places, really see them, through his words, like a picture postcard. I've apologized to him for not appreciating his efforts. It's not enough, though. I'm going to have to find an olive tree that will grow in

Iowa. Charlie might be able to help me—he seems to have a knack for obtaining items no one else can get.

For some reason, I'm now comfortable with Charlie's possible criminality. Maybe it seems such a small offense in the grand scheme of things. Irene doesn't agree. She's downgraded her relationship with Charlie to "friendly acquaintance" status. They do seem to be genuine friends, and the only change I've noticed is they've stopped holding hands at lunch. Still, it bothered me that I hadn't been in my right mind when Irene made her decision. I showed up unannounced in the library yesterday afternoon, and convinced her to take a coffee break. It took a while to get her talking—it always does with Irene—but after a little prodding it all came tumbling out.

"I fell in love with the idea of having a man," she explained. "I realized a war was going on, and I was still sitting at the same desk, surrounded by the same books, living the same life I'll probably be living in twenty years. At first I was just excited. Then I thought he could save me from boring myself to death."

"I don't think you're the first to think it, hon," I said, patting her arm.

"It wasn't fair to make someone else responsible for my life. Especially someone I don't love. As much as I've tried to force it, he's not right for me. I couldn't keep on pretending he was." She paused, took a sip of her coffee. "I know you'll tell me the truth, Margie. Do you think I'm stupid? I'm thirty-nine this year—how many more chances am I going to get?"

I couldn't answer that question. How much do any of us know the future? I did say this: "You're very brave, and I don't want anyone to save you from yourself. I like who you are."

She smiled and went back to work. I hope she knows I meant every word.

Well, please write and tell me what the doctors said they could do for Robbie. I just adored the dove he drew. That boy is sure talented. I've stopped posting his work on my fridge and place it in a real frame instead. He's turned me into a real art aficionado!

Love,
Rita

P.S. The beans went over really well at the USO. I've got one for you. Mrs. Hansen from down the block brought it over a couple of weeks ago when I came up for air.

Mock Veal Cutlets
1 pound ground veal
6 tablespoons fat (or something oily)
2 cups cooked rice
1 cup thick white sauce (Some milk with butter and flour to thicken it—don't forget to season with salt and pepper. Can't anything be made better with a dash of S and P?)
6 stuffed olives, minced
1 teaspoon salt
1 egg, beaten
1 cup fine bread crumbs

Cook veal in 2 tablespoons fat until well-browned; mix with rice, white sauce, olives, salt and egg; cool. Form into cutlet shapes; roll in crumbs. Fry in remaining fat until lightly browned. Cover; cook slowly ten minutes. Serve with tomato sauce.

May 30, 1944

*V-mail from Marguerite Vincenzo
to Seaman Tobias Vincenzo*

Dear Toby,

I'm looking at the moon. The one you just sent my way.

Love,
Ma

June 6, 1944, D-Day

ROCKPORT, MASSACHUSETTS

Rita,

Are you listening to the radio today? I am. Everyone is. I can fairly hear the echo of the voices from one home to another. And the church bells, they woke me this morning. Can you believe I felt annoyed at being woken? Just for a moment, before I realized what was going on.

And did you hear him, our president? "Our sons," he called them. Hairs lifted all over my body as he spoke. It's as if I understand all of it for the very first time.

I've had a pen in my hand all day. Snatching up scribbles of profundities. How will this be remembered? I want to take it all in. Absorb every moment.

I know Robert's there, Rita. But then again I suppose all of us feel like all our boys are on those beaches. But I feel like it's just so close to the part of Europe where he was stationed. It'd make logical sense.

And I'm so PROUD! I'm proud of them. So proud of Robert. And worried. More than I've been. I'm proud and worried about all of them. That being said...

I can feel this war turning. We'll win this thing. Can't you feel it?

And I just can't shake the feeling that Sal is part of it. Some great swirling force changing the tide. He'd do that, your Sal. He'd win this war for everyone.

I guess there's nothing left to do but wait. The whole world is silent. We are all sitting here, listening. Listening and taking moments to run into town for a cup of coffee and some rehashing of news.

Speaking of news... I have wonderful news about Robbie! There is a medicine called penicillin that we can give him the next time he gets the fever. It should kill the bacteria that is hurting his heart. And though he won't ever be one hundred percent well, his chance of dying is greatly lessened. Those doctors at Yale are brilliant. Mad scientists, yes. But brilliant all the same!

I feel... Today I FEEL...some of that worry I was talking about rolling off my shoulders.

Oh, I can't stand this letter writing anymore. My nerves tie themselves into knots while I wait. Please write soon.

Love,
Glory

June 6, 1944, D-Day

IOWA CITY, IOWA

Dear Glory,

The Allies have liberated Rome!

I'm as proud as if Sal had opened the city gates himself. (In my imagination he did.)

I've spent the day glued to the radio. Is it wrong to feel relief even though the future is still not certain? I do, though. Immense relief. I slept soundly for the first time in ages last night.

And now I'm curled up in Sal's chair with paper and pen, writing to you while I wait for the president's speech. Roylene and Little Sal are here, keeping me company. The baby lies on a blanket examining his toes. Roylene is stretched out on the floor next to him, slowly writing her own letter—to Toby. She shields her words with one bony hand. I wonder what she's hiding.

What she doesn't realize is I don't mind if she's writing words of love. It's her job to remind Toby that he is alive. If she slips in a photograph of herself wearing a polka-dot bathing suit—or less— well, I'm all for it. My boy could use something illicit to think about, even if it is flat-chested, ninety-pound Roylene. Look at me! All this talk of liberation is turning my mind salty!

Charlie and Irene are coming for dinner (together, but not together), and afterward we're going to listen to the radio and pray. I'm sure you're doing the same in Rockport, as is everyone else in this great nation. It's got to have some power, right? Enough to give our boys the wind at their backs and solid ground beneath their feet?

Later…

Oh, Glory, he sounds worried. Still, the strength and intensity of his words made me want to crawl into the radio and grab hold of his magnificent voice. It could carry me to a better place. It could carry the world.

Our boys will hear it as they push forward. They'll hear the sounds of our prayers and feel the strength of our love and gratitude. They have to.

Fred Waring's group played "Onward Christian Soldiers" after the speech. Did you hear it? Usually that song makes me want to roll my eyes, but not this time. Charlie started crying, in the convulsive, soundless way that men do. "Don't you understand," he said after composing himself, "that's a funeral dirge for the first wave." We all thought about that, the many lives lost before we even opened our eyes this morning. I squeezed Charlie's hand, but he left the room shortly thereafter. Irene stood up and sat down and stood up again, unsure of what to do. Then Charlie came back, eyes red, looking miserable.

We all sat, frozen in place, as the radio droned on.

After a bit Roylene walked over to Charlie, the baby on her hip. Without waiting for permission, she plopped Little Sal down on his lap.

Charlie held him gingerly, using only his fingertips, as though the baby might break if he wasn't careful. He didn't give him back, though, and after a few minutes, Charlie's smile returned, and he drew Little Sal closer to his chest.

Seeing that baby in a man's arms did me in. I bolted for the kitchen sink, splashing cool water on my face so I wouldn't vomit. Before I could lift myself, I felt a consoling hand at my back, soft and warm against the thin cotton of my dress.

It was Roylene.

She wrapped her skinny arms around my midsection and

squeezed. "This is from Toby," she mumbled against my bosom. She held on while I cried, this wispy little sapling supporting a rubber-limbed, fully grown weeping willow.

It's dark and quiet now here in Iowa, bedtime for most, though something tells me I won't sleep quite as well tonight.

Love,
Rita

=======

June 7, 1944

*V-mail from Gloria Whitehall
to Sgt. Robert Whitehall*

Darling Man,

I've listened to our president and heard the news of D-Day. There is a fire in my heart that I can't smother. A worry...a knowledge I carry with me. I've kept my worry, my fear, my love for you, all locked up. And I've hidden behind so many things. And as I sit here, with the dark falling all around, I realize the rabbit holes I've dallied in. I'm sorry for evading you and all you do. I'm back on the topside of the earth now...and you have my whole heart.

I hope it's not too late.

Come home to me, Robert.

Love,
Ladygirl

[Letter never sent.]

June 11, 1944

ROCKPORT, MASSACHUSETTS

Dear Rita,

I went to town today to do my shopping at the open-air market and there were these men sitting around playing chess. They were having a wonderful discussion and I lingered over the cabbages and strawberries to listen. The gist of their conversations was this: "This is everybody's war, now." And I agree with them—it's never been so true.

I got your letter and was thrilled to see that in actuality we were listening to the radio at the same time! It's the little things that thrill me, that's what Levi always says. A certain slant of light, a delicate white trim on a previously red rose, a dear (as of yet unmet) friend listening to the same words at the same time.

I feel less alone. But really, I've felt less alone since all those moons ago when we began this lovely correspondence.

Day by day news drips in...too quickly. It must have been bad during those invasions, because the secretary of war has been efficient with those telegrams. So far, so good, here at our house. And the only issue is that we haven't had a letter from Robert. I'd feel better if we had a letter.

Truth is, we weren't even due for one, he writes so infrequently, so I wouldn't even be worried if those damn church bells weren't tolling every hour on the hour.

I've been thinking about all of you so much. With each ringing of that damn bell. I think of Sal and Toby. Roylene and Irene. Charlie and Mrs. K.... Of course, Robert is the first on my mind, but the rest of our collective brood wriggle their way in. How I wish I could meet everyone in your world. What do you think about a possible reunion of sorts? Can you use the term *reunion* when we have yet to meet? Well...that's what I want to do, that's what I want to look forward to at the end of this damn war. A meeting. All members of both our clans. Here, by the sea. Can we plan that? Let me know. Sal will be with us in spirit—I just know it.

All is wonderful here, Rita...as good as it can be. The garden is thriving. Robbie is better. He laughed. And there was no coughing afterward. I am so blessed.

Claire (my mother-in-law), came by the house the other day and I decided to practice a little of what I like to call "Rita's Good Sense."

I smoked my contraband cigarette and leaned against my porch while I quietly listened to her huff about all those "Artists" who didn't have any "Moral Compass."

You would have been so proud. I yessed her to death and, before I knew it, she was gone. Silence is a powerful tool. I need to practice it more. Much more. The funny part was that I (for the first time, God help me) watched her play with the children. She does love them, Rita. That's all that really matters, right?

How are you? Any word from Toby?

All my love,
Glory

June 13, 1944

IOWA CITY, IOWA

Dear Glory,

Our letters must be synchronized now. I got yours probably about the same time you got mine. There's something very comforting about that.

I've been thinking about Robert all day. Have you heard any news yet? The bravery of those men continues to astonish me. I don't think I really understood the word *hero* before now. And they are, each and every one.

I feel in my bones that Robert is alive. Don't ask me how I know—I just do.

I was so glad to read about the medicine for Robbie. It will make you all breathe a little easier. I would put my faith in a mad scientist without question—they certainly keep the world moving forward!

So…news on the Iowa front: Dr. Aloysius Martin promoted me to executive secretary. I'm not exactly sure what the new title means, though I have my suspicions he wants me to learn shorthand. Still, his wife used precious sugar to make a cake, and the Martin children came in to sing "For She's a Jolly Good Fellow," which made me laugh and laugh. It felt good to laugh, Glory. I don't do much of it.

In bigger news, Roylene and Toby are getting married.

Next month.

I'm not pulling your leg. Here's the story:

Last Thursday, Roylene snuck away from the tavern long enough to stop by for lunch. She looks even thinner, if that's possible. It seems Roy expects more from her now, maybe as a punishment, maybe out of general meanness. But being a mother changes a woman, and Roylene is no exception. She's sick and tired of Roy working her to death, but she's not going to hide out in that dingy kitchen waiting for her circumstance to change for one more minute—Miss Roylene is going to take action.

Over tuna fish sandwiches (extra mayo—I make mine with corn oil), I told her about the children's center at the USO—volunteers provide care while war wives help out in the factories. Plenty of gals around here make use of it, all in the spirit of helping out. Well, I used my pull to get Myra Mezick on the phone—she heads up our local program.

Roylene got to talking with Myra, asking questions and feeling her out, and everything seemed fine until our girl went silent. "No, ma'am? I mean, yes, I understand," Roylene finally whispered. "Thank you much." She returned the receiver to its cradle and turned to me, eyes brimming. "They only take married women. I can't lie about something like that."

What could I say? The world is not a fair place when you don't follow its rules.

We sat down for fruit pudding (recipe to follow). Roylene bowed her head and got to work putting away the dessert, but I think she didn't want to look me in the eye. I was too far inside my own head to console her, running through all the ways I could talk Myra into bending the rules.

Roylene was scooping seconds on her plate when we heard a sharp rap on the front door. It was Mrs. K., her mouth jammed into an expression I refer to as "early Mussolini."

She pushed past me without a how-do-you-do and made a beeline for a shocked Roylene. "You can get married," Mrs. K. announced. "You call that woman back and tell her to make a place for Toby's baby."

We're still on a party line, Glory. Mrs. K. must spend half the day with her ear glued to the phone, listening in on other people's dramas. She breathes so heavily I'm amazed anyone can hear themselves talk. Once, I interrupted my conversation to ask her if she needed medical assistance.

So Mrs. K. heard Roylene's entire conversation with Myra, and it got her goat. She remembered a human interest story she read a few weeks back in one of her magazines. Down in Kansas City is a lawyer who will marry young, war-separated couples by proxy. It's not legal in Iowa, but our fair-minded state will recognize the marriage nonetheless. It's on the up-and-up, according to Mrs. K., and only costs fifteen dollars.

"But that's not a reason to marry someone," Roylene said after Mrs. K. finished her explanation. "I don't mean no disrespect."

I spoke before really thinking. "It's not a reason, but it's a good excuse to bring it up. Did you want to marry Toby before this afternoon?"

Roylene smiled broadly. "Yes, ma'am. More than anything."

"Well, then, you might as well ask him."

You should have seen Roylene's face. She ran for paper and pen, and started writing out her V-mail proposal to my son.

I guess if you're going to break society's rules, why not keep breaking them?

I still haven't quite sorted out my feelings on this. On one hand, I did mean to encourage her. The marriage will be good for the baby and good for my boy—he'll have something to keep his spirits up. On the other hand...well, this isn't the way it's supposed to happen. I hope that's enough of an explanation.

Love,
Rita

Chilled Fruit Pudding
2 cups berries or cherries
1/2 cup sugar
2 1/4 cups water
1/2 teaspoon grated lemon rind
1/8 teaspoon salt
3 tablespoons cornstarch

Put fruit, sugar, 2 cups water, lemon rind and salt in a saucepan. Bring to a boil, simmer 10 minutes. Mix cornstarch with remaining 1/4 cup of cold water and slowly stir into hot mixture. Simmer 5 minutes, stirring constantly. Cool. Pour into individual dishes or baking dish. Chill and serve with freshly whipped cream.

June 27, 1944

IOWA CITY, IOWA

Dear Glory,

Loneliness is built into the fabric of this war, isn't it? When it gets bad I say a little prayer before I stick my hand in the mailbox, hoping against hope for something glorious. The "Rockport, Massachusetts" stamp on the front of an envelope means the clouds will part, revealing a brilliant sun.

The funny thing is, I don't really need the letters anymore to talk to you—we have whole conversations in my head. Do you hear me over there by the sea? Someday after this crazy war is over, we will meet. I look forward to that day, but to be honest the thought fills me with anxiety. What if you hate the way I pluck my brows? What if my voice blasts your ear like a foghorn, or I screech like chalk against a board? What if I have a horrible habit of interrupting or absentmindedly picking my nose? I'd be the last to know, right? What if…what if you just don't like the looks of me?

It's strange, isn't it? I'm familiar with the contents of every chamber in your aching heart, but I have no idea what your hair looks like in the sun.

We will meet someday. I know it, too.

But in the meantime…news from the Iowa front. We haven't heard anything from Toby yet. As far as I know, he's contemplating Roylene's proposal when he isn't scrubbing latrines and avoiding enemy fire. Roylene's been dodging her own bullets lately, so she hasn't had much time to pine.

Last Saturday morning, she showed up on my front porch with Little Sal and a shiner the color of dried prunes. It seems Roy overheard her discussing possible job opportunities with one of the waitresses and lost what's left of his mind. He gave the poor girl a good thwomping in the alley behind the tavern when she stepped out for a breath of fresh air.

Sal always said it takes a true coward to hit a woman, but I think it just takes a regular old son of a bitch. "That's enough," I said when I saw her face. I picked up my pocketbook and my sweet, rosy-cheeked grandson and walked over to Mrs. K.'s door.

She opened it wearing a housedress and pins in her hair. "Can you watch him for a while?" I asked. Mrs. K. began mumbling excuses in German, but I kissed that baby's soft head and handed him over to her awkward embrace. "He's no trouble. Roylene's got a bottle made and he takes lukewarm oatmeal."

We hit the pavement before the old warhorse could say *"nein."*

On the way to the tavern we stopped at Charlie's boardinghouse and Irene's apartment and asked them to back us up. Ted, the boy with the eye patch, ran into us near the co-op and asked what's what. When we told him he joined in, and I'm sure we were a sight marching down the sidewalk, kind of like Our Gang all grown up.

We had so much energy, Glory. It filled my lungs and reached every corner of my body, all the way down to my toes. I thought there was a distinct possibility that I could take on Roy myself, if that's what it came to.

Only he was nowhere to be found. We pounded on the locked door and called him out, but the bar stayed dark. Roylene hadn't brought her key, so we kept at it, shouting his name and demanding he come out and apologize. He didn't care one bit about marking that girl for the world to see, so we didn't give a hoot about airing his dirty laundry for all of Iowa City to inspect.

It was the middle of the day, so we didn't notice the flashing lights until the squad cars nearly swerved into our legs. Well, most of us didn't notice. Irene went white and tugged Charlie into the alley. That left Ted, me and Roylene.

The officers outnumbered us by two. It was only then that Roy came out of the tavern, his ruddy face crumpled up like a spent pack of cigs. "These people are trespassing on private property," he growled, his hair blindingly white in the sun. "I want them arrested."

Roylene squared her shoulders and stepped in front of him. "Pop, you're gonna need to change the way you treat me," she demanded. Her voice had a steel beam running through the middle. I didn't know she had it in her.

Roy stuck his hand out, like he needed to protect himself from an onslaught. "Arrest these vagrants," he said, spitting each word into the hot, humid air. The young cops gazed uneasily at each other. Roy pulled out his wallet and extracted a worn card with some signatures on it. "I hand over an envelope full of cash to the Officers' Fund every year, you understand me?"

"Yes, sir." The boys nodded. They talked to Ted for a few minutes, then sent him on his way because they wouldn't arrest someone who'd "already paid a great debt overseas." That left Roylene and me.

Well, we spent the next few hours locked up in the city jail, until an officer came to tell us we could leave with a fine and slap on the wrist. His sergeant didn't like the idea of two ladies sleeping on smelly, urine-stained cots like hardened criminals. Once I gained assurance Roylene would not have a spot on her permanent record, we accepted a ride to my house in the back of a squad car.

Of course, Mrs. Kleinschmidt stood watering her front yard as we pulled up. She held Little Sal tight against her bosom with one thick hand, the hose in the other. Her hard blue eyes stared at us as if she were etching the scene onto a photo negative for later developing.

I thanked the officer—who was really quite nice and old enough to be my father—and Roylene and I headed up my walk.

"Thank you much, Mrs. Kleinschmidt," Roylene said. She smiled weakly, her features etched with exhaustion. Mrs. K. reluctantly handed over the baby. Roylene thanked her again and headed into the house, Little Sal watching over her shoulder with round gray-blue eyes.

"You are not a good influence on that boy," Mrs. K. scolded over the fence. "Causing trouble. Working with a married man. Spending time with war profiteers." She clucked her tongue. "You don't act like a widow. Where is your black dress? Why are you wearing lipstick?"

I didn't have any fight left in me. "Thanks for watching our boy," I said tonelessly, and went into the house without a look back. Roylene put the baby down for a nap and I fixed the girl some cold chicken salad with sliced beets. I left her to eat in the kitchen and pounded the stairs to my bedroom. I found my gold lamé dancing dress and put it on, holes and all. I did my hair up in an elaborate twist, and put on a full face of makeup. Then I sat barefoot on my front porch and drank strawberry wine with Roylene until the sun fell all the way down. Mrs. K. was watching through the blinds. At least, I hope she was.

Roylene and Little Sal spent the night. This morning I asked if she wanted to move into my guest room. She said yes. I told myself it was for her and the baby's benefit, but who am I kidding? I've been cultivating solitude, as carefully as I do my garden and the sunflowers growing past my gutters.

I don't want to live alone, Glory. I'm afraid I'm getting used to it.

Rita

P.S. I haven't heard from you, and I hope everything is all right. I also hope this letter acts as a distraction if that's what you need at the moment. It's the least I can do for you.

———

July 1, 1944

*V-mail from Seaman Tobias Vincenzo
to Roylene Dawson*

Tire swing. Front porch. Whitewashed and sun-baked. Not a hint of sorrow in it. The three of us. Together.

Yes.

Of course I'll marry you.

Toby

July 7, 1944

Rita,

My telegram came. He's alive. Seriously wounded in action. In the hospital.

I was swimming down in the cove with Levi and the kids. It was Corrine's first time there…a baptism of sorts. She took to the water right away like a little chubby mermaid. Her hair has grown (finally) and the blond curls turned the color of caramel when wet. Just like Robert's. I was thinking of him. Wishing he was there to watch his children—Corrine so like him, Robbie so like me…. And Robbie was swimming, too. It was like a miracle. We were laughing and healing in the deep salty ocean.

The bicycle on the road above glinted in the sun. Caught in my eye like sand.

I swam for the rocks, and took the trail up the road. I ran fast, hiding behind trees…pretending I was a forest fairy. I kept thinking, *He'll go past the house, he'll go past the house,* but no one else on our road has anyone in need of a telegram.

I met the boy before he got to the door.

Has it ever happened to you, Rita, that you see a young person that you think you recognize, only to remember that it couldn't be that person at all, because you are all grown up? Well, for a moment that boy looked exactly like Robert when he was fourteen. Shaggy-haired, too-tall, graceless teenage Robert. All arms and legs. My love. But it wasn't him at all, was it? No. It wasn't.

In the time it took for him to meet me with his outstretched hand I lived two lives. One without Robert, and one with him wounded.

I'd not stopped (for fear of losing him in my sight) to towel off, so when I reached for the telegram, drops of seawater fell from my fingers and wet the paper before I could grasp hold of it.

Salt from the sea, not from my eyes as it should have been.

It's punishment is what it is. It's my fault.

I should be dead. Or in a hospital in France. I can no longer face Levi or this house or this town.

I'm going to Connecticut to be with my mother.

Glory

———

July 14, 1944

ASTOR HOUSE

Dear Rita,

It's cold in Connecticut. I won't close the windows and the wind feels more like March than July. How is it that this bed still smells of her, after all this time? I keep burying my head deeper and deeper into the down pillows to find her. What a rabid mind I have, that makes cheese out of everything I think I know. I'm a ninny. Did I have babies? Ninnies shouldn't have babies. Nor should whores. Only women like you, Rita. Only women like you should be allowed to have and raise babies. Maybe people like me shouldn't be allowed to even live among the rest of society. Maybe it would be better if the rotten apples fell from all the trees. I have holes in me. All over me like a moth's been at a sweater. I wonder where Robert's holes are. Through his eyes? His arms? Leg? Heart? Head?

Oh, my. I suppose I should begin again. You must think I've gone around the bend.

Do you like the stationery? So fancy. Just like my mother. She liked fancy things. I'm sitting up today (in her bed…but upright, which is an improvement and allows me to hold a pencil). I somehow managed to get from Massachusetts to Connecticut with myself and the children in one piece, though I don't recall much of the drive. I'm beginning to feel a little better this morning, though it's been a hell of a couple of days.

I hope my letter to you about Robert made sense. I jotted it down and handed it to Levi to post. He begged me not to leave. I couldn't even look at him. Looking at him seemed as bad as touching him. I thought I'd vomit and faint at the same time. So I did the only rational thing—I put the kids in the car and drove off like a mad woman. And even as I was driving—even in my grief over what has befallen Robert—I still could not get Levi's burning gaze out of my mind. God help me, Rita…if you could see him, perhaps you'd know why. The depth in his brown eyes. The smolder just beneath the surface. How is it that the mind and the body can crave two different things? I keep trying to talk to my mother, but she won't talk back. She's not a good spirit. Or she's stubborn. Either way, she's quiet. Maddeningly so.

I'd not been back here since her funeral. And you know when you revisit somewhere you remember being large, and then you go and it's much, much smaller? Well, that isn't what happened. The opposite, really.

This house—it's enormous. I think I had a better handle on its size when I ran through its halls as a child. It even has a name. Not overly original or creative. *Astor House.*

I couldn't believe how well kept the place is. I mean, I sign the checks for the caretakers each month, but I thought it'd be overgrown and dusty. Like a secret place or something. Dead like my mother and father.

Not so. It's perfect. It's like we never left it. Spooky, really.

When we drove up there was no one there to greet us, as I hadn't called or written ahead. So I opened the grand front door, my hands shaking, convinced the key wouldn't work. I was holding Corrine in one arm and Robbie was clinging on to the bottom of my spring duster. They were so quiet, both of them. No trouble at all. And then there we were, in the grand foyer. All the air came out of my chest. I sat down on a small chair by a marble-topped side table. The children sat at my feet. I don't know how long it was until the car was noticed and Michael and Gwen (the couple who takes such good care of the estate) came fussing. But I felt as if we were statues, the three of us. Me in my hat and gloves...hands folded properly in my lap. I stared off up the sweeping staircase, waiting for my mother to come down. And my babies sat so still. Little marble garden gnomes...quiet as clouds.

"Miss Astor, are you all right?" asked Gwen. I didn't know her well. I hired the couple after my mother died. But she seemed sweet in a ruddy sort of way. I didn't know how to answer her. I tried to form words with my mouth, but none came out. Michael cleared his throat.

"Gwen, why don't you see to the children while I put on a pot of tea?"

That's all it took. They are good people. People who realized I needed to sit there. Good enough not to ask me any questions.

Gwen swept the children upstairs with superb grace. They were laughing with her, I think. Glad to be away from my hand-wringing. Michael backed away from me. I think he wiped tears from his eyes as he left. I couldn't fathom why, but then I lifted my gloved hand to my own eyes and realized my whole face was wet with tears, wet enough to seep through the cotton. I had a dizzying moment where I thought perhaps I was still reaching for the telegram, but I wasn't. I was home.

I sat there, with my ankles crossed (the way Father always asked me to sit) and with my handbag on my lap and my driving hat pinned on. Like a visitor. And I stared at the staircase for a long time. Waiting for her to linger, lovely on the landing, and welcome me home. The stained-glass window on the landing soon caught afternoon light and the colors danced across my feet. I used to practice ballet here in this hall. Chaîné, chaîné, plié…and again.

I don't know what finally moved me. Boredom? The smell of something cooking? But my legs were stiff so I must have been there a long time. I walked through the drawing room on my way to the kitchens. Lifting a white sheet off my piano on the way. I touched the keys. Out of tune, sour. Like me.

The servant's kitchen, on the other hand, was warm and inviting. Michael tried to get me to eat some toast with my tea. But I couldn't. It was then that he asked me what had happened, and though I tried to tell him, I opened my mouth and the words wouldn't come. The tears. Only the tears. How disgusting it was. I don't know why I couldn't just contain myself.

Kind Gwen came down and then brought me back up to my childhood rooms. I stayed safely outside the door frame, just close enough to see my babies happily at play…so comfortable among all my old things. And just close enough for them to see me there, to know that I was still with them. But I couldn't go back into those sweet pastel rooms. Baby rooms. Rooms for my babies, not for me. I am no longer an innocent.

And to be quite honest with you, Rita—my thoughts went wild

as I watched them. I was thinking, *Who are those children? How does Miss Gloria Astor have children?* I thought I was going to be a ballerina, in France. I quit dancing years ago. After mother died… but still…maybe I should run away to France. Would everyone be better if I were just gone? Plenty of people I grew up with left their children in the care of other people to live lives abroad. Why not? Oh, but my heart wants to kiss butter off Corrine's chubby fingers. And kiss sweet Robbie on the forehead after he's gone to sleep. He smells of honey and cut grass, that boy. How did I get here?

I'd never leave them. And France is different now, I suppose. The world is forever changed by war. We are forever changed.

I walked toward my mother's quarters. "Are they made up, or empty, Gwen?" I was able to ask, though I didn't recognize my voice.

"You never told us what to do with her things, so the room is just as she left it. It's fair dusted, though, and clean as clean could be. I'm sorry, miss, if that doesn't please you."

Miss? I chase chickens. Really. I touched her face. "Please call me Glory."

"Yes, miss," she said before she left me in front of the double doors that led to my mother's suite. And then she turned around. "Don't worry about the children. Michael and me love children and we'll keep them safe and fed until you feel well again."

The first thing I did was open the windows. Because the smell in the room was about to make me faint. My mother, concentrated. Tea rose. Glycerin. Cigars. (Yes, she had that man's vice. Though she didn't smoke them outside her rooms.)

I didn't know what to do. And she wasn't there. And even if she was, she wouldn't council me, would she? So I crawled on her big four-poster bed, like I did when I was a little girl and they were in Europe. And fell asleep. With my gloves on.

The next few days were a blur. Gwen brought me coffee and

soup. But I had her draw the curtains. Make it dark. Like a cave. And I kept on sleeping.

But this morning? This morning I feel better. And I said to myself, "Glory, if there is stationery in your mother's bedside table, then you must write to Rita!" and low and behold when I opened the drawer, there was her stationery set. *Violà!*

So here I am. I have a lot to think about. I told Levi to phone me here as soon as he gets a letter from Robert or another telegram. I need to know the extent of Robert's injuries. I need to prepare for the worst.

I also need to know if I'll be able to care for him. Am I doomed to be the caretaker of the sick forever? Is that a selfish question to ask? Of course it is.

But the question haunting me more than any other is this: "How will I tell him about Levi?" I'm a harlot just like Claire Whitehall always thought.

I think I'll dress like her today, my mother. Wear her things and look in the mirror. Conjure her and demand advice.

I believe I'll be here for a bit. Feel free to write me here. The address is on the envelope.

Please don't worry too much over me. I'll be fine.

I also want to say that I read your last letter at a rest stop on the way here. I swept it into my handbag before I left Rockport. Tell Roylene congratulations! I am so, so proud of her. What a monumental decision. She's in my thoughts. Her bravery.

I'm trying to learn from her. I'm trying to be brave.

The sun plays games with its shadows here. My mind is working in waves. There's no more air left inside today. Maybe there will be more tomorrow. Rita, does the air have favorites? Does it choose to blow life into certain people and not others? Does God have favorites? How does He choose? How do any of us choose?

Glory

July 21, 1944

IOWA CITY, IOWA

Dearest Glory,

I am worried.

I know what it's like to draw in the sketchbook of memory. Everything is recreated with fine lines and precision, though the models are not in front of you, only remembered through the haze of fantasy and longing. It's real, but then it isn't. And it lies to you sometimes.

Don't get stuck there, hon.

Your letter made me think of that Fitzgerald novel, *The Great Gatsby*. Toby read it in school and loved the book so much he left it on my pillow for me to read. It crushed me. Oh, that Jay Gatsby, standing on his pier with arms outstretched toward the green light he never could quite touch. He hooked his hopes and dreams on to things unworthy of pursuit. That's the tragedy of his story.

Toby always said Gatsby was about the inability to accept change. That idea and the image of you wandering through the lifeless Astor mansion made me think of him, but that's where the similarity ends.

Unlike poor Gatsby, you already possess the green light—it's just buried under memories, fear and a war that has covered this entire world in ash.

It takes and takes, this war. But it has to give in some ways— it's the law of nature, isn't it? To keep balance in the world? Your husband lost something on the shores of Normandy, but you, you have been given an opportunity to see what you're made of.

I think you'll be pleased to find it's not just sugar and spice.

Thinking about you,
Rita

P.S. Thank you for your lovely words about Roylene. She's settling in nicely with Little Sal, and is seeking a job in earnest. We hadn't heard from Roy, but a few days ago he left a moldy apple crate on my front porch, filled with Roylene's personal effects: a few worn summer dresses, a hairbrush and a pair of wool socks with some lace trim she won't take off even though it's hot as Hades around here.

I doubt Roy's done with her. He doesn't seem the type to give up without having the last word. I just hope he sticks to words, you know? Words we can handle.

July 23, 1944

IOWA CITY, IOWA

Dear Mrs. Whitchall,

I heard you had quite a shock and I'd like to say I'm very sorry your husband was wounded in France. Can you tell him I'm proud of him? Even though he doesn't know me from the fence post?

Mrs. Vincenzo said you're feeling low, so I hope this next part doesn't seem crass given your circumstances. I'm getting married on August 9 in Kansas City (the one in Kansas). Mrs. Kleinschmidt set it up. I think she's scandalized by my unmarried state, to tell you the truth.

Anyway, I'm writing to cordially invite you. I know you can't come, but if I could have the world the way I want it, you'd be standing next to Mrs. Vincenzo in a fancy dress, watching me become a Mrs.

If you have any advice about living as a married woman, I'd be glad to hear it.

Regards,
Roylene Dawson

———————

July 30, 1944

OLD LYME, CONNECTICUT

Dear Rita,

The very day your letter arrived at Astor House (slapping me out of my self-induced lethargy and fruitless ghost hunting), something so ridiculous happened that I hesitate to write about it. But I have to tell you, because I need your level head now more than ever. I feel so awful that I rely on you so, and don't seem to be able to give you anything in return. From chickens to love, I ask and I ask. And you always answer. Not like my silent mother at all. More like the mother I wish I'd had. It's terrible to wish you had another. One should always be happy that they have whatever it is the Lord sees fit to provide them with. I'm just a greedy little Able Grable.

Well…guess who comes driving up to the front gates of Astor House in his blue Ford pickup? Levi. Levi looking like a movie-star tough guy ready to take on the world. His eyes were shining. He was so happy to see me.

My heart leaped and sank at the same time. I think it shaved ten years off my existence, I truly do.

And the strangest part was that I was sitting on the grand front porch steps, drinking my coffee and wearing one of my mother's long chemise nightgowns. The children were playing on the front lawn. Even before we saw Levi open the gates and then drive up the circular drive, I was thinking about how we were sitting out in the front of the house like visitors. Strange interlopers in a strange land. The children ran to him. He scooped them both up in one movement and held them close. That's when I realized what I've done. Will they run to their father like that? Have I replaced him completely with my playacting? I felt sick. And undressed. The chemise I was wearing was a pink-and-silver layered thing, chiffon and high-necked. But she was taller so I took some of her jeweled broaches and pinned up the hem, weighing down the fabric and draping it in a crazy fashion (also tearing it a bit). I knew I looked crazy. But not as crazy as I felt. Corrine Astor rose inside of me like a wild beast.

"Put them down, Levi," I said, rising to my feet.

He put them down and they returned to me like ducklings.

"I got the telegram from the war department, Glory," he said, clearing his throat. "And a letter from Robert, too."

I ran down the steps then. "Give them to me!" I shouted.

He gave me the telegram.

Oh, Rita, he's been paralyzed. My darling Robert no longer has the use of his strong, tall legs. But he's alive. And his mind is intact. I was relieved and broken in the same moment.

When I finished reading I looked up at Levi. "Now the letter."

"That was for me, Glory. Not for you."

What's that term men use when they've been tricked? Is it a sucker punch? Well, that's what it felt like. A punch in my gut.

"What did he say?" I asked, holding my breath, not wanting to know the answer.

"He wrote and told me that maybe you'd made the wrong choice all those years ago at the Sadie Hawkins dance. He asked if I thought you could fall in love with me. He said you deserved a real husband."

"And how do you feel about those words my wounded husband wrote to you, Levi?" I asked, a rage I didn't understand beginning to clog my throat.

He cocked his head, aware that he was entering dangerous territory by the tone of my voice. Then he looked off toward the horizon and scratched his head.

"I don't know how it makes me feel, Glory. He's my best friend, too. All I know is he's hurting. We have to make some decisions here…whether you like it or not," he said.

"And what decisions are those?" I asked. I wanted to hit him, Rita. Really. Why did I want to hit him?

"We need to decide what we will tell him and when. We need to decide how we'll welcome him home. And we need to decide if he's…"

"What? If he's WHAT?"

"If he's right," said Levi. "Right about you making a different choice. This is horrible news, Glory. But maybe there's a light in it. Maybe we can all have what we want in the end."

"You can't be serious," I said. And then, as I turned my back on him, "Get out of my sight, Levi."

"But, Glory…"

I returned slowly to the stone steps of Astor House with Robert's children hanging on my legs and ripping further the pink chiffon of my mother's moldy shift. And then I dashed the shine out of Levi's eyes by shrieking at him and making him leave. I made him go. I said horrible things.

You are right, Rita, we do need to go home. To Rockport. That's where I will face Robert and try to repair all the damage. The question becomes, will they both forgive me? Will Robert forgive my transgressions? And how on earth will Levi ever forgive me? I won't list all the terrible things I said but I'll give you an example: "Lazy good for nothing leech" might have been one of them. God help me.

Love,
Glory

July 30, 1944

OLD LYME, CONNECTICUT

Dear Roylene,

Congratulations! I'm so, so happy for you. Honestly.

I can't think of anything more I'd rather do than attend, but I have to wait for news as to when Robert might be coming home. And I received the news of what has happened to him, so I will have to prepare the house. He's been paralyzed, Roylene. He no longer has the use of his legs. But no matter what, his heart and his mind are alive and intact. So I'm lucky. We all are. I almost felt guilty writing to Rita. How can I have a husband alive when hers is dead? It does not seem fair.

Especially when I've been such a wretched wife.

Which is why I'm the LAST person on God's green earth to give you any sort of advice.

All I can say is…love him. And stay true. Remember, the past is the past. You can't live in it. You have to think forward.

I wish I'd known that.

I'm enclosing a little gift for you. I found it in my mother, Corrine Astor's, things. It's a bracelet. I know it's old-fashioned, but I thought it was beautiful. The blue sapphires in the centers of the silver flowers are the blue you need for your "something blue," and the antiquity of the thing covers "something old." But it's not borrowed. It's yours.

I hope you like it.

All my best,
Glory

P.S. Kiss that baby for me.

———

August 1, 1944

Dearest Robert,

I am here waiting for you. No matter what. Yes, we will struggle… but you are needed. I need you. The children need you. Don't give up, my darling. If you can't walk, I will walk. Your legs might not be moving, but your heart beats. And the last time I checked, that heart belonged to me.

Get well and come home. We will get through it all. All of it. Like we always have.

What you wrote to Levi is nonsense. You are still a man. You are Gloria Astor Whitehall's man.

I love you,
Ladygirl

P.S. I made the right choice at the Sadie Hawkins dance. Don't ever guess at that again.

———————

August 7, 1944

IOWA CITY, IOWA

Dear Glory,

This war is intensifying, and our world sits atop the roller coaster again, hoping this time to free-fall into peace. It's going to be a hard landing, though. Cherbourg, Saipan, Florence—I can feel the push and pull all the way in Iowa. Does it infiltrate everything? Are all of our lives becoming about surrender and liberation? Is that how it works?

It appears so, at least for us.

Robert has surrendered. So Levi is then liberated. But where does that leave them? Where does it leave you?

Levi will not be angry for long. He loves you too much. Do you still have tender feelings for him? He will deserve gentle treatment, because in many ways you are asking *him* to surrender. Would you be able to give up your chance at love without a fight? This situation is a lot for a man—even a man like Levi—to take.

Also, please be understanding of Robert's frame of mind. It's only been two months since he was wounded. That is not sufficient time to adjust to this new life. He sits in a hospital bed, in a room with other men whose lives are irrevocably changed. Every one of them can't help but think of the world as a very different place, so it's natural he'd devise new rules for dealing with it. You must acknowledge his offer to Levi as being rooted in desperation, and admire the selflessness of the idea.

But...I think I know what's in your heart. Worry. Guilt. Sorrow.

Put them to the side for now. Let things settle. Let Robert come home and the children reacquaint themselves with their father. Let Levi and Robert come to terms with their feelings while looking each other in the eye. As this is going on, go into that sunflower room and shut the door. Think. Think hard. How can you make this new life work? Is it necessary to wound Robert yet again to clear your conscience? Or, do you dishonor him by withholding the truth? These questions must be answered from the place in your heart that no one has access to, because then you'll know the answers come directly from who you really are. If they may make you uncomfortable, or hate yourself a little, you'll know you're finally getting at the truth.

Love,
Rita

P.S. Robert's legs will be compromised, then, like our dear president? If accommodations must be made, such as building a wooden ramp to the outdoors, I think it's a good idea if you help construct it. (Unless Levi is doing the building. If that is the case, then proceed with caution.) I'm being bossy, as usual, but I think the exercise will help you to understand the magnitude of what you are undertaking, and the enormity of Robert's sacrifice. You once told me about the differences between active and passive individuals. I'd like to add another to the list—active people understand that the mind heals faster when the hands are occupied. Build. Garden. Write.

P.P.S. After I post this I'm going to pack for tomorrow's trip to Kansas City. Roylene is nearly beside herself with excitement, her slim body vibrating like a tuning fork. The fine bracelet you sent arrived just the other day, much to our collective shock. It's a stunner, hon. Roylene can't stop admiring it. Thank you ever so much for your generosity. I'll write soon with details of the big day.

———

August 7, 1944

IOWA CITY, IOWA

Dear Mrs. Whitehall,

Thank you for the bracelet. It's nicer than anything I've ever owned. I'm not writing that so you feel sorry for me. I just want you to know it's extraspecial when a gift is something you've never had before and never expected to have. I hope I'm making sense.

I understand your mama passed a while ago. Mine didn't, but she might as well have, so I have an idea of what it feels like. She took all her things with her when she left, so I wouldn't have anything of hers to give someone if I wanted to. I would, though. It'd be like passing her spirit on.

I'll be careful with it. Mrs. Vincenzo got all bent out of shape when I washed dishes yesterday with the bracelet fastened to my wrist. I tried to explain—it feels like part of my skin. Did so from the first time I put it on. I don't know why.

Well, thank you much. Next time I write I'll be signing off…

Mrs. Toby Vincenzo (Thought I'd try it out.)

August 9, 1944

KANSAS CITY (THE ONE IN KANSAS)

Dear Glory,

What a day.

We arrived in KC last night, after a long bus ride. We're staying at a quaint hotel near the impressive county courthouse. I'm sharing a lovely pale yellow room with Roylene and Little Sal, and Mrs. Kleinschmidt, who Roylene asked to be an official witness, is adjoining. The desk clerk gave us the twin rooms as a courtesy. Mrs. K. is speaking to me again, but I don't think she's very pleased to have her privacy compromised. She's dead bolted her side of the door.

Roy is across the hall. Yessiree. He surprised us all by showing up at the bus stop carrying a satchel and wearing a cheap, shiny suit the shade of day-old coffee. I was about to unleash my sharp tongue when I saw Roylene's face flush pink with pleasure. "Pops? Are you really coming?" she asked, her voice suddenly sounding very young.

"Wouldn't miss it for the world, dolly," he answered brightly. But his sharp eyes never left that bracelet dangling like catnip from her slender wrist.

He whistled. "Now that's a nice bit of rock."

Roylene's face took another turn on the color wheel, toward crimson. "It was a gift."

"Then you're moving on up in the world, ain't you?" Roy threw his arm around her, not caring that Little Sal was in her arms, making her stance awkward. I took the baby from her, and Roy shifted his attention to me. "This better be legal."

Oh, that man's gall! "It's—"

"Toby sent the paper back," Roylene interrupted. "It's legal, Pop. Don't make this bad. Please…not this."

His hand twitched. If we weren't standing in a public place, it would have found its mark. "Well, then, we better hop to it," he said. His mouth moved into a false smile easily, like it was a well-greased piece of machinery.

The bus ride was uneventful. Roy behaved himself for the most part, but then, we didn't pay him all that much attention.

We got up really early to set Roylene's hair in a back wave. Poor Little Sal fussed—he wanted in on the festivities. His mischievous hands pulled Roylene's hem so many times Mrs. K. had to stitch it up. I could have easily done it, but the woman swatted me away anytime I got near her creation. I'm not complaining—it was a vision. A two-piece, draped dress in raw silk of the deepest rose, with a chocolate-brown ribbon accentuating Roylene's tiny waist.

The dress is something new. Your bracelet took care of the old and blue, but we were stumped for something borrowed. Roylene had everything she needed, and loaning her a handkerchief or a penny for luck seemed rather uninspired. She looked a bit worried (all brides are superstitious, are they not?) but I told her it would make no difference once we got to the courthouse.

Mrs. K. and I got dressed (plain day suits to keep the attention where it belongs!) and we wrapped the baby in his christening gown at Roylene's insistence. A sharp rap on Roy's door and we were off.

The lawyer who met us in the judge's chambers was older than I expected but dashing, his dark hair graying at the sides, bringing one's attention directly to his soft, cornflower-blue eyes. He introduced himself as Bill and greeted us warmly, then addressed Roylene. "I'm just a stand-in for your groom, but your man loves you and wants this day to be special even though he can't be here in the flesh. A proxy wedding means the same as the real thing in the eyes of the law. When we walk out of the courthouse doors, you'll be married to him body and soul. Are you prepared for that level of commitment?"

Roylene swallowed. "Yes, sir."

The man nodded and called over to an adorably petite, red-haired woman standing in the corner with a bouquet of magenta dahlias. "Mary Ann?"

The woman handed the flowers to Roylene, who added them to the sunflowers I brought from home. "You're the twenty-fifth girl my husband's married." Mary Ann giggled. "Best of luck to you."

The ceremony began. When the judge mentioned the ring, Roylene went white and my stomach flipped. We'd forgotten.

"We need something to keep going." The judge sighed. He was balding and his eyes looked tired.

"Oh, dear," Mary Ann said, fanning herself. "This has never happened before."

A heavy silence fell over the room. I could see the sweat gathering on Roylene's upper lip.

"Borrow the goddamn handcuffs from the bailiff if you have to," Roy muttered.

Something borrowed. I twisted the gold band off my finger and passed it to the lawyer. The judge started up again, and when they got to the "I do" part, Roylene caught my gaze. We held each other that way for a long moment. Because, when it comes down to it, she is also marrying me, and I her.

My desire to do so surprised me, Glory. I had to turn away and choke down the emotion clawing at my throat. I held my grandson so tightly he squirmed.

Lawyer Bill gave Roylene a fatherly kiss on the forehead, and then it was over. My son was a married man.

Afterward, we went to lunch with Bill and Mary Ann, and we all signed a card to send to Toby. Even Roy scribbled his congratulations. We rubbed Little Sal's hands with sliced beets and pressed them onto the V-mail. I don't know if it'll go through, but the sweet gesture made even Mrs. K. smile from ear to ear.

We're heading back to Iowa City first thing in the morning. Roylene just wondered aloud if she'll feel like a different person tomorrow.

I feel like a different person today.

Love,
Rita

P.S. Even with all the commotion, I've been thinking about you all the time. Write soon, hon. I can't wait patiently for news of your homecoming. I just can't.

August 15, 1944

ROCKPORT, MASSACHUSETTS

Dear Rita,

I'm home.

I will never be able to thank you enough for your last letter. I've folded it and put it in a small silk satchel that I pin to the inside of my slip (or overalls when I'm in the garden). I hope this letter gets to you quickly. We are always waiting, aren't we? All in a state of hesitation and held breath. Sometimes it's glorious like a storm at the end of a hot day. And sometimes it's like waiting for a vaccination. Perhaps the greatest gift this war has given us is the anticipation itself. Such things out of the ordinary lead to the most inexplicable extraordinariness.

Extraordinariness in the form of a married woman who's been untrue. Who's fallen into false love with an old option and then kicks that option aside like a flat tire. Yes, at least my time at Astor House gave me a little clarity about what it is I've done. And I was scared. So scared to face Levi after all the things I said. After refusing him that one final time without any warmth or apology. But there he was, waiting for me with an open heart and a hammer.

And we did as you said, Rita. We began the project of making a comfortable reentry for Robert. My husband, his best friend. We sawed and hammered side by side, with the children helping with the smaller things, taking breaks to steal some sunlight for their souls. As we worked I realized something else. I do love Levi, Rita. In some ways, I've married both of them. Robert and I were married by our similar histories and by a priest, under God. Levi and I were married when we were eleven years old, by the goddess of the sea. But I'm not a pagan princess...I'm a human wife. And it's time to let my childhood go. I pushed it away with every "bang" of the hammer.

You gave me this gift, Rita. The gift of time. And this war gave me you. Such sweetness out of such sorrow. (And I'd throw it all away, all of it, if we could travel back in time so that you could have Sal back and Toby safe.) We don't need to have the answers. We'll never have them. They'll come and go and change. And all we can do is figure out the best way to behave when life comes at us. Even if society says it isn't right. Right is so subjective, after all.

Robert is scheduled back home in the fall. He thinks late September. The house will be ready for him. Now I just have to work on myself. Will I be ready for him? Who knows.

I love you, Rita. Have I told you? Is it too odd for me to say? When do you think it would be proper to begin planning our grand "reunion"? I think if I had that to look forward to, it might make the trying days ahead less trying.

AND there is a new painting from Robbie enclosed. It's of his family. Me and Robert (note his wheelchair), Levi and Corrine. Don't go thinking my boy is a genius. Robert wrote to him and asked him to paint it just like that. He's a very, very good father. I wept when I read the letter to Robbie and helped him with the wheels on the wheelchair. But Robbie told me, "Don't cry, Mama, the world is good to us. Look how big the sunflowers are! Only lucky people have sunflowers like that!"

Our boy. He loves you, too.

Your account of Roylene and Toby's wedding was lovely. I wish I'd been there. You are a wonderful woman. Roylene is lucky to have you. And do I dare say that YOU are lucky to have her? Oh, I envy her at times.

And one more thing: we took the kids to the outdoor market and I bought the most delicious "fudge." I told the woman there I wanted to send the recipe to my sister in Iowa and she was flattered that it would travel all that way, so she kindly jotted it down. Here it is:

Carrot Fudge
Ingredients:
Carrots
Gelatin
Orange essence

Method:
Finely grate carrots and cook four tablespoons in just enough water to cover for 10 minutes. Add flavoring with orange essence, grated orange rind or orange squash/cordial.
Melt a leaf of gelatin. Add gelatin to mixture. Cook quickly for a few minutes stirring all the time. Spoon into a flat dish. Leave to set. Cut into cubes.

All my love,
Glory

August 23, 1944

IOWA CITY, IOWA

Dear Glory,

Thank heavens you're home. Really home.

I have to be honest—I can't predict what is going to happen once Robert returns. I suppose what I'm trying to say is be open to failure. Given what's at stake, well, *everywhere,* it feels like some sort of betrayal to even write that word. But once you accept it as a possibility, you can make plans for the event it does happen.

Okay, I'm done being serious. Are you sighing with relief?

Tell Robbie his family portrait is hanging in my dining room above the buffet, a place of honor. It's lovely. His legs may not be nimble, but his fingers are. I'm thrilled you're cultivating this. When the body is not working so well, it's key to keep the mind moving. (This will hold true for Robert, as well.)

So…news on the Iowa front: my garden could feed all of General Bradley's men and then some. The tomatoes have taken full advantage of all the sun we've been getting—passersby could mistake my backyard for a children's party full of red balloons. Roylene is going to help with the canning this year, and I'll send you some of Sal's famous sauce. His recipe is the best kept secret in Iowa City! As the torchbearer, I feel it is my duty to pass it along, and since I now have a daughter-in-law Roylene is the lucky recipient.

Oh, Glory, she's such a dear. I've finally broken her of the habit of standing while she eats—the girl has the dishes done before the

238 SUZANNE HAYES & LORETTA NYHAN

food's even hit her stomach! She's shy about hanging her underthings outside, but laughs uproariously at Groucho's best innuendos, her back against the sofa, ribs bobbing up and down at every witticism coming from the radio.

The other day I arrived home from work a bit early and found her and Little Sal in Toby's closet, nestled between his pressed shirts and old spelling bee trophies. Her face turned the color of rhubarb jam! I told her not to worry—she could have easily caught me among Sal's things, sniffing for a trace of him like an old hound dog. And Little Sal should start getting used to his father's scent—this war can't last forever, right?

I also wanted to tell her I'm grateful she's brought new love into the house, but I didn't want to embarrass her further, or remind her that Toby's not here. She's got enough to think about.

Roylene's building herself up to go see Roy. They had words when we switched buses in Des Moines. I was minding Little Sal so I didn't hear much, but Roy seethed until we got to Iowa City. Charlie and Irene met us at the depot, and amid the chaos of congratulatory hugs and bag retrievals and settling into Charlie's car (He's gotten his hands on one somehow. Don't ask—I surely don't!) Roy slipped away.

Whatever transpired is playing on that girl's mind. Roy left the argument unfinished, and she's wrestling with it, I can tell. She talks about heading down to the tavern to "Say hello," but never quite makes it out the door.

I offered to accompany her, but she refused. Charlie said he'd drive her and stick around, but she's turned him down as well, gently, saying she's got to do this for herself or she'll always question her ability to do so.

The world could certainly learn a lot from Roylene Vincenzo.

Well, take care and know that I'm rooting for a smooth return of the hero Robert Whitehall.

Love,
Rita

P.S. School is back in session, and Charlie, Irene and I are again eating lunch on the greens. Sometimes I bring Little Sal, who pulls on the grass and delightedly points at ants with his pudgy fingers while I try fruitlessly to brush them away. It's enjoyable because my subconscious has stopped trying to play cupid. I find it hard to believe I couldn't see they are two perfectly fine puzzle pieces that just don't fit. It's a mystery, isn't it? How that works?

———————————

August 23, 1944

IOWA CITY, IOWA

Dear Toby,

I love you, too. And yes, it was strange but not wrong, if I'm making sense.

I've been a wife for two weeks now. I'm living in your home, which through your ma's kindness feels like my own. My life in the tavern seems far away, like it happened to someone else. My days are quiet, one tumbling into the next.

Work's hard to find unless you live in Des Moines or Cedar Rapids. The USO center said they'd take Little Sal on the days your ma has to work, but the factories around here don't need me. Everyone who can wants to help, which is nice, but it don't help me none. The other day, I thought I'd take one more walk into town to check for openings. If I didn't see anything, I'd start asking at the local farms. I figured they could always use another set of hands.

When I got to Clinton Street I saw the enlistment office. My feet walked in before my brain caught up. I was flappin' my eyelids like a real country bumpkin when an officer asked me if I needed anything. She stood at attention while she waited for my answer. Her uniform was crisply ironed and the deepest, prettiest blue I'd ever seen. "I'm just looking for work," I said. "But I haven't found nothing yet."

"Yes, you have," she answered right back. "Your country needs you to work for Victory. Join the WAVES and free up a stateside guy to go overseas. The training center is in Cedar Falls. That's just a hop, skip and a jump from here." She took me in, her eyes bright. "You look perfectly suited for it. What do you say?"

I said yes. Scrawled my name on the dotted line.

Oh, Toby, don't be mad. Do you remember the first time you sat on the counter while I chopped onions and washed dishes? I asked why you enlisted and you said it was an opportunity to see the world and meet history face-to-face. You also said you believed this war to be one of the only times you'd get into a fight and know for certain you were on the right side of things.

I barely finished high school. Kansas City was the farthest I'd ever been from home since leaving Oklahoma. What can I offer Little Sal? What kind of wife will I be to you, if the only thing I can talk about is how to make a good corned beef sandwich?

I'll be gone a year. I'll miss Little Sal something desperate, but my mind will rest knowing he's staying with your ma. I want to give him to her for a short while. She's not easy with him yet—when he bumps his head on the crib or topples into the coffee table she cries out like he lost an arm. If she has time alone with him, maybe she'll be more comfortable.

I haven't told her yet. She's lonesome, and having us around helps. I've seen lots of lonesome people in the tavern, so I can spot it even when they try to hide it. Telling her will be harder than breaking the news to Roy, that I know.

I probably shouldn't, but I'm gonna go see him and tell him why I'm leaving. I have to. My mama never did.

Your wife,
Roylene

———————

August 26, 1944

IOWA CITY, IOWA OR THE BANKS OF THE SEINE!

Madame Gloria!

Paris is liberated! *Viva la France!*

Because Sal is nowhere, he is everywhere. I imagine him atop the Eiffel Tower, waving French and American flags. We always talked of going to Paree to drink champagne and eat the stinkiest of cheeses. He would wear a beret and I a silk scarf.

But, as de Gaulle said, "These are minutes which go beyond each of our poor lives."

So, in honor of this victory I'm revealing my best soufflé recipe! Here goes:
Spinach Soufflé
3 eggs, separated

1/2 cup medium white sauce
1 teaspoon grated onion
1/2 cup grated cheddar cheese
2 cups finely chopped cooked spinach

Beat egg yolks until thick and lemon-colored. Combine white sauce, onion and cheese. Stir egg yolks into white sauce mixture. Add spinach. Fold in stiffly beaten egg whites. Set in a pan of hot water and bake in a moderate oven (350°F) about 50 minutes, or until firm. Try not to open the oven before it's done!

Cordialement,
Rita

P.S. I think Roylene is ready for her big confrontation with Roy. She's got a look about her that says she's made up her mind. I'm worried, but that girl has already proven she's got a backbone, so my money's on her.

⸻

August 26, 1944

ROCKPORT, MASSACHUSETTS

Oh, Rita,

Can you believe it? France. It's as if Robert did it all by himself, I swear. I feel him everywhere. His grace and his strength. His almighty altruism. It's as if he WILLED them to win. The tide

is surely turning now. I can't wait to talk to him about all of this.
I hope he'll remember it. I hope they tell him, blow by blow, what
happened.

The bells are ringing, only they aren't mourning bells!

Levi and I fairly ran into town with the children to spend the day
on the beaches stopping by all sorts of impromptu picnics. There's
nothing but smiles and tears today. So many mothers and sisters
and lovers full of hope now. And pride. Flags everywhere, like it's
the Fourth of July all over again!

We lit sparklers tonight. Just the four of us, and we sat and
looked at the moon.

"I miss Daddy," said Robbie.

My throat closed. I couldn't speak. "Soon, Robbie...so soon he'll
come home. And when he does, the whole world will be thankful."

"I think that's my cue to leave," said Levi. And he did.

I didn't watch him go, and the children didn't whine. We
snuggled there, the three of us on our back porch, and lit more
sparklers.

All I could think about was Sal.

And Toby. And Robert. And you and Roylene. How we find
love in the strangest places. And how it never plays by the rules if
it's right.

Did I ever tell you I spent a whole year in France? It bothered
me to no end when it was occupied. How can you occupy anything
so free, so brazen and bold. How do you take over a people so in
love with life?

The answer is, you can't.

I'm thinking of your boys, Rita. I'm thinking of Sal ushering the
lost souls into the gates of heaven. And of Toby, who is celebrating
just as we are at this very moment.

They are fireflies in my eyes.

In hopes of peace,
Glory

P.S. I love being a woman. A woman among amazing women. Women who understand just how much we need one another.

P.P.S. In that spirit, I leave you with thoughts of my mother's favorite song. Do you know the singer Billie Holiday? My mother traveled down to New York to see her sing in nightclubs. Once she brought back a recording of "It's Like Reaching for the Moon" and she sang it so much we all committed it to memory. I think she felt it defined her relationship with my father. I think it defines this beautiful day!

———————

September 6, 1944

ROCKPORT, MASSACHUSETTS

Dear Rita,

How lovely and amazing and QUIET it's been. I'm spending a good deal of time gardening. Well, you can hardly call it that, I suppose. It's more like reaping! Oh, holy dear LORD, the sheer volume of tomatoes!

I've become a veritable domestic goddess. Sewing and cooking. Mothering. Preparing for Robert's arrival. (Which could be any day. The army is so disorganized for such an organized army...well, you know what I mean!)

So I've been making a lot of things with tomatoes.

Tomatoes and cream and sugar for breakfast.

Tomato omelets for lunch and dinner.

Tomato soufflé.

Tomato SOUP. (So much soup.)

Tomato sauce, as well.

But here is why I am writing to you. This recipe. Oh, Rita. Make it and feed it to our Roylene!

Tomato Soup Cake
(I know! But it's good. Trust me. SO GOOD!)
1/2 cup shortening
1 cup sugar (substitute 3/4 cup honey per rations)
1 cup tomato soup (best used if sitting in icebox for a few days)
1 teaspoon baking soda
2 cups flour
2 teaspoons baking powder
1 teaspoon cinnamon
1/2 teaspoon cloves
1 teaspoon nutmeg
1 cup raisins
1 cup chopped nuts (of course, if you can get them!)

Blend shortening with sugar. Stir baking soda into tomato soup. Make sure it dissolves. Add to shortening and sugar. Sift dry ingredients and add to the mix. Stir in raisins and nuts. Pour into a greased and floured 13x9-inch cake pan and bake at 350 degrees for almost an

hour. Glaze or frost or simply butter. Good toasted, too.

As for your new pal Roylene. I'm so happy for both of you! And more than a little bit jealous. I'd give anything to sit in your kitchen.

And I know your voice. It's deep and rich and full of laughter behind all that. So don't you worry. Me? I sound like a bird who got caught in a fan! And if you have any bad habits I'll just love you more. You've been doing the same for me.

Love,

Glory

P.S. Guess who gave me that recipe? Remember the woman who lost her boy and yelled at me in the coffee shop? Yes. She gave it to me! She just walked up to me while I was at the drugstore picking up Robbie's medicine.

"I've heard your Robert's coming home to us," she said.

"Yes, ma'am," I said (ready to duck, I tell you...).

"This is for you, it's a comfort."

And she walked away. You could have knocked me over with a willow wisp.

I'm just a bubble of hope these days, I swear. Any word from Toby?

September 17, 1944

IOWA CITY, IOWA

Dear Glory,

It's an angry moon this night and last. I like to think Toby sent it my way as a warning.

My mother always claimed a moon like this one—washed with crimson and violet—brings to the surface all the things we wish to hide.

Maybe that's why Roy showed up on my front porch this afternoon.

We'd gone to late mass, Roylene and me and the baby, and came home to a lazy, warm afternoon. I'd invited Charlie and Irene over for lunch and a Monopoly tournament (we've been building up to it the past couple of Sundays) and the four of us sat around my dining room table, spooning chili con carne into our mouths and vying for Boardwalk and Park Place.

The insistent pounding on the door shrunk my heart to a stone. My body followed suit. I was immovable, barely breathing. Charlie got up, and I heard him turn the knob and something in his greeting told me it wasn't the worst. Turned out to be pretty close, though.

Charlie's body filled the door frame, forcing much shorter Roy to duck under his armpit. He shouted for both Roylene and me, calling out names that aren't fit to write much less say.

The second I could clear my head I stepped forward, but Roylene put an arm out to stop me. "This is my fight," she said, and tapped Charlie on the shoulder. "It's okay. I'll talk to him."

Charlie let her pass but didn't budge from the door frame. She met Roy on the porch. Irene crept up to the front window alongside me. We wanted Roy to know he had eyes on him.

He glared at his daughter, sneering and vicious. I watched him open and close his fists, but they stayed at his side. Instead, he beat her with words. Slapped her with every insult a man uses to bring a woman down until she can't rise again.

In one fluid motion, Charlie stepped forward and landed a right uppercut on the south side of Roy's jaw. Roylene screamed and I pushed myself onto the porch, taking the girl in my arms.

"You get on now," Roy yelled at her, blood dripping from his mouth into his cupped hand. "I mean it—get! Bull on all this nonsense. Pick up that kid of yours and move on home. You don't run out on your responsibilities. Not while I'm livin'."

"Roylene is welcome to stay in my home as long as she likes," I said, managing to keep my voice steady.

"Liar," Roy snarled. "If you hadn't kicked her out she wouldn't have made an ass of herself trying to join the WAVES. A married woman with a baby." He said the word *married* like it was a dirty joke.

Roylene's spine straightened. "You got it all wrong. I didn't *try*, Pop. They took me. I'm goin'."

"Why would they? All you're good for is giving the Japs a laugh."

My feet felt a little unsteady beneath me and I took a step back. I placed a hand on the small jutting bone atop Roylene's shoulder. "You're joining the WAVES?"

Roy snickered, a horribly wet, phlegmy sound. "Ah! You didn't know, did ya?" He turned to Roylene. "What kind of game are you playin'? You're gonna stick her with the kid, ain't ya?"

I couldn't speak. Even if I could, I didn't know what to say. The more it dawned on Roy that I hadn't a clue, the bolder he got, spitting on the ground at Charlie's feet and then grabbing at Roylene.

She shook him off and took my hand. Her face was full of so much—shame at keeping the secret, embarrassment with her father, pride in herself. "I was going to tell you when the time was right," she said softly. "I just told Roy last week, but it's not like he's making it out to be."

"She's runnin' just like her mama," Roy hissed.

Her grip on my hand tightened. "It ain't the same. Not one bit. I'm coming back, and when I do I'll be a better mama, and a better wife, and a better person." She met my gaze, her eyes clear and determined. "I hope more than anything you can understand. You can, right?"

What could I do, Glory? Of course I was frantic at the thought of her leaving, but she was standing in front of me, this half-starved, determined girl with her father's bloody handprint on her arm. *What could I do?*

I held her. I told her she'd be a valuable addition to the United States Navy and I was proud as could be. I said I'd welcome the opportunity to mother my grandson for a while. I said I'd miss her.

And, oh, I will. I most certainly will.

Roy finally left after Charlie backed him into the sunflower patch for a man-to-man talk. I don't know what he told him. I don't think I want to know.

When Roylene sat with me tonight for the late-news hour, she laid her head on my lap. I didn't say a word, just stroked her baby-soft hair. She fell dead asleep on the couch, and I came out to where I'm sitting now, on the back patio, to watch the moon and write to you.

The air still holds the day's heat and my dress is sticking to—
Later...

Charlie stepped into the backyard a few minutes ago, surprising the bejesus out of me. He'd been sitting at the dining room table looking over Roylene's enlistment papers, but I think that's an excuse not to leave me alone. I caught him glancing at Irene when I said I'd be fine, thank you very much, so I suspect they think I'm going to take a dive into the deep end again.

Sorry if the words above are smeared, but I stuck my hand over the letter the second I saw him. For some reason I didn't want Charlie to spot his name. Like I was talking about him behind his back. Silly, right?

He must have sensed my nerves because he didn't sit down. "She's really leaving, huh?" He winced as he finished the question, like he felt sorry he asked it.

I tried to keep my voice lighthearted. "No changing your mind when it comes to Uncle Sam!"

Charlie looked me in the eye, but he didn't smile. "I'll drive you gals to Cedar Falls when the time comes," he said, and squeezed my shoulder. "And you're going to need some help once she's gone. I may not look it, but I can cook a meal and mind a baby."

I didn't turn him down. I probably will need the help. "Thank you."

He nodded. "I'll leave you to your writing," he said before heading out. "That's going to help, too."

He's right about that.

But I am glad Charlie's coming with us to the WAVES camp. It'll be nice to have someone else along in case my heart gives out halfway through the trip.

Love,
Rita

P.S. Since I haven't heard otherwise, I'll assume Robert is not home yet. It must be driving you crazy, the waiting. Chin up, Glory. I'll be thinking about you and your family in the coming weeks.

September 24, 1944

ROCKPORT, MASSACHUSETTS

Dearest Rita,

He's home. My Robert is home. His homecoming was so strange. No matter how hard I tried to make it not awkward, there was just no getting around the surreal quality of the whole event. Waiting at the station with the children (I'd told Levi to stay away). And then there Robert was being helped into his waiting wheelchair by two other officers. He wheeled toward us with no hesitation and stopped about four feet away. He held out his arms to the children and they ran to him. He scooped them up and nuzzled both of them close. Then, he looked up at me and do you know what he said?

"I thought you might have brought Levi," and in his eyes, I saw he was grateful I didn't. I wondered what he could read in mine. Could he tell what I'd done just by looking at me?

I dropped my handbag. I went to pick it up but he rolled himself forward fast, maneuvering the chair and giving the children a ride. We almost knocked heads trying to grab that darn bag. But I grasped it first and stood up straight.

"You're a quick one, aren't you," I said, and then wanted to gobble the words back into my throat.

"Give us a kiss, Glory," he said, and turned his head tapping his cheek. "It's been a while since a pretty lady kissed this soldier."

And I should have turned his face with my gloved hand. I should have cupped his chin and kissed him full on the lips, because that's what I wanted to do. But I didn't. I kissed his cheek like a sister would have. A cold sister. And then we made our way home. Marie helped by driving us, and the wheelchair was easy to maneuver. I thought it would be clumsier. Turns out the only clumsy part of the whole equation was me.

When we got home Robert marveled at all the new accommodations for the chair. And at how Levi lowered some of the cabinetry in the kitchen and bathrooms so he can reach things without having to ask for help. Levi met us there and the two embraced like brothers. I felt ill and sweaty.

"Why don't you go to bed for a bit, Glory?" suggested Robert. "It's been a hell of a war."

It's been a hell of a war, he said. I'll never forget it.

Of course, what kind of a woman would go to bed? I went directly to the kitchen. I left the two of them with the children outside and didn't pop my head out again until I had a four-course meal for all of them. It's all I could do. It's the best I could do.

That's how it's gone. It's only been a few days. And we all walk around with our own thick clouds hanging in the air. Father would have called them "elephants in the room."

And then, when I got your last letter, I acted like a childish fool. Robert was newly home and I was taking a moment to myself on a fine, blue sky September afternoon. I strolled down to the mailboxes and on finding your letter ripped it open. I've missed you and I wasn't going to wait to sit in the house with a proper letter opener. Then, when I started to read the tale it wove...I folded it up again and fairly ran back to the house! I swept past Levi and Robert, who were talking on the front porch and supervising the children as they painted. (There's another picture from Robbie. It's of a Christmas tree. He's a little impatient for the holiday season, that boy.)

Anyway, I must have been flushed because Robert reached out and caught my skirt pocket. "What's the rush, honey? What you got there?"

Levi answered him before I could. "It must be a letter from Rita. If those two ever meet, we'd never get another second with Miss Glory." Then they laughed a little.

I flushed, deeply. There are some things...some things that should not be known. How much of myself have I given to these men? Anyway, I held my head high and said, "Yes, Robert, Levi is correct. It's a letter from my dear friend and it holds some very important news. May I be excused?" My sarcasm must have bitten because both of them looked down and then Robert cleared his throat and let go of my pocket.

It was odd, standing there. Wanting to say I was sorry and wanting to be gone all at the same time. So I left and grabbed a glass of iced tea on my way up to your sunflower room. I sat on the bed and read your tale. Oh, Rita. How awful and wonderful, too!

I'm so glad you are safe and that Charlie was there. What a terrible man he is, that Roy. And how marvelous you were, truly, to give her that peace of mind...that moment of pride when you looked at her and hid your own sorrow in order to help her self-confidence. Once again you prove yourself to be of the finest stock of human there is. I swear it.

And the way you wrote it all down. It was like I was there with you. Right there under that warning moon. Please tell Roylene I'm proud of her, too. What a wonderful, selfless thing to do.

My heart, though, aches for you. Yet another loss. And you love her—you opened your home to her and now she's like another child to you. I suppose life is all about one loss after another. Anna used to say that the Buddhists meditate about reactions. That we cannot control WHAT happens to us, only how we react to it. Well, my darling Rita, you have been a supreme being in that department. I on the other hand have failed miserably.

I suppose Robert's homecoming is going to take a lot of time and healing. A lot of careful steps.

When I was little and my father took me out on the large rocks that jut out into the sea, he'd say, "Gloria, take off your shoes and socks. You must feel each foothold and make sure it is sound before you place the next in front of you. There are some paths you cannot trust with your eyes, test them always to make sure."

And then he'd add, "Don't be afraid of walking on the barnacles. They hurt, it's true, but at least you know you have stable footing. Barnacles aren't slippery."

So here I am…walking one foot in front of the other…on my own private patch of barnacles.

I miss you.

You still haven't answered my plea for planning a meeting, Rita. I'd love to plan one. Even if it never came to be, at least we could look forward to it.

Love,
Glory

October 3, 1944

IOWA CITY, IOWA

Dear Glory,

Oh, hon. This is unexpected. I didn't think you'd be the one jostling for position in your own home. I don't mean that as a slight—it's just that this particular scenario never entered my mind. I thought for sure those two would give each other a wide berth.

I've been sitting cross-legged in front of my garden for the past half hour, trying to put myself in Robert's place. The only conclusion I can come to is this—Levi is the *easy* one to deal with. You, on the other hand...

You're not the woman he left, Glory. I guess none of us are the same people we were before this war started, but even if Hitler had never stepped foot in Poland, over the years you'd show Robert aspects of your personality he'd never thought were there. We're all so multifaceted, and it's impossible to see all the sides at once.

I suppose some people would say he left a girl and came back to a woman, but I think that's oversimplifying things. You were a woman a year and a half ago, just a *different* kind of woman.

Robert needs to figure out this new Glory. I've got to say, being sassy and petulant isn't going to help; however, he's going to have to learn to accept all your emotions, as you're freer now, and they rise to the surface more easily.

And you're going to need to accept Robert's quirks. He may move quickly in that chair, but acclimating to this new lifestyle will take time.

I'm not an expert, but I believe marriage is about loving someone enough to accept whatever comes, be it pleasant or unpleasant without a thought of giving up. Sal taught me that.

Oh, Glory, I wish I could tell you these things with my arm around your shoulders and my head leaning against yours. The sun is brilliant this afternoon. And unlike the cement patio, the earth miraculously still holds the warmth of summer—I can feel it through the denim of my overalls. I've got my back against the wheelbarrow, and my paper is supported by some magazines Roylene left behind. On the back of one some Hollywood type is telling me to wear Victory Red lipstick to keep our troops safe. If only it was that simple.

And yes, you read that right. Roylene is gone.

Charlie and I brought her to Cedar Falls last Thursday. We acted like two worried parents dropping their youngest off at sleepaway camp. Charlie kept asking her if she needed anything, and I think if she'd requested a samurai sword he would have hopped on a plane and fought General Tojo for one.

Roylene was quiet and contemplative when we arrived—I'm sure she was thinking about Little Sal (we thought it best he stay in Iowa City with Irene, after much teary back and forth). She jammed her fingers in her mouth, a habit I thought she'd long since given up.

The camp was an impressive sight to behold. It's located on the stately grounds of the Iowa State Teachers College, and I couldn't help but think, if this were another life, we'd be dropping Roylene off in the students' dormitory. But this is the life she's been given, I told myself, and I can only help her live it. I slipped my arm around her shoulders as we took in her new home. Lines of girls dressed smartly in navy blue, sharply tailored suits marched by where we stood. Roylene's eyes were glued to a gal holding the flag in front—

she stood nearly six feet tall and held her figure as fine and elegant as the Statue of Liberty.

"We best get you checked in," Charlie said, and picked up her small suitcase.

"I can't," Roylene whispered, and abruptly turned on her heel and started walking, away from us and away from the camp.

I turned to follow, but Charlie stopped me cold. "Give her some thinking time," he said, and we wandered the campus for ten minutes or so, until I was just about ready to jump out of my skin.

We found her sitting on the hood of Charlie's car, shoes kicked off, her eyes puffy and red. "What am I doin'?" she moaned when we approached.

I wasn't sure I had a good enough answer for her. While I stood there with my mouth hanging open in the breeze, Charlie scooted up next to her and calmly said, "Why'd you go and sign up?"

"I come from nothin'," Roylene said. "Worse than that, when you really look at it." She stopped, took a breath. "Did you ever catch a glimpse of what you could be, if you really tried at life? The woman at the enlistment office gave me a peek. This war is terrible, she said, but that doesn't mean it doesn't give us some opportunities. I could find a place for myself serving my country. Little Sal could always have something to be proud of, instead of feeling like he had to make up for where I came from. I just don't know if I can leave him. Does that make any sense at all?"

Charlie sighed and asked if he could tell her a story. Then he told a tale I'd been waiting to hear for a long time. It came out in a torrent—his jailbird father, alcoholic mother, juvenile delinquency. He grew up in the back of a pool hall, was arrested for the first time at twelve years old when his father talked him into driving a getaway car after he'd robbed a drugstore.

"I got plenty to be ashamed of, and I've spent the past few years

SUZANNE HAYES & LORETTA NYHAN

trying to catch my own glimpse of what I can be," Charlie said after he'd finished. "I wanted the war to help me get there, to make me whole. That didn't play out, but it might for you. I don't have a child, but if I did, I'd do everything I could to make sure I could look him in the eye when he asked what kind of man I was. Now, you got nothing to be ashamed of besides being born to a real SOB, but life is long, and if you feel you'll look back on this experience and see it's made yours a better one, then you need to consider it."

I wanted to object. Roylene was already whole in my book. But some kind of understanding passed between the two of them, something outside of my comprehension, so I didn't say a word. After a moment, Roylene slid off the car and walked up to me. "I need to do this, for Little Sal and Toby…and me," she said, her eyes full of conviction. "I don't take it lightly, and I know I'm taking a risk. I need your permission for leaving, though, or it won't feel right. I trust your opinion more than any other, Mrs. Vincenzo. Do you think I should go?"

Every part of me wanted to scoop her up and take her back to Iowa City, to her son and the life I wanted her to live. She gazed at me expectantly, her eyes clouding up a bit when she guessed my answer.

"Every day I'll tell Little Sal about his brave mommy and daddy," I said, and pulled her trembling body close. "It's only a year, hon. You go. Jump off some cliffs for both of us."

I kissed her forehead and promised to send weekly updates of Little Sal's progress. And then I let her go. It's the third time I've given someone to this war and, oh, Glory, in some ways, it was the hardest.

On the way home, Charlie pulled over onto an embankment about three miles past Waterloo.

"Everything I told her was true," he said, cutting the engine. "There's more to the story. I want you to hear it, is that all right?"

The next decade after the drugstore robbery was one of petty (and not-so-petty) thefts and consistent arrests. He did some adult time in the Oklahoma State Pen. That's what doomed him to 4-F status. "I thought if I could serve," he admitted, "I could make up for what I'd done."

Then Charlie went on, from the sordid mess of his mother's death to his father's final incarceration, to the guilt and pain and regret that tug at his pant leg like the unhappy, attention-starved child he was.

Given his bravery, I'm not proud of what happened next. As he talked, mean thoughts zipped through my head like bolts of lightning. Why was Charlie sitting next to me and not Sal? Why is my husband—a man who read Shakespeare and never harmed a fly—decomposing under a mound of Italian soil while this man wears shiny shoes and drinks hooch and plays Monopoly at my dining room table?

Charlie must have sensed something. He dropped forward, gluing his forehead to the steering wheel, arms slack at his sides. The droop of his shoulders announced his defeat.

His total immobility prompted me to act. I gently pushed him upright. I combed through his tangled hair, wiped the sweat from his brow, curled his fingers over the wheel. I turned the radio on to something low and melodic. "You are a respectable man out for a Sunday drive," I said. "I believe it, so you should start believing it, too."

"Do you?" he whispered. "Do you really believe it?"

I did. It was a side of him I had seen, and one I knew to be true. "I do," I said, and we drove off into the heart of Iowa, two people under the wide expanse of cloudless sky.

This is the thing, Glory—sometimes it takes so long to see the best sides of a person. I'm not certain Robert has seen all you have to offer. I don't even know if *you're* aware of your many attributes. They lie in wait, like a tower of brightly wrapped gifts hidden in a cedar closet. When the door finally opens you have to be certain they won't come tumbling out, overwhelming him.

Anna has the rare talent of seeing more than most. Levi, too, in his own way. Now it's time for Robert to have his chance. Let him discover you, and you him. Take the time you both deserve.

Good luck, my friend.

Love,
Rita

———————

October 13, 1944

ROCKPORT, MASSACHUSETTS

Dear Mother,

It's been five years since we said our last goodbye. Do you remember that October? The Indian summer stayed and stayed. I felt that somehow, if it lingered...so would you. How O. Henry of me. Sophomoric, you'd probably say.

I'm writing this letter because I couldn't find you when I went home. I felt sure I'd see your ghost. To be honest, I've been a little mad that you haven't haunted me. I suppose you and Father are dancing at some infinity ball.

I've taken to writing letters, you see. I've made a friend through paper and pens and envelopes and postage. A true friend. Not like the girls at school or the silly geese you dressed me up to play with as a child.

Her name is Rita and she lives in Iowa City, Iowa. Her husband just died in the war last spring. He was wonderful even though I didn't know him.

Are you engulfed up there, with all these spirits coming through? Or do you have box seats?

Anyway, I've learned a lot through writing things down. So I figured I'd let you go this way.

I'm letting go of the ache for you. The desire that wasn't filled even when you were here on earth. I'm letting go of the idea that I can still please or displease you. I'm letting go of the horrible fear that I'll turn into you someday. And also letting go of the fear that I won't.

When I came home I wanted to confess all my sins. I needed you to tell me what to do. You see, I love two men. I love Levi. I love him very much. And to make everything more complicated, Robert loves him, too.

Every day I worry about losing one or the other (or both!) of them. I wake up with an ache that won't go away. It throbs inside of me all day long.

I can't wait until summer comes around the bend again. I'll be able to run down to the cove and dive into the deep waters there. Somehow I think those icy waters will calm this heart that is on fire. You liked the cove, didn't you, Mother? Or have I made that up in my mind?

I'm thinking so much of you lately. Of you and Father both. The love you had together. Perhaps that's what I've been looking for. That combination of fiery passion as well as stable commitment. Maybe you two were the lucky ones. I suppose the rest of us need to pick one or the other and then try our best to create the other portion of that amazing equation as we live our lives. Yes, that seems to be it, doesn't it? Wake in the stability of a proven, time-tested love and then create the passion that can exist inside of it.

Look. See what you've done now? You're not even here walking on this earth and you've helped me make my decision.

I can still see you, the way you looked at me when I came home from the Sadie Hawkins dance. You were sitting in that red velvet wing chair wearing your glorious taffeta night robe and reading.

"Who did you choose?" you asked without looking up.

"Robert," I said, and sat on the ground leaning my head against your knee.

You didn't say anything else, but you did the most incredible thing. You let your hand find my hair. And then you stroked my head. Do you remember? It was the most affectionate you'd been with me in years.

Would you stroke my head now, Mother? Now that I've made this decision? I'll dream that you would. I'll dream your soft hands are all around me.

I love you, Mother.

All best to you in heaven,
Gloria

[Letter stuffed into the side pocket of Glory's jewelry box.]

October 16, 1944

ROCKPORT, MASSACHUSETTS

Dear Rita,

Has the world ever been so beautiful and terrifying as it is right now? I never thought I was a person who was afraid of much. But boy, I'm scared.

Your letter arrived not a moment too soon (as they always seem to do!) Just when I was beginning to doubt that I could maintain this entire farce. And that's what it started to feel like, a farce. Shakespearean (so Sal would have loved a retelling of the story) and forced. Every morning I felt I pasted a lipstick smile across my lips and hoped the day would rush by. Afraid to lock eyes with Levi, whose longing seeps from him. Or even look too hard at Robert, whose eyes hold the same longing. Like the other night when I was clearing the dinner dishes and Robert came in to help me. Levi grabbed the dish from him.

"I've got it," said Robert, holding firm to the plate.

"Let me," said Levi, not letting go either.

They both pulled at it and then it fell to the floor. Crashed into a million pieces. Then they both just stared at me. I'm so exhausted by all the tension. Something has got to be done.

Or Robbie, who needs so much, and Corrine, whose little life has been turned upside down more than any of ours, I guess.

So many sets of eyes pleading for me to be more than I am. Frankly, I'm exhausted. And then? Then I get your letter.

I was walking back from a glorious outdoor rally. I'd just made a speech about "Maintaining Our Autonomy When the War Is Over" (the irony of this was not lost on me, but I was persuasive, anyway). We were on the green, near the beach, but I'd decided to take the long way home. So I walked through town.

It's lovely here when the tourists leave. Don't get me wrong, I love the jumble of new people during the late spring and summer months. They give this place a newness that it needs. But when they empty out, it's like the sea at low tide. An acquired taste. And yet…a treasure trove of tide pools and deep-sea shells. And the water is always so peaceful even if it's laden with seaweed.

Anyway, I was walking through town and Sam comes running out of the post office waving a letter. He gave it to me and then held my hand. "Someday you'll have to tell me all about these letters, Mrs. Whitehall," he said. "I get almost as excited as you do when they come in and I don't even know why!" Then he went back into the post office.

I liked that. Feeling like our friendship has gone beyond us. It is one of the only good feelings I have these days. Can you tell I'm trying to skirt around an issue here? Because I am. My words fail me here almost as much as they did the very first time I tried to write to you.

It happened. All of it happened. And now? Now I'm lost. Here goes, the whole shebang of it.

When he first got home, Robert was doing exceptionally well. But as the elation of homecoming began wearing off, reality sunk in. He needs help to bathe, Rita. And help to dress. He tries, but falls. His upper arms are so strong…but I think there's a part of his brain that assumes his legs will work. So he tries to make them move, and when they don't…he finds himself on the floor. He won't let me see him like that, so he yells and grabs for the bottoms of doors, trying to slam them shut. To close me out.

It was the sneaking out of bed at night that was the worst. And it led to all the trouble. I'd lie there and pretend to stay asleep. Pretend I couldn't hear him struggle from the bed to the chair. I told myself I pretended because I wanted him to have that little bit of grace. Truth is, I knew what could happen in the dark night, just the two of us and some crickets. Honesty. The kind that turns your stomach.

One night, though, I was so restless I followed him out of the bedroom. He wheeled out onto the back porch to smoke. When I got to the door and looked out, I could see the back of his head, the smoke curling into the darkness.

You were with me in my mind at that very moment, as if you were standing right next to me.

"It's now or never, Glory…" you said.

So out I went.

"Got one of those for me?" I asked.

He didn't turn around right away. I walked around to face him and sat right up on the weathered wooden table we keep out there. That way, my head was a bit higher than his. I needed some kind of power in the situation or I'd never do what had to be done.

He shook a cigarette out of his pack and lit one for me.

"When did you start, Ladygirl? Not too ladylike…"

I took the cigarette and lingered over my first drag. "Not very ladylike to sit on a table in your nightgown, either," I said.

"Maybe we lost all the *real* ladies to the war," he said.

"Maybe so," I said, but then I got quiet because I was losing my nerve. Thank God he knows me. Thank the good Lord.

"You got something to tell me, Ladygirl?"

"Yes," I said.

"I knew it," he said, slapping his knee and laughing. "I could feel it from the day I got off the train. It's been written all over your face.

Spit it out, quick. Who is this new Gloria I'm married to? The old Gloria Whitehall would have told me anything."

"It's not that easy, Robert. It's about the hardest thing I've ever done."

"It's serious?" he asked.

And that was it. I wasn't going to bruise his pride any more by making him play twenty questions with me. I let my weakness with Levi fall out of my mouth. The flirting, the kiss, the—you know. I won't write it.

Nothing but crickets were heard for a long, long time. So long I helped myself to another three or four cigarettes. He didn't offer to light those.

"Do you love him, Glory?"

That's what he asked when he broke his silence. Do I love him... do I love him.

I thought I'd say no. But when I opened my mouth, I said, "Yes, I do. But not how I love you, Robert. Not like a wife loves her husband. I love him like a dear friend. Like a long-ago love. Not up close. I love him from years and years away."

"Will you leave me be for a bit?" he asked. His voice cracking and breaking my heart.

"You want me to go to bed?" I asked.

"Yes. Go to bed. I need to be alone, okay, Gloria?"

Gloria. Not Ladygirl. Maybe never Ladygirl again.

I went to bed but I didn't sleep a wink. I heard him come in the house and then I heard some things breaking. But I didn't get up. After it got quiet I went to check on him. He was in the living room, asleep in his wheelchair, holding a picture frame. I eased it out of his hand, careful not to wake him. It was a picture of the three of us—me and Levi and Robert, our arms around one another from when we were kids. The three musketeers.

Our wedding picture was on the floor, glass broken. I took the photo out of the frame and eased that one back into his hands. He would wake up holding us as a couple. And I would put the picture of the three of us high up on a shelf, where it belonged.

The next morning I woke up to shouting.

"She's my wife!" yelled Robert.

I ran to the porch and out the screen door in time to see him throw his coffee cup at Levi. I froze.

"What part of that did you not understand, Levi? Were you still so angry at me for winning her heart? Were you angry at me for being healthy enough to fight in the war? Well, look at me, man! Who wins? WHO WINS NOW? You get the girl and you get to walk. You get a nice house and two kids, too. Happy? Are you happy?" He was pulling himself up by the porch columns, his legs slipping, but his arms holding strong.

Levi was white. Pale as if he was dead. I could tell he wanted to help Robert, but knew he mustn't get too close. Because in Robert's face was a rage neither one of us had ever seen. A rage that came from a dark, black place, Rita. The war was inside of him...ready to come out.

"I didn't get the girl, Robert. I might have got her attention for a second...but I didn't get her. She's always been yours, we all know it," said Levi, loud enough to be heard over Robert's roaring tenor. Just yelling without words.

That's when Robert fell. He fell to the ground, down the two small steps from the porch to the grass.

Levi couldn't stand it, so he reached down to help him up. But then Robert's arms shot up and before I knew it he'd turned Levi over and had him pinned to the ground. He was punching him, over and over again. Levi was struggling to get up...and that's when I unfroze.

"Stop it! STOP IT!" I cried. I threw myself on Robert's back, and he shot up his elbow. It clocked me right in the eye. I fell to the ground next to them, and I must have screamed because the children were out and on the porch, and then on top of me in a heap.

Robert turned to me, "Oh, Jesus, Glory! Are you okay?" He was at my side in a flash. "What did I do…? What have I done? What the hell is happening to us?" he choked out through his enraged broken heart. His eyes were absolutely frantic, Rita. I think it wasn't until that very moment that I understood the full ramifications of my transgressions. He fell back and leaned his body against the lattice of the back porch. The children went to him, trying to hush him. How they've fallen in love with their daddy so quickly. It's been a natural adjustment for them. He shines in their eyes.

Levi got up and backed about a yard away from the pack of us. There was crying and soothing and cooing going on for the children…and soon, believe it or not, there was laughing. All of us. Levi, too.

My eye hurt, but my heart was starting to heal.

When all the fuss quieted down, Levi was the first one to talk.

"I came over this morning to tell you I'm leaving. I'm going to California. I got a cousin out there who bought some land. He fought in the war, fell in love with grapes in Italy, I guess. Wants to start a vineyard."

"What do you want me to say?" asked Robert, smoothing back his hair. His hair that was growing in again, but there's gray there, Rita. And he was squinting at Levi. There were tears for that lost friendship, too. So many tears.

"Nothing," said Levi. "There's nothing to say. I'm sorry, Robert.

I'm sorry I tried to take something from you that we all know was always yours."

The wind blew through the trees. I heard my heart beating in my ears. This was it. He was leaving. He looked at me, into me and then past me like he'd seen a ghost.

"You leavin', Levi?" asked Robbie. "I don't want you to leave." He ran to Levi, who scooped him up. My thoughts and eyes went to Robert, who I know longed to do the same thing, but couldn't.

"Hey, little man. You got your dad back now. You don't need me around anymore."

He tried to set Robbie down, but that child's legs went to jelly.

"How about this, how about I go out to California and make a pretty penny. Then you and your mother, your father and baby Corrine can come out and visit me. Whaddaya say?"

The invitation seemed to do the trick. Robbie squirmed away and took off chasing Corrine, yelling, "She's no baby! She's a big old sore thumb!"

"I guess that's that," said Levi.

"Seems so," said Robert.

Levi rubbed some dirt off his pants and walked away. Down the path that I'd seen him run up a thousand times, and I knew I'd never see him there again.

"Damn, girl. Just go to him if you want to…" said Robert, noticing my stare. "I can't stop you, and right now I don't know if I want to."

I ran down the road after Levi. It was an easy thing to do because for the first time I knew what had to be done. There were no more questions in my heart.

"Levi!" I shouted. "Wait up!"

He turned to face me. The trees along our road arched over him, framing his masculine perfection. It's a vision I'll never forget. His nose was bleeding and he was wiping it away with a handkerchief. One I'd made for him.

"You coming with me?" he asked, his eyes shining.

For a moment I was sorry I'd run after him. It seems that all I do is hurt that man.

"No, Levi. I just wanted to tell you a proper goodbye. And a proper 'I'm sorry'—and a proper 'thank you.'"

"My ma always told me that true friends don't have to say those things. Are we still friends, Glory?"

"Always and forever," I said.

He began to walk away again and then turned around.

"Just so you know," he said, "I always knew it would be him. I knew it that night long ago at the Sadie Hawkins dance, and I knew it before we even kissed each other while he was gone. I knew this couldn't happen to us. Seems to me there are people in the world that you love…but that love isn't meant for the real world. It just can't work out. It was like a fairy tale, wasn't it, Glory?"

The tears were hot, the tears on my face. They stung and pulled at my swelling eye. "No, Levi. It was a lie I wanted to tell myself. A lie I made myself believe and it was so, so selfish of me."

We just stood there, looking at each other.

"Do you mind if *I* think of it as a fairy tale?"

I didn't know what to say, Rita, so I borrowed a line from when we were kids.

"I'm not the boss of you," I said.

"Damn, girl," said Levi, shaking his head and laughing. "I'd kiss you on the cheek, Glory, if I didn't think that would be dangerous. Better I leave now, okay? I'll write. I promise."

The "promise" lingered in the air between our bodies.

Then, in one of those fine moments that make up the tragic quilt of life, he was gone.

I walked back up the road and sat next to my husband on the ground.

"Can you ever forgive me?" I asked as we watched the children wander around the morning garden.

He didn't answer. My breath started to come out all shallow.

"Did he ask you to go with him?" he asked, finally breaking the silence.

"Yes," I said.

"And you came back to me?"

"Of course I did," I said.

It seemed as if Robert didn't know how to react. I wanted to reach out to him, Rita...but I knew it was too soon.

"And you want me to forgive you?" he asked, not able to look me in the eye.

I took a deep breath. "Yes. I want you to forgive me. I want you to forgive both of us."

We sat there for a long time listening to the children play. Letting the sun warm us.

Finally, he broke the silence. "I don't know. That's all I have, Glory. Is that good enough for now?"

"Yes. Anything that lets me stay here with you is good enough, Robert."

And it is. It IS good enough for now. Isn't it?

Love,
Glory

October 21, 1944

ROCKPORT, MASSACHUSETTS

Dear Rita,

Life is strange here. Robert hasn't said a word about Levi, or my confession. And I haven't brought it up, either. But it hangs between us. It tugs down at the end of our smiles.

We went into town for the first time as a family to get some shopping done. Robert is so strong. I can get the wheelchair in and out of the trunk of the car, but as soon as he can he takes over for me and wheels that thing around like nobody's business. He's so handsome. I think he's even better-looking now than before. I told him so. I think he believed me.

We couldn't get much done, as the local hero (Robert) garnered so much attention from everyone. I'm surprised there wasn't an impromptu parade. I'd have welcomed one, to be honest. I felt some cold eyes on me. Robert felt them, too, but that's when he grabbed my hand and kissed it.

That night he snuck out of bed again. But he wasn't gone long…

And when he came back inside I turned to him and kissed him like a wife should kiss her husband. I didn't know what else to do. And it felt right.

Anyway, that's what's going on here.

Love,
Glory

P.S. You know what Robert wanted me to make him for lunch yesterday? A sandwich on white bread with peanut butter and...get this...jelly! Have you ever heard of such a combination? I tried it, though. It's good. Reminds me of the sweet-and-sour chicken at the Chinese food pagoda.

—————

October 31, 1944 (Full moon tonight...spooky!)

IOWA CITY, IOWA

Dear Glory,

I haven't written in a few weeks because I'm giving you and your family a rest from outside meddling. Still, I find myself thinking about your situation every day. I'm not sure I would have told Robert, but, as my mother always said, "The truth comes out, whether you like it or not." It was rising to the surface, anyway, right? You just stuck your hand in the water and yanked it up, saving it some time.

Healing takes patience, which is something I'm trying to come to terms with.

Tonight, I've been sitting on the front porch passing out oatmeal cookies to the neighborhood children (recipe to follow). Before the war, the local schools hosted apple dunking contests and the neighbors gave candy treats to the children on Halloween. Now, the little ghosts and goblins traipse from door to door, asking for bits of aluminum and tin, shouting, "Scraps to beat the Japs!" instead of "Trick or Treat!"

But the children are snug in their beds at this hour, and I wouldn't be surprised to see a tumbleweed blowing down this deserted street. It's chilly, but I'm wrapped in a heavy quilt. The porch light aids the moon in providing light. I don't want to go inside. If I didn't worry about the baby waking in the middle of the night, I'd sleep out here with the rabbits and squirrels.

Little Sal is keeping the loneliness at bay, to a certain extent. On the days I don't work for Dr. Aloysius Martin, I lose myself in my grandson's eyes, which have finally found their color, a deep gray. It's been a while since I've taken care of such a young child, so when he settles in for his afternoon nap, I sneak one in as well. Some days I awake with a start, forgetting the year or where I am. My eyes search the room for proof that Sal existed. If I don't spot any, I convince myself I'm still in Chicago, still the kind of woman who sneaks into back alleys with gangsters. I lay there trembling, wondering if I really did find my way to the tailor shop, or if that was all a dream and I made the wrong choice and ended up with nothing.

Maybe it's easier to imagine the past two decades never happened than deal with the events of the past year.

Writing to you helps immeasurably. Roylene also helped, though she seems farther and farther away each day I don't receive a letter from her. I weave romantic tales for Little Sal, stories he won't remember, though I hope hearing about his parents will keep them present somehow. I tell him epic tales of Grandpa Sal's heroism, which strangely has a distancing effect for me. Was he really mine?

Tomorrow is All Souls Day. I don't think I'll go to mass. I need to spend the time remembering Sal's soul is with me. It's getting harder and harder to remember that lately.

I also think I'm going to head to the American Legion to see if I can be of more assistance. Funny how Victory seems within our grasp, yet there appears to be more work to do than ever. Mrs. Kleinschmidt is so enthralled by the single-mindedness of her purpose she's shaking like a Model T.

And…I very much like the idea of a visit, Glory. It gives me something wonderful to wait for. Now that's a change, isn't it?

Love,
Rita

Oatmeal Drop Cookies
1 cup flour
1 teaspoon baking powder
1/2 teaspoon salt
1 1/2 cups rolled oats
1/2 cup seedless raisins
1/4 cup brown sugar (firmly packed)
1 egg, beaten
1/4 cup dark molasses (I like to use blackstrap, but some can't handle the strong taste)
1/4 cup orange marmalade
1/2 cup shortening, melted

Mix and sift flour, baking powder and salt; stir in rolled oats and raisins. Stir brown sugar into egg; beat well. Beat molasses, marmalade and shortening into egg mixture. Gradually stir in oatmeal mixture. Drop from teaspoon on lightly greased baking sheet. Bake in moderately hot oven (375°F) for 12–15 minutes.

October 31, 1944

V-mail from Marguerite Vincenzo
to Seaman Tobias Vincenzo

Toby,

Remember my stories about the man who lived in the moon and ate Swiss cheese all night? He'll take care of you. Draw your soul into a tight ball and toss it to him. He'll keep it safe.

And that way, I'll be able to see it smiling down on me on nights like this.

Don't die. Refuse to. Come back to Iowa and let me fix what the war has broken. Sleep in your bed with your baby snuggled against your chest. Eat the meals I prepare. Sit on the front porch and watch the new world unfold. You have a place in it. I'm counting on that.

Happy birthday, baby.

I love you.
Ma

[Letter never sent.]

November 6, 1944

CEDAR FALLS, IOWA (WAVE TRAINING CAMP)

Dear Mrs. Vincenzo,

I'm going to Hawaii! Well, I'm going to California and then to Hawaii. It's mostly the yeomen (clerical gals) who get to travel, but when the lieutenant found out I had kitchen experience, she decided to send me to work in the Officers' Club. Doesn't that just float your boat! Ha! Another girl, Maxine, grew up in her granddad's diner. She's going, too. We get along all right, so I have high hopes.

Maxine says pineapples grow everywhere on the islands. If that's the case, I'll have to learn to cook with them real fast. I've never had one, have you? I bet they're sweet. It'll be nice to eat something sweet all the time. I thought about sending one to Little Sal if they'll let me, but I don't think I'll do that. I don't want his teeth to rot before giving them a fair chance.

Basic training hasn't been too tough. Lots of marching, cleaning and even marksmanship! You know, when I joined up the officers said I could free up a stateside navy boy so he could go help Toby fight in the Pacific. I am doing that, but I feel I'm doing much more. The officers keep telling us we're "vital" to the war effort, in so many ways. I like that word—*vital*. It makes me feel better about leaving you and Little Sal. I had some dark days after you dropped me at the camp. I'll tell you about it sometime, but let's say I was just about ready to go AWOL again. I made it to the fence and turned around.

I don't know what brought me back. I did think about what Charlie said when you sent me off. I also think about how puffed up with pride you get when people ask you about Toby. I want Little Sal to think about me that way someday, when he gets older and can understand things.

So thank you, Mrs. Vincenzo, for everything you've done for me. I won't ever let it slip my mind. Please give my sweet boy a kiss from his mama, and know that this letter is a hug for you.

Love,
Roylene Vincenzo (I like to write it)
Officer's Cook, SC, U.S. Navy

P.S. I've enclosed a letter for Roy. I know we left things real bad, but he's still my pop and I'm going far away. You can just slip it under the alley-side door of the tavern, so you don't have to see him. Thank you in advance.

=========

November 6, 1944

CEDAR FALLS, IOWA (WAVE TRAINING CAMP)

Dear Pop,

I had to go. You know that, don't you? I'm not Mama. I'm not running from you, though I have good reason. You got to admit it.

If you let yourself, you can be proud of me. I'm doing a good job, everyone says so. I'm a hard worker. You taught me that way of living. And that's something I have to admit.

The navy is sending me to Hawaii. I can hardly believe it. I wonder if it's going to match the place I already built in my head. I hope so.

Well, I want to say I'm leaving with no hard feelings. I'm going to walk on the plane thinking you feel the same. Even if you don't. I've got my own mind now.

But if you do feel the same, why don't you walk over to Mrs. Vincenzo's house and visit with your grandbaby? She might not be happy to see you at first, which you got to understand, but if you put in a little effort, she'll match it.

Well, take care of yourself, Pop. I'll see you after the war.

Your daughter,
Roylene

November 19, 1944

ROCKPORT, MASSACHUSETTS

Dear Rita,

Did you know that it was a woman who started the tradition of Thanksgiving as a set day and a national holiday? I didn't. I learn so much, every day. It's amazing what happens when you open yourself up to the world. It has so much to give. My cup runneth… as they say.

After I got your last letter I went back through my box (I keep all of your letters in this pretty tin candy box that my father gave me ages ago. It has vines and flowers all over it and it reminded me of you) and I looked back to last year's All Souls letter. So much has changed since then. So many hopes and dreams shattered and built back up. We're both changed now, you and I. For better or worse. But I couldn't love you more. Or ache for your letters more, either!

How I feel so lonesome in this house with Robert home, I will never understand. I feel like a tree in the backyard, all bare now with no leaves. Waiting, waiting for the snow to bury me so I can sleep for a little while.

What an inappropriate time for all of these somber feelings. The war is going well, and the holidays are…well…here already. My goodness. Time flies and stays still in the same breath.

I'm sad that you are missing Roylene, but I'm certain you are so, so proud of her. She'll be back, Rita. And you will have this time to bond with Little Sal. How lucky she is to have her baby being held in such safe arms.

What are your plans for Thanksgiving? I'm preparing for a proper meal this year. And I'll have a full table. I have so much to be thankful for. Robbie's improving health. Robert home alive. And my friendship with you.

I wish you could be here. Or I could be there. I want to cook next to you and be able to reach out my hands if you need one to hold. When you think of Sal, please try not to miss him too much. He's alive in the eyes of your grandson.

I worry about you all alone. Will Charlie come? Mrs. K.? Have you had word from Toby? Or Roylene? I'd rather be there in your world than here in mine.

You know, now that I think of it, that's exactly how I feel. Like a tree. Rooted in some ground I can't quite figure out. And all these things go on around me all the time. I provide shade and comfort and oxygen. People admire me or simply take no notice. I'm neither here nor there.

But my branches? They reach for the sun. Oh, Rita, how my arms ache as if they were reaching and reaching.

I'm always searching Robert's eyes for some sort of redemption. And I want to simply tell him that I'm more in love with him than I ever was. That I don't think about Levi anymore. I mean, besides a fond memory of when we were all kids. But I'm afraid he won't believe me. But I know you do. God, how I love my Robert. It's as if I forgot who he was, or something. I can't believe I ever thought I had a choice. He's my love. My one and only love.

I was giving Robbie a bath the other evening. We were listening to music on the radio. I was singing and humming along. I suppose my mind must have wandered off because he asked me the most astounding thing. He asked, "Mama, why do I miss you and you are right here with me?"

I need to find my moment here inside this life with them. I need to leave all those other things behind and look to the future.

We all do. Right? Our whole country needs to do that. I suppose I'm in good company!

This year, after taking time to emulate you, dear Rita, my mother-in-law and myself have formed a tentative friendship. And I'm giving her the highest of all honors by sharing her sweet potatoes with you. Claire never cooked a day in her life, but her cook, Nancy, swears by these. We'll see!

Sweet Potatoes
4 to 6 sweet potatoes
2/3 cup dark corn or maple syrup
1 orange, sliced
1/2 teaspoon grated orange rind
2 tablespoons butter or margarine
1/3 cup chopped nut meats
1/4 teaspoon salt (to bring out the sweetness!)

Peel sweet potatoes; then slice into a buttered casserole, arranging them in layers with orange slices and chopped nut meats. Dot each layer with butter and season with salt and pepper. Pour syrup over them. Bake in moderate oven for 1 hour. A little water or orange juice may be added if needed. Serves 4 to 6.

Love,
Glory

November 28, 1944

Dear Glory,

Your sweet potatoes were a big hit at the USO. And that's where I spent my Thanksgiving, passing out meals to those ready to head out, with Little Sal strapped tightly to my back, like a papoose.

It seems everyone is going to the Pacific now. This makes me both worried and hopeful.

Donna Reed stopped by Iowa City for the holiday. That girl is on a constant USO tour. She looked a little tired, but the boys went gaga for her, drooling all over their turkey dinners. She was sweet, and I'd kill for her legs, I'll tell you that much.

Oh, Glory, I couldn't stand to be in my house for Thanksgiving dinner. I would have been like Roylene, eating my meal standing at the kitchen counter, while the baby pushed mashed potatoes into his mouth. That's why I jumped at the chance to help out when Mrs. K. asked. I think my enthusiasm took her by surprise. She kept narrowing her eyes at me as we rolled bandages for the three hundredth time.

There was a certain feeling of excitement while we cooked— the ladies saying surely the end will come soon. I kept pretty quiet. We're still sending boys overseas, and people are still dying. The war will only be over for me when Toby comes walking through my front gate. And the war will never be over for Sal. He'll not see the ticker tape parades or hear Mr. Roosevelt's voice ringing over the land.

My blue mood kept me in a daze as I scooped potatoes and

poured gravy, so I didn't notice the tall, imposing sergeant talking to Mrs. Kleinschmidt until Mrs. Hansen elbowed me in the ribs and pointed him out.

As he spoke with Mrs. K., she pushed out her chest in an effort to match his military stance, her face reddening from the effort. "No!" she shouted. "No! No! No!"

He took a step closer and she kept her ground. "I am an American. I will not say one word to those…Krauts! Not a one!"

"But your country needs you," he said, and I've got to admit, it sounded a bit monotone and scripted. "The U.S. Army takes full responsibility." His nostrils flared as he stifled a yawn.

Mrs. K. pointed one arthritic finger at the sergeant's very decorated chest. "They are Nazis! Huns! Animals! You should lock them up and let a horse eat the key and shit into the river!" And then she stormed away, shouting epithets to anyone who cared to listen.

The sergeant shrugged and picked up a plate, coming down the chow line. When he got to the potatoes, he studied me for a long moment. *"Sprechen sie Deutsch?"*

Mrs. Hansen, fork paused midair with a hunk of dark meat hanging from it, looked at him as if he'd suddenly grown a second head.

So I answered him in English. "Yes, sir," I said. "My mother and father were both from Munich."

"May I speak to you privately?" he asked, with a stiffness that didn't suit him. "Army business."

I handed my spoon to a wide-eyed Mrs. Hansen and walked to the corner of the room with the sergeant, whose name I learned later is Friedrich, or Freddy, as he prefers.

Turns out the POW camp in Algona needs some translators. The prisoners write a weekly newsletter—in German—and the army translates it into English for approval before allowing it to print. With everyone stateside scrambling for leave over the holidays, they're short a few translators this December. Toss a coin in Iowa and you'll hit a German, but the thought of working with the enemy gives most people the heebie-jeebies. We were the fifth USO the sergeant hit up for volunteers.

"I'll do it as long as this guy can come with," I said, pointing to Little Sal. He'd fallen asleep, his soft head resting at the nape of my neck.

The sergeant smiled. "Junior soldiers are welcome, too."

He meant to be cute, but his words turned my spine to ice. Am I crazy for saying yes? Maybe. Mrs. K. spit on my shoes when she found out, and Mrs. Hansen said you can never really know your neighbors. I said that means I probably shouldn't watch little Vaughn anymore while she runs errands. She took it back.

Charlie thinks it's a great idea. He suspects the U.S. Army wants to keep our prisoners so well taken care of they'll go home to whatever's left of the Fatherland and tell everyone about the hospitality of the generous Yanks. "Brilliant public relations strategy," he called it. Irene's a bit more practical. With all the Iowans overseas or working in the factories, we're desperate for farmhands. Perfect work for POWs, as long as we keep them warm and well fed. "Necessary evil" was what she called it.

Dr. Aloysius Martin is convinced I'm a spy. When I mentioned visiting the camp in Algona, he winked at me, entranced by visions of his devoted secretary working for the OSS. Actually, that thought entered my head, as well. I must admit, as Freddy explained my duties, I fantasized about somehow recognizing the man responsible for Sal's death. I'd slip a knife into his liver and skedaddle before anyone was the wiser.

But I think the real reason I'm doing it is much more mundane— to keep my mind busy over the Christmas season. Hopefully next year, when Little Sal can run and talk, I won't need to keep devising ways to distract myself from reality. Or I'll learn to make a life from my distractions, I guess. That just might be the only way to keep on.

Anyway, hon, I wish your mind was more settled as well. I'll be thinking about you.

Love,
Rita

P.S. I got word from Roylene! She's headed to Hawaii after training. Every time I get a little down I picture that girl hula dancing in a grass skirt with flowers in her hair and some native boys fighting with each other to feed her chunks of pineapple.
P.P.S. I forgot to address the peanut butter issue. I have heard of those sandwiches, though I don't think I'd ever make one, especially for guests. Occasionally they're served in the university cafeteria. Sal always called them "cement mixers."

I have been making use of peanut butter recently, though in a pudding recipe. Irene really likes it! Let me know what you think.

Peanut-Honey Pudding
2 cups milk, scalded
1 cup soft bread crumbs
1/2 cup evaporated milk
1/2 cup peanut butter
1/4 cup honey
1/4 teaspoon salt
1/4 teaspoon ginger
1 egg, slightly beaten

Combine milk and crumbs; let stand 15 minutes. Add half of evaporated milk to peanut butter; beat smooth. Add remaining milk, beat

smooth. Mix honey, salt and ginger; add to peanut butter mixture.
Combine crumb mixture and peanut butter mixture. Add egg; mix
well. Pour into casserole; set in a pan of warm water. Bake in moder-
ate oven (350°F) 1 1/2 hours or until inserted knife comes out clean.

―――――――――

December 10, 1944

ROCKPORT, MASSACHUSETTS

Dearest Rita,

"Make a life from distractions…" Do you even know how wise you
are? How did I get so lucky, to pick you from that hat? (Well, your
name WAS the last one in there…so I suppose it was all meant to
be.)

I am thrilled to hear you will be translating. You must write and
tell me everything.

And, is it bad that I've fallen a little in love with your Mrs. K.?
I kind of wish she lived next door to me.

My Thanksgiving was lovely. Truly. And I thought of you all
day. Was it too awful, Rita? This first Thanksgiving without Sal?
Or did baby Salvatore help ease the pain a little bit? I love thinking
of you bouncing that baby on your knee.

My mother-in-law was able to come this year. I don't think I ever
told you what transpired the day I picked Robert up at the train
station. She wasn't there, you know. Robert hadn't seen her until
Thanksgiving evening when she came up the drive.

I'd just assumed that she and I would go together to pick him up, but when I rang her, she said, "Don't pretend you don't know he doesn't want me there!" and hung up on her end.

Later that night when we were settled in, I asked Robert about what she may have meant. He placed a hand on mine and looked into my eyes. "Glory, I wrote her from the hospital and told her not to come. I told her I couldn't have her meddling with us anymore. That you were my girl and if she wasn't going to let you alone, I'd just assume not know her anymore."

"Robert Whitehall!" I shouted. "That is your mother. You can't choose, you know." And that was that. I never really pushed the subject again.

Then, a week before Thanksgiving she called. They had a hushed conversation and when Robert came into the kitchen he asked if she could eat with us. I have to say I was relieved and frightened at the same time. Must life be such a confluence of juxtaposition ALL the time? It's so confusing! I wondered if she knew about Levi. Had heard the rumors in town. I wondered if she'd asked Robert about it. Did he defend me? He didn't mention anything at all about it.

So I said yes, of course. And I do think the reunion was successful. He seemed a little bit more whole after seeing her. God knows I can relate to having a mother you love, yet don't agree with. And in the surprise of all surprises, Claire Whitehall helped me with the dishes. And only broke two.

I lit the hurricane lamps and set up tables in the living room. That's the room downstairs that faces the sea, and with the trees bare there was a direct view. There was a warmth and an informality to the gathering that I most likely can't convey properly. There we were—me at one end of a long table, Robert at the other. The kids between us. Then there was Anna and Marie and Claire on the other side of the table. What a motley crew! We talked and reminisced about "Franksgiving" and how glad we are that the day is back where it should be. Though I didn't mind it earlier for those few years. I wonder if it really did make for a different set of sales in retail? Did it in Iowa City? Christmas isn't big here in Rockport in terms of retail.

Robert made a toast and there was an awkward moment when everyone, even Robert himself, thought he would stand. It was terrible for a moment and then he raised his glass.

"To Victory," he said. And I could almost see your Sal rising up behind him. He's with all of us now.

Happy holidays to you, my dearest friend,

Love,
Glory

P.S. Enclosed is Robbie's latest painting. It's of the Christmas angel, only it's a soldier. I asked who it was and he said, "Uncle Sal." XO

―――――

December 20, 1944

IOWA CITY, IOWA

Dear Glory,

It sounds as though your Thanksgiving dinner was held in the true spirit of the holiday. The most disparate personalities can manage to come together when a good meal sits on the table. I raise my glass to Robert in absentia. To Victory, yes, and to those who've brought us to its threshold.

In all likelihood this package won't arrive at your doorstep until after the holidays. It's a good thing I don't work for Santa, as it seems I am unable to send Christmas gifts on time! The recipe included with this letter is for you. And I do hope Robbie likes his present—the beret was Sal's. All artistes should look the part, right? Mrs. K. helped with the dress for Corrine.

And speaking of my next door neighbor...

Breaking news on the Iowa front: Mrs. K. is NOT a widow!

Is your mouth hanging open? Mine was surely catching flies.

Let me explain...

I hated to think of Roylene wearing those worn feed-sack dresses when not in uniform, so I decided to refashion a few of mine as a Christmas present. I knew I'd have trouble with some of the new necklines, so I bit down my pride and knocked on Mrs. K.'s door. I expected she'd turn me away. To my surprise, she didn't do much of anything. The door opened and she made a sound and disappeared into the depths of her home.

An open door is a sort of invitation, so I followed.

Mrs. K.'s living room appeared normal—spotless, orderly, smelling slightly of onions—but something was off. In the kitchen, the morning's newspaper covered the table where Mrs. K. usually sat copying V-mails. With a sigh she pulled out a chair and dropped herself heavily into it.

"What's wrong?" I, of all people should understand blue moods, but the sight of a depressed Mrs. K. brought an unexpected surge of irritation.

Her face remained blank.

"For the love of God, what is it?" I wanted to shake her.

The old woman's fingers crawled across the tabletop and slid a yellowed photograph from underneath *The Daily Iowan*.

It was a wedding portrait. The man was well-built and serious of expression, the woman stout and dreamy-eyed. Two strangers.

"It is our anniversary," she whispered.

Funny, I'd forgotten Mrs. K. had to be married at some point to be called a widow. I couldn't imagine her waking up to this man, nuzzling his shoulder, cooking him breakfast, ironing his shirts. Standing there, I realized that I'd always wondered about her past—but never found the right moment to ask. The question was about to jump from my rude tongue when she offered the information herself.

After her parents died, Mrs. K. opened a fabric and notions shop with her small inheritance. To offset the cost of doing business, she worked as a seamstress on call for the University of Berlin.

Every spring she kept busy repairing and sewing *talars*—those black, voluminous gowns professors wear at graduation ceremonies. One Saturday morning Helmuth Kleinschmidt pushed open the door to her shop and demanded she whip one up for him. He sighed and drummed his fingers on the counter while she finished with another customer, ill at ease in a place reserved for women. His manner bothered her, and Mrs. K.—*Bruna*—questioned him, saying he did not look old enough to be anything more than a student.

He barked his résumé at her. Helmuth was a prodigy of sorts, lecturing at the university before he'd even finished his degree. "In the time it takes you to walk around the block," he said to her, "I'll have earned my doctorate."

Though she knew how to read and write well enough, Mrs. K. was intimidated by erudition. She silently bent at his feet with her measuring tape, and began preparing the order.

As she slid the tape up his inseam her hand began to tremble. She prayed he wouldn't notice, and he didn't, until she looped it around his muscular neck. He teased her about it. She smiled and forced herself to meet his gaze. They were married within the year.

Helmuth Kleinschmidt was twenty years old on his wedding day. His bride was thirty-one.

People laughed. They said Helmuth wanted a nursemaid, not a wife.

Which was true enough. Helmuth finished his graduate studies in record time, mostly because his wife cooked and cleaned and worked tirelessly to support him. While he fought in the Great War, she worked. When he resumed his low-paying teaching job at the university, she worked. When he said they were moving to America, that he had been offered a tenure-track position in Philosophy, she was so busy it took her a week to ask where.

"Iowa City," he said.

"Is that near New York?"

"Dummkopf," he said.

They settled in and enjoyed the social life of an up-and-coming scholar and his wife. Mrs. K. reprised her job sewing and repairing graduation robes, and nearly doubled their income. She was happy. So much so that she didn't notice his absences, the late-night "German club" meetings held in their cavernous basement, the last-minute trips to academic conferences she's now certain never existed.

When she returned from installing some curtains at the university one afternoon in the summer of 1927, he was gone. A rather curt note lay on her pillow. "I've returned to Germany," it said. "I trust you'll be fine, Bruna."

Few people asked, but when someone did she always said he'd gone back to visit his parents in Berlin and got hit by an omnibus. She didn't care if it was bad luck to create someone's death story. She figured he deserved it.

After a year or two she'd convinced herself he really was dead.

Then, in 1938, a letter from her cousin Adele stopped Mrs. K.'s heart. Adele had seen Helmuth in Stuttgart. He looked dashing in his high-ranking Nazi officer's uniform. He hadn't the time for conversation, but it appeared as though life in Germany had been good to Herr Kleinschmidt.

After eleven years, it finally hit her that he had left.

Anger became Mrs. K.'s constant companion, and later, as the war unfurled, fear.

"This is why I can't go to the prison camp," she said after I'd digested her story. "HE might be there. Bastard."

I nearly said, *No, HE is probably lying facedown in a ditch with Uncle Sam's footprint on his back*...but I didn't. She still thinks about him, which means, in some way, she still loves him.

I put my hand on her shoulder, which I don't think I'd ever done. "How about we get you all dolled up so you can flirt with Sergeant Freddy," I said. "Make Helmuth crazy jealous."

I got the tiniest movement in her upper lip. *"Hure,"* she called me (it means what it sounds like). We were back to familiar terrain.

We spent the rest of the afternoon creating dresses for Roylene that would put anything in *Harper's Bazaar* to shame. Mrs. K. said my sewing would horrify Sal's mother, but I think I did all right!

And you know, I didn't think I wanted any more surprises in life, but I was lying to myself. The world can change on a dime, but I guess that isn't always a bad thing.

Have a joyous holiday, Glory. Please send my good wishes to everyone in Rockport.

Love,
Rita

P.S. Mrs. K.'s admission got me thinking about how tightly we hold on to things, even when there's no harm in loosening the grip a bit. It's about time I shared some more of my family with you, hon, so Merry Christmas. This one's for you. I think my husband would be pleased to know it's in good hands.

Sal's Favorite Minestrone
(Most people start with meat stock, but Mama Vincenzo always used vegetable, which is ideal now. She said it was "cleaner," whatever that meant....)

Dice an onion. Cook it up in a pot with a little butter and olive oil until it softens. Add some chopped celery, garlic, oregano, basil, parsley. Add a dash of salt and pepper. This is tonic for the blood.

Slowly pour 5 cups of vegetable stock into the pot.

Chop up some potatoes and add them to the soup. Then add three times as many tomatoes. This is to keep a person connected to the earth.

Add some chopped carrots and diced courgette. This is to keep a person bright-eyed.

Toss in a handful of spinach, and as many green beans as you like. This is for strength.

Add some salt for the women in your life, and some pepper for the men—but not too much! Turn the heat down low.

If you let the minestrone simmer for less than two hours then Mama Vincenzo will haunt your kitchen for years....

If you don't cover it in parmesan before you eat it, Sal will!

———

December 25, 1944

ROCKPORT, MASSACHUSETTS

Dear Rita,

Today was a wonderful day. I feel like my old self again, sort of. Nothing strange or magical occurred. It was just a perfect Christmas

Day. Robbie and Corrine are getting so big. Their absolute excitement was a joy to watch.

I knelt with them on the floor as they tore open their gifts. The house was full of glistening Christmas lights and the smell of the Douglas fir.

A sense of peace and normalcy permeated the whole, quiet day. And the snow! How it sparkled and fell down on the world, coating it in a pure white blanket. It was as if there was no war going on at all.

I made a plum pudding and a roast. Everything was delicious. And I invited absolutely everyone, but in the end it was only us because of the snow. My quiet little family. Robert and the children.

I can't say there isn't a sad sort of tension between us, Robert and I…but I can say that we love each other.

We've had word from Levi. Robert got a letter and he left it unopened for two days on the kitchen counter. I didn't touch it, even though it killed me not to. Finally, I noticed it was gone and I waited. Robert told me about it the next morning over breakfast. Seems Levi is doing well. He's found a girl and he is going to give working on that vineyard a try. He's happy. And I'd be lying if I said I didn't feel a little bit of my heart is there with him. But I am filled up here. Finally.

He sent his love to all of us. I knew that part was hard for Robert to share, and I loved him for it. One woman does not deserve so much love.

I'm thinking of all the letters I've sent complaining about my life. They embarrass me. I hope you have never thought of me as ungrateful. Well…I suppose I've thought of myself like that, so I guess you are allowed to, as well.

One thing I want to mention is that I thought of you all day. I know this is your first Christmas without Sal someplace in the world. I pray you were not alone, that Charlie and Irene came. Or Mrs. K. I wish you would just pack everything up and come live in your sunflower room. Goodness. My life would be perfect then. But I know Sal is with you. I know he is showering you with love and kisses and he's also filling up Toby with strength and courage so that he'll return home to you safe and sound. And soon.

Also, I've thought a lot about the possibility that Sal sent you Roylene. The heavens must work like that.

Merry Christmas, Rita. And Happy New Year. I am busy daydreaming about our meeting. I can almost smell Little Sal's fuzzy head! (Does he have hair yet? My children took ages to grow hair.)

Glory

===========

December 25, 1944
(Late, late at night—way past lights out!)

ALGONA, IOWA (POW CAMP)

Dearest Glory,

Merry Christmas!

I'm writing from a narrow cot in the visitors' barracks of the Algona POW camp. As you can imagine, this room is pretty empty. Tonight, only three beds are full. Well, three and a half. Irene lies snoring on one side of me and Charlie is stretched out on the other, his feet hanging off the edge. They drove me here with plans to drop and go, but the heavy snow changed their minds. I'm glad to have them, and you know, I think they had a good time.

Little Sal is sleeping at the foot of my bed in a soldier's trunk we converted into a makeshift crib. Charlie kept calling it a manger, which cracked everyone up.

The men here are surprisingly dear. Most are around Toby's age, but the youngest prisoner is fourteen years old, and the oldest is sixty-five. Hitler must be desperate indeed to draft children and the elderly. Heinrich, the older man, crafted an American army vehicle of scrap wood and canvas. It hung on the tree in the officer's barracks. Sergeant Freddy gave it to me for Robbie, along with a sculpted angel for Corrine. I'll ship another package to you as soon as I can. Heinrich carved der Weihnachtsmann (Santa Claus) for Little Sal. The baby blinked his long lashes at the elderly gentleman, and then promptly shoved the sculpture in his mouth.

It's hard to imagine, but the first time I came to Algona I had no contact with the prisoners at all. I thought that was just fine. I didn't know if I'd be able to speak with the POWs without my sharp tongue coming out. How could they be so stupid as to follow a madman?

On my start day, Sergeant Freddy met my bus at the gate and walked me through the officers' club. Those fellas know how to live. The OC has a bar and waiters in formal white dress, and—get this—slot machines! Charlie spotted them at the Christmas party tonight and his eyes glowed brighter than the brass band playing "Blue Skies." Irene and I steered him toward the bar. We figured it was the safer vice.

Anyway, that first time I reported for duty I sat in a small office and, armed with a cup of coffee and a typewriter, began the translation. Sergeant Freddy had me attack some of the older issues for practice. At first I found some of their writings offensive; using haughty tones, they discussed an immense longing to return to the Fatherland and reveled in their "Germanness." They complained about what I considered to be minor things in comparison to what I'm sure the American POWs are enduring. But as I read on, I began to realize one thing: these men are happy. Yes, they are working hard (mostly on farms, but also in canning plants and nurseries, and even the hemp plant near Eldora), but they're getting paid AND enjoying themselves. When not working they hold concerts and boisterous physical competitions. They recite poetry and play organized sports. They make use of the lovely library filled with donated books.

It should have made me angry. Instead, it filled me with the most glorious sense of pride. This is what Sal and Robert fought for, and what Toby and even Roylene continue to defend. This is America. The generosity of spirit, the understanding of human dignity, the concept of allowing our enemies to partake in the bounty of our land, because we are faithful to our promise when we signed the Geneva Conventions and because, quite simply, it's the right thing to do. These men, our prisoners, see all this and like what they see, believe me.

One sweet boy, his cherry cheeks and golden hair identical to Toby's, told me he wanted to stay in the States when the war was over. Unsure of whether this was possible, I simply smiled at him and asked, in German, "Won't you miss your mother?"

"My mother died," he explained in fairly good English. Then he swept his arm toward the window, at the great fields of northern Iowa. "And now I have a new one," he added, a note of finality in his voice.

And for the first time I could really see the end of this war, Glory.

Later...can't sleep...

I was going to save this for another time, but my mind is whirring and I don't think sleep will come tonight. Strange place, strange noises—and I don't think it's Santa Claus pushing his chubby self down the chimney.

I keep assuring myself that every man is tucked in his bed, including the camp, which is now covered by a blanket of snow. Maybe my nerves are still humming from the Christmas party I attended just hours ago. It was one of great cheer. I know we're in what is essentially a prison, but the men put on the most touching Nativity play (where Little Sal really did lie in a manger), and afterward we were treated to a festive art show. There were prizes, and the competition grew so intense it could've heated this entire barracks.

The only problem was most of the men painted the same thing—a family farm. It was impossible to tell if they used memory as a model or if they were simply painting what they've been seeing every day working for the local folk. Irene skipped the competition in favor of taking Little Sal to investigate the library, so Charlie and I strolled past the paintings, one after the other, giggling at the prospect of Sergeant Freddy trying to come up with a winner.

As we made our way back to the Officers' Club, we passed through a door frame hung with mistletoe. I wouldn't have noticed—who expects to see mistletoe in an all-male POW camp?—but Charlie gently placed his hand on my arm to slow me. He pointed to the hanging leaves and shrugged, then swooped down for his kiss.

I'm not exactly sure why I didn't stop him. Maybe because underneath the officers' whiskey, his lips tasted of the honey-rich smoothness of kindness and adoration. When he pulled away he stood close but didn't touch me. "I'm not saying it has to include me, but you have a future, Rita. It might not feel right to think it, but know inside yourself that it's there waiting for you."

We started walking again and my eyes darted around the room, looking for Sal. I was certain he was hiding somewhere in the room, watching us. Of course he wasn't there, not even his ghost.

I wanted to cry. Did I cross over some great divide? Is the first step in moving on the moment when you can separate the here and now from what was?

I'm crying now, hon. For my husband? For myself? For the sweet babe lying at my feet, who will never feel the comfort of his grandfather's strong hand holding his?

I'm not sure yet. But then I guess I don't have to be.

Rita

January 9, 1945

ROCKPORT, MASSACHUSETTS

Dear Rita,

I remember learning in school, that in some ancient societies when people died, they believed there were three heavens. One for the body, one for the soul and one for the personality. The body was taken care of by burying the people with their things. Worldly goods. The soul was thought to fly above and become part of what the person's soul most dreamed of...and the personality? Well, that was up for interpretation.

I suppose your letter, particularly the part about Charlie under the mistletoe, made me think about this. You are still alive, Rita. And you can feel safe building a life around you that feels wonderfully solid—because all who know you, know that your Sal is the person who exists in the heaven for your soul. He's with you. You will be with him again. But I have to believe that when we die, we are able to see things clearer. Free from all the burdens of what society thinks are right and wrong.

Are you pure of heart? Of course you are!

Finally, I think I can say the same of myself. Sometimes, Robbie asks for Levi. He's clever, though. Like his father. He only asks me. He only asks in a whisper. "Where is Levi?"

And I tell him, "Levi was here to help us when we were so, so worried about Daddy. He was our war angel. Now he's gone to have his own wife and maybe his very own little boy someday."

My son seems to accept that. And I accept it, too. Even though I know it's far too simplistic a way to explain what really happened here, time lets us lie a little to ourselves. Time does indeed heal.

Our holidays were lovely. And thank you so, so much for the Christmas package. It arrived on New Year's Day and the children had another Christmas. What a gift, truly.

On New Year's Eve, I must admit…I had a moment. Thinking about all that has transpired in the course of one small year. It takes my breath away.

And you. Helping those lost souls. I can only hope Sal and Robert found the same kindness when they were overseas.

Happy New Year, my friend.

Love,
Glory

P.S. Can we begin to plan our meeting? I find myself daydreaming of it all the time.

February 24, 1945

IOWA CITY, IOWA

Dear Glory,

Oh, busy days, busy days. How is it that the war is winding down yet we're moving faster and faster, as if God is cranking up the wheel Himself?

On Saturday we had a birthday party for Little Sal, with a festive Hawaiian theme. Roylene sent a very colorful shirt from the islands, along with a tender note. Irene baked a coconut cake and Mrs. K.—I kid you not—attempted a hula dance in my living room. I don't know if I'll ever recover from the sight.

Charlie brought a tricycle. Little Sal is much too young for it, but the thought was sweet. Mrs. K. said Charlie must have conjured it up from 1940, as no kid around here has seen a new bike in years. "I made it myself, with scrap parts," Charlie said, and, you know, I believe him.

"I suppose the war effort could do without a few pieces of metal," Mrs. K. said, so I think she believes him, too.

Little Sal stared at the shining bike like it had dropped from heaven. He scooted over to it on his tush, and then held the seat to push himself to standing. I worried he'd lose his balance and fall onto the handlebars, but before I could scoop him up...he took a step, then another, and one more before crashing to the floor. Little Sal froze, startled, until what he'd accomplished dawned on him, sparking a grin from ear to ear.

Then he pushed himself up and tried again.

And I let him.

What do you think of that?

Rita

═══════════

March 15, 1945

ROCKPORT, MASSACHUSETTS

Dear Rita,

You are right about the busy, busy new world. Don't get me wrong, I'd never wish those long days of waiting and worrying back again, but time did seem to stand still—almost suspended—before Robert came home.

Now, between raising two children, taking care of Robert (though he's gotten so good at taking care of himself), the housework and my Women to Work meetings, I can't get a moment to myself.

It's bittersweet, really. No more long teas in the sunflower room pouring over your letters. No more time to write pages and pages to you.

Which is why we need to plan our meeting. I go to bed at night counting the pies I'll make. Three blueberry, four peach. It's fun. I can't wait to see your face. Hear your voice. Hold your hand. You've gotten me through some of the roughest times in my life, Rita. I hope I've been a help for you, as well. Sometimes I worry that I've just been one more thing for you to take care of. I'd like to give something back to you. Something that time will withstand. A friendship that won't end.

Our friendship won't end, will it? Please not that. I won't let it.

Anyway, I do have NEWS!

I was speaking at a (freezing cold) outdoor rally the other day. We are trying to work with factories all across Massachusetts. You see, as the men come home…the women are losing their jobs. There has to be a way for all of the workers to keep their jobs. How can we expect women to return back to the lives they lived before? It isn't possible.

So there I was, flyers shaking in my gloved hands. Speaking about positive and professional protest. And I looked all the way to the back of my small, brave crowd…and guess who was there?

Robert. Somehow, Robert had convinced Marie to help him into town so he could watch me speak. Can you imagine?

After, we went into town and I bought hot chocolate from the local soda jerk. Then we went down to the pier where we used to go as kids to play pirates. We sat close together on a bench to keep warm. Oh, Rita. If you could have seen the sparkle in his eyes. It was like he was falling in love all over again. I know I was.

"You were wonderful!" he said.

"Thank you. I was worried you wouldn't like me sticking my nose in all this," I said.

"Nonsense. It's the part of you I love the most."

I kissed him then, tasting the cold on his mouth. Letting his kiss warm my own. And then I pulled away….

"I'm so, so sor—" I began. He held his fingers up to my lips; our faces were so close that my nose pressed up against those strong fingers. He leaned his forehead against mine and closed his eyes.

"Don't say it, Ladygirl. You were lost. I was lost. We've found our way back now. And people who survive, they don't look back. It's a rule of war. Keep moving ahead."

Oh, Rita. He called me Ladygirl.

Love,
Glory

P.S. HAPPY BELATED BIRTHDAY, LITTLE SAL!

I am so happy he is such a big, brave boy. I've sent a basket for that bike. Let him ride like the devil, but tell him that sometimes he must stop and pick some flowers for his grandma.

—————————

April 11, 1945

IOWA CITY, IOWA

Dear Glory,

One year. How is it possible?

Here I am, getting my garden ready, washing the dinner dishes, mending a skirt, writing—so much the same, yet so much different. Now a sturdy toddler helps me plant my sunflowers. And dear friends place bouquets on my front porch, a reminder that sorrow can bring sweetness as well.

One year.

I woke up this morning and asked Sal to give me a sign, something to let me know he was still present, still watching over me. I dropped Little Sal at the USO and walked to work, eyes bright, searching.

I came up blank.

Dr. Aloysius Martin asked me into his office after lunch. The university has begun preparing for increased enrollment when the boys return from overseas. Florence met a naval officer in San Diego, so they'll be looking for me to go full-time during the school year, when Roylene returns, of course. My performance has been exemplary, he said.

I stood there looking at him for a minute. Was this it? It was the only extraordinary thing to happen to me all day. Was this Sal's sign?

Then something struck me. It's time for me to stop asking Sal to give. He gave me everything when he was living; why do I keep asking him to pull double-duty?

I decided right there to take the doctor's offer. It was a sign, but not from Sal. It came from me. You once said I honor Sal by taking care of Toby. What you also meant was I honor him by living. Which I intend to start doing.

It's time to start jumping off some cliffs.

As part of my pay package, I'll be eligible to take courses free of charge. I'm going to take advantage of this. Charlie thinks I should take Advanced Psychology. Irene votes for Creative Writing. I might take both, thank you very much.

With all this consideration of the future, I can't help but get excited thinking about our reunion. Hopefully by next summer this war will be over, and I can bring my family to meet yours. It simply will happen—the soul meeting the body, so to speak.

Love,
Rita

May 8, 1945, VE Day (very late at night)

ROCKPORT, MASSACHUSETTS

Darling Rita,

This should be (and is!) a day of great celebration. And celebrate we did! Impromptu parades and rallies and cheering commenced almost in conjunction with the sunrise. What a day. A day for the history books. A day for the ages. I'm sitting here in my nightdress curled up in your sunflower room and I can still hear the people on the beaches with their bonfire celebrations. The smoke and laughter floating in with the night breeze. I can feel it trying to coax me into its wonderfulness.

But it can't. This day is such a sad day, too. I think that's what I was feeling all day. Relief, yes. And pride. I'm so, so proud of our fine soldiers and our wonderful country. But I'm so sad, Rita. Too sad to let anyone know about it but you. It makes me feel selfish, this sadness.

Just yesterday I bought the *Life* magazine with the photographs of the concentration camp at Buchenwald. Did you see it? That woman photographer Margaret Bourke-White took them. (Part of the reason I wanted it was because she's a woman in a man's world creating amazing things.)

Did I ever tell you that Anna is Jewish? Marie, too. So there I was with it spread open on my lap, sitting in the small meadow that separates my property from Anna's, and it was surreal looking at those horrific photographs of bodies piled on one another while there I was in real time with the meadow just blooming with clover and sea grass. Marie walked over to me and sat down on my blanket. I thought of hiding the magazine but didn't have much time, or any hiding place.

"Don't worry, doll. I've already seen it," she said, and I breathed a sigh of relief.

"Just awful," I said, and wanted to choke on the sterility of those words. Of course it was awful. What was I thinking?

Marie put a hand on my shoulder. "Have you ever heard of *tahara?*"

I told her I hadn't and then she explained. It seems that there is this amazing and ancient Jewish tradition, part of a burial rite, actually, wherein women gather and wash the bodies of the dead repeating, "She (or he) is pure, she is pure, she is pure," and then they drape the body in pure white cloth, like a heavenly outfit. Well, the point is that none of the people who were killed by the Nazis were given the right of *tahara*. She said it was one of the things that bothered her the most.

I left the meadow after speaking to Marie and felt an aching for the world that I can't describe. And then earlier today when everyone else was celebrating I was thinking about them. All of those who died in this war. All who will die yet.

Oh, Rita. The absolute injustice of it all. Something must happen from all of this loss. A tide will turn. I'm thinking of things I see in my own sweet town. Hatred of Negroes, fear of the Jewish among us. A misunderstanding of any culture different from what we are accustomed to. I'm thinking of my childhood caretaker Franny... and how if we were in Nazi Germany or occupied by Nazi Germany how many of us would be killed? Would I know the faces in the piles of bodies? Would I be in the piles because I speak out for women's rights? Would my children be in the piles? Would you be in the piles because of a last name like Vincenzo?

This must be a day of celebration but also a day of reckoning. A day to remember human rights.

I love you, dear Rita. I love you and I pray that someday you come to me, because I don't think I can do all this work without you. And there is so much work to do in a world that's gone mad. So many rights to fight for and preserve. I don't feel like I can do it alone. I need you. I'll always need you.

And I know, in reality, that you have a full life there in Iowa. So forgive me this moment of weakness. But in all sanity I'm telling you right here in black and white (and on a day that ends in so many ways the beginning of our relationship…) that this room is always here for you. It will be yours forever. And I will always be here, waiting.

Love,
Glory

June 9, 1946

ROCKPORT, MASSACHUSETTS

Dear Sal,

Remember the time we got up in the wee hours to drive to the county fair in Marengo? I balanced my famous strawberry-rhubarb pie on my lap the whole thirty miles, only to drop it in the dirt ten feet before the judging table. I bawled so hard I scared Toby. But you…you picked up the mess and started eating with your hands. I think I called you a damned lunatic—I don't remember, but I know my mouth and what came out wasn't nice. I clearly remember what *you* said. "I'm not tasting this pie. I'm tasting all the pies you've made since you cut me a slice and passed it across the counter at the Mondlicht Café. I know what you can do."

Oh, you wonderful man. You saw everything inside me, every pathway to my heart. Every thought, profound to petty. You laughed away the bad and celebrated the good.

To be known, really known, is the essence of love. To live without love is a shadow life. I crept in that darkness when you left for training, Sal. And it nearly swallowed me whole when you died. In a way, I wanted it to.

Until someone decided she knew me well enough to point out why I had to live. I'm sitting in the room she painted for me right now. The sunflowers on the wall reach for a heaven that's lucky to have you. She's stenciled your name on one flower, and mine on another, and Toby's, Roylene's and Little Sal's on the leaves tying them together. She knows what's in my heart. And she knows because you taught me how to let myself be known.

We arrived yesterday, a two-car caravan—one for us, and another for Mrs. K., Charlie and Irene. The ancient road slowed the wheels, and we chugged up the path like a cab heading to the peak of a roller coaster. So, so slowly. My breath went shallow, then stilled in my lungs. My heart pounded louder than the struggling engine.

The house was smaller than I'd imagined, and painted a peaceful shade of off-white, like fresh milk in a saucer. A woman stood in the screen door, her figure outlined in shadow. She cried out as she skipped across the porch, the wind lifting her dark curls in welcome. I pushed out of the still-moving car and tripped into the brightness of a New England sun. We'd both shrugged off our shoes, though we didn't know it. Our feet barely touched the ground.

I took her in, no words, no sound, nothing but her steady gaze, a balm to soothe what the terrible war had ravaged. Her capable hands called to me. They held the pen that kept my soul afloat when I wanted to drown it in a bathtub full of grief, and still they reached, their strength holding me up yet again.

We pulled at each other, tugged even—making sure we were real flesh and blood, a dream come to reality. We laughed. We caught tears with the pads of our fingers.

It was glorious.

I'll remember this moment forever, I thought. *I will take its beauty with me.*

She was the one who told me I could do that. When I felt you slip from my grasp, she showed me how to dance cheek-to-cheek with my dashing soldier. She taught me how to take the past and press it carefully onto the present moment, so, so gently, as to not mar the future.

It is in these moments, when the past gives the present its rosy glow, that we will find each other.

So I'll be seeing you, Sal. When your grandson laughs delightedly as his mother pulls a face, I'll be seeing your sense of humor. When your son sits under an oak tree, scribbling epiphanies in a composition notebook, I'll be seeing your erudition. When I catch myself swaying to a tune on the radio, I'll be seeing your grace.

And as I sit here in a room warmed by the sun, in the house of a woman you brought me to, I see your love.

I'll be seeing you, Sal. Always and forever,

Rita

PUBLISHED IN
THE DAILY IOWAN,
JULY 28, 1946

War Bonds
by Toby Vincenzo

A recounting of the poet's mother meeting a wartime pen pal

There was a waiting time,
when the people made sense of God's mess
A nightmare objective
Fields of the dead
And through it all, two women wrote
intentions
dreams
loss
on paper with steady hands.
Trusting friendship and humanity they wrote
as the pages flew across time and space
Little by little
pace by pace
a war bond grew
Something new
and green among the red fields of war
And somehow, she here, her there
It became a bigger thing than even all their lives
And a triumph was no good without the other

tragic things come and go
nothing was real that wasn't written
Down
She here, her there
they forged a mighty thing
a garden all its own
to grow and sing
Soon the letters couldn't be enough
The long dry seasons in between
she here, her there
and in the air
a buzz of wonder:
Does her hair shine?
It was time.
She here, her there
to be together in the everywhere
A date was made
To mark the big event
Families, long known but never seen
gathered like chickens to the fence
here there everywhere
They met at the ocean place of one
where the sunflowers carried the name of the other
And the car couldn't chug up the gravel road
fast, fast enough
She was out and running
as the other slammed the screen door,
flowered dresses,
hair askew
High heels tossed in tandem.
Nothing else but them.

Family gathered around
no sound
to watch them touch each other's faces
and link arms
silent now no words
turning away from all the rest of us
Walking down the path to where the ocean meets the whale rocks
of the sea
Flowers blooming in their wake, they walked.
What miracle is this?
That they didn't notice.

* * * * *

ACKNOWLEDGMENTS

Loretta Nyhan

I'll Be Seeing You, a book about the power of friendship, would not exist without the generous spirits and open hearts of my friends listed below:

To my fantastic agent, Joanna Volpe, the miracle worker, who always knows how to take a sad song and make it better. You're the greatest, Jo! Huge thanks to Nancy Coffey, Kathleen Ortiz and the incredibly smart, hard-working team at New Leaf Literary and Media Representation.

To the talented Erika Imranyi, the best editor two writers could possibly hope for, whose sharp eye and kind heart truly brought this novel to where it needed to be. I can't imagine Rita and Glory's story in anyone else's hands. Thanks also to Leonore Waldrip, and the entire team at Harlequin MIRA.

To my early readers and writer buddies: the kindly assassin Kelly Vaiciulis, my walking partner Kathleen Bleck, Jenny Kales, Mike Callero, Erin Nyhan, Anna Maria Koch and photographer extraordinaire Alexa Frangos—thanks for your wisdom and good advice.

To my LGP ladies, especially my book club, Baby's Got Paperback, for their kind support, and for welcoming me with open arms. Thanks also to the Terry Family, especially Margaux, for her enthusiasm.

To all my New Leaf agency sisters, who cheered me on from the start, especially Erica O'Rourke, Holly Bodger, Kody Keplinger and Amy Lukavics. The Team Volpe retreat needs to happen, and soon.

To the patron saints of novenas and prosecco, Lisa and Laura Roecker, who always held me up from afar—I'm forever grateful.

To Jean Lawlor, who never laughed when I added Cherry Coke to my beer, and always partnered up with me for square dancing in gym class. Thank heavens for Wendy's salad bar, circa 1984.

To my wonderful in-laws, Tom and Maureen Nyhan, and the rest of the Nyhan clan, especially Mike, Dan, Ann, Seamus, Liam, Erin and Alex Sinvare. I am a lucky girl to have married into such an amazing family.

Special thanks to my brother, Steve Roach, his wife, Lori, my godson, Liam, my brother-in-law, Brent Georgi, my nephew, Alex, and my sister, Joyce, who knows me better than anyone, and still loves me. Thanks, my sista.

To my parents, Henry and Maxine Roach, who have always supported me, even when they probably thought I was a little crazy. They've given me the most important thing parents can give a child—the knowledge that she is loved. I can't thank them enough.

To the three great loves of my life, my heroes, Tom, Dan and Jack, who have brought me so much joy.

And to Suzy. Oh, Suzy. Someday we will meet, and I'll take your hand and never let go. Thank you, my friend. For everything.

Suzanne Hayes

I'd like to send my sincerest thanks to my husband, William, and my three daughters, Rosy, Tess and Grace, for being so patient and for cheering me on.

And to the readers of the many incarnations of this project: Jan Nichols, Michelle Esposito, my mother-in-law, Margaret Palmieri, and my great-aunt, Rita Palmieri.

To my agent, Anne Bohner, who changed my life.

To our amazing editor, Erika Imranyi—what can I say? Your vision for this novel was mightier than mine, and it carried me through. A great editor is an artist, and you, my friend, are indeed great. Thanks, also, to the ever fearless Leonore Waldrip, and the entire Harlequin team, whose tireless efforts brought this book into fruition.

To my mother, Theresa Cooper, and to my grandmother, Fay Barile. Two independent women, so stubborn and so beautiful, this is really for you.

To both my fathers, Robert Mele and James Sterling Cooper. Sometimes there are no words....

And, of course, to my writing partner, Loretta Nyhan. Oh, friend. Though I have yet to meet you (upon the writing of this note), you are the keeper of my heart, and the friend I dreamed about when I was a little girl. Without you, this novel wouldn't exist—but more important, I wouldn't know you, which would be the greatest tragedy of all. Thank you.

1. Rita and Glory's friendship was born of intimacy, even though they don't know each other before they begin writing. The definition of intimacy is "shared fear." How does this explain the depth of their friendship? Have you ever had a close friend with whom you shared fear? If so, how is that friendship different from others you have?

2. Rita and Glory are very different people. They are from different parts of the country, they are not the same age and they come from different social classes. They also share similarities with each other: motherhood, community, a strong sense of women's rights. Did you identify with one or the other character because of their similarities, or because of their differences? Which one, and why?

3. Glory and Rita spend a lot of time in their letters talking about their victory gardens. The gardens become a metaphor in the novel. What are some of the things the gardens represent? Was anyone inspired to plant their very own victory garden?

4. The romance between Levi and Glory is complicated. They were friends, childhood sweethearts, and then they were both left behind when Robert went to war. Why do you think Glory let the romance go as far as it did? How did she show her remorse? Can you sympathize with her actions? Do you

forgive her? How do you feel about how the love triangle was ultimately resolved?

5. *I'll Be Seeing You* explores the many types of sacrifices people make during wartime. What did the characters in this novel sacrifice? How did they feel about their personal sacrifices? About the sacrifices of others? Would you have made the same sacrifices under the circumstances in the book? Why?

6. Social historians have often noted the importance of the women who went to work during wartime, seeing them as the root of the women's equal rights movement later in the twentieth century. How do the female characters in *I'll Be Seeing You* illustrate this? In what ways is it similar or different today?

7. The recipes in the book are real wartime recipes. Did you try making any of the dishes? If so, do you have a favorite? (We hope you brought them to your book club meetings!)

8. To a certain extent, most of the characters are waiting for something (oftentimes, multiple things). Besides waiting for their men to come home, what else are Glory and Rita waiting for? How about some of the other characters? Do you feel the wait is worth it?

9. A few of the letters are marked *Unsent*. Why do you think the women decided not to send these particular letters? How would their stories change if they had? What do the unsent letters reveal about Glory and Rita's characters?

10. In Rita's final letter to Sal, she writes that Glory taught her "how to take the past and press it carefully onto the pres-

ent." Discuss the importance of memories in the novel and how memories of the past impact the present action. How do they shape the characters and their actions, the decisions they make?

Is it really true that, as of the date of this interview, you've never met each other in person? How did you connect initially, and how did you come to write a novel together? What has that experience been like for each of you?

Yes! It's true. We haven't met yet. Sometimes this surprises us. It feels like we have, but we only know each other through phone calls and email conversations.

Suzy: *I was blogging and connecting with other writers online. I remember the day that Loretta launched her blog. It was announced over a set of other writer blogs. I clicked on over...and there she was! Writing about organic food and the Beatles. I commented on her posts, and she started commenting on mine. A friendship was born. I think it took us about a year to shift over to phone conversations, and it was during one of those conversations that we expressed our desire to write something completely for ourselves, for fun. I suggested letters back and forth via email. We agreed on setting the letters in WWII, and then I sent off the first email, in character, and hoped for the best. When I got the first email back, I was elated. Soon the letters were flying between us. A story was forming as a friendship was growing. It was a very exciting time.*

Loretta: *The way this novel came together is a classic example of the "happy accident," which, of course, means it was meant* to be. When the first letter came it was like a shock to my system. I was consumed with the need to write back, and that feeling never changed throughout the whole process. This experience has been one lovely surprise after another.

What was your inspiration for I'll Be Seeing You? How, if at all, have your own personalities and experiences informed the characters of Glory and Rita?

With both of us trying to get writing careers off the ground, we were spending a lot of time thinking about what it means to wait. We were talking to each other almost daily. It was the support that we needed, someone else going through the same experience. It seemed only natural that we would write about two women who were in a stressful situation and leaning on each other for support. I don't really think we discussed that part of it, though...I think we stumbled into it. We both share a passion for similar historical eras, and we both like the research part of the writing.

Suzy: Glory is younger than I am, but she looks at life the same way. Her idealism, her sometimes selfish-without-knowing-it behavior is a lot like my own. The part of her character that is most related to me is the house and town where she lives. I grew up visiting Rockport, Massachusetts, every summer. It lives inside my heart. When I was thinking about where I wanted to spend my time in these letters, there simply was no other choice.

Loretta: Rita is bolder and more outwardly opinionated than I am; however, I do love to give advice (sometimes when I probably shouldn't). I also have a husband and two sons, and though it was disturbing, I forced myself to imagine what I would feel *if I had to send them off to war. It certainly wasn't fun, but it helped give those letters a necessary emotional depth. There were tears, though, lots and lots of tears!*

You've created such a rich and memorable cast of characters in this novel—particularly Glory and Rita, but also Levi, Robert, Roylene and even the incomparable Mrs. K.! When you started the book, did you have all of the characters and their journeys mapped out in your heads, or did they reveal themselves to you as you wrote? In what ways did the characters surprise you along the way? What was the greatest character morph as you wrote and revised the novel?

Suzy: *I didn't have anything planned. I wrote a letter (the first in the book) and sent it off. When I received Rita's first letter, and real characters were starting to emerge, I responded to her in character. Soon, my own cast of characters came through the keyboard. They surprised me as they showed up. They had so much to say! For me, the character that changed the most was Glory. She grew up during the revision process. It was an amazing experience, helping her grow from spoiled child to wise adult. (Well...maybe not always so wise...)*

Loretta: *When I got Suzy's wonderful first letter, Rita appeared and just started talking. I know how that sounds, but sometimes characters show up with fully formed lives. I knew Rita would have a crazy neighbor. I knew she would be overprotective of her only son. I knew her husband would be a real sweetie, and I knew what would happen to him. Her story was there; I just discovered more and more of it as time went on. The only real surprise for me was Roylene. Just like Rita, I didn't expect her to become so dear to me.*

I'll Be Seeing You is, above all else, a novel about the triumphant powers of friendship. How did your unconventional friendship with each other influence Rita and Glory's story, and vice versa: how did Glory and Rita's friendship influence your own?

We grew closer as Rita and Glory did. For the first ten letters or so, we didn't talk about our project at all. We let the friendship unfold naturally, for Rita and Glory, and for us. When we did finally decide to negotiate plot points and discuss character arcs, we took our relationship to a deeper level. How would we deal with the division of labor? What happens when we disagree? Working through difficulties strengthened our friendship, just as it did for Rita and Glory in the novel.

In *I'll Be Seeing You*, you explore what it meant to be a woman during a specific time in U.S. history. What drew you to this time period, what kind of research did you do and what do you want readers to take from Glory, Rita and Roylene's experiences?

We have quite a collection of WWII-era women's magazines—so much can be learned about women's lives during wartime by thumbing through an issue of Woman's Day *circa 1943. We watched interviews with women who served in the WAVES and WACs, and listened to Roosevelt's D-Day speech countless times.* Since You Went Away: World War II Letters from American Women on the Home Front *by Judy Barrett Litoff and David C. Smith was invaluable. It's a collection of letters women sent to their men overseas. The letters offered more than a wealth of period details; underneath the sometimes* mundane details of family life, you can see the worry, the strain, the desire to keep their husbands and sons connected to their lives at home through words. There's an admirable nobility in that.

We thought it was important to underscore that all women (whether they label themselves feminists or not) share the same reality in our culture. And because of that, we struggle for the same rights. We wanted readers to see the independence and power that Rita, Glory and Roylene shared—a fearless determination to give back to their communities, their families and their country. Not for any other reason than it was the right thing to do. Women are a community, and there's a lot of untapped power there. Not divisive power, inclusive power. We hope readers can feel that, and we hope our characters inspire our readers to want to go out and make new connections with people (other women, organizations, etc.) that might need them.

Can you describe the process of writing a novel as a team? Does each of you write your own cast of characters (and if so, who wrote which characters in *I'll Be Seeing You*)? Do you each take turns with the manuscript, passing it back and forth to each other, or is one of you the organizer (if so, who)?

Suzy writes from Glory's perspective; Loretta writes Rita's letters and those from the Iowa City characters. The only exception is Toby's poetry—those are all Suzy's.

We sent letters back and forth to each other via email. In the beginning we didn't know when a letter would come—we wanted to experience the anticipation, just as Rita and Glory would. Loretta compiled all the letters into one continuous document.

What can you tell us about your next novel?

We want to tell you EVERYTHING about our newest novel! It's so exciting to write about new characters. The historical era we chose was the progressive era: 1917-1920 America. It's about two sisters, Pasadena and India Adams, who find themselves cast out by family misfortune. They end up in Manhattan with two very different agendas: Pasadena is determined to earn enough money to buy back their family home, and India just wants to grab up everything the city has to offer.

The girls find themselves living on the top floor of a tenement in the overcrowded Lower East Side. They quickly learn that survival will be more difficult than they planned. Instead of finding solace in each other, the sisters search for their brother, Kingston, who disappeared into the chaotic city. As the girls' separate lives begin to intersect in ways they'd never imagined, it's Kingston who they hope will sort things out—if they can only find him.

An unforgettable story of two
courageous women brought together
by one extraordinary little girl

Betty Jewel Hughes was once the hottest black
jazz singer in Memphis. But when she finds
herself pregnant and alone, she gives up her
dream of being a star to raise her daughter, Billie.

Now, ten years later, in 1955, Betty Jewel is
dying of cancer and looking for someone to care
for Billie when she's gone. With no one she can
count on, Betty Jewel does the unthinkable:
she takes out a want ad seeking a loving
mother for her daughter.

www.mirabooks.co.uk

PARIS, 1919. THE WORLD'S LEADERS HAVE GATHERED TO REBUILD FROM THE ASHES OF THE GREAT WAR.

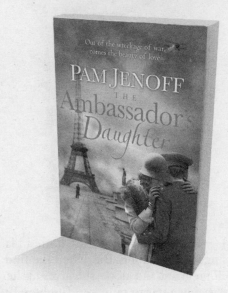

For one woman, the City of Light harbours dark secrets and dangerous liaisons, for which many could pay dearly.

Against the backdrop of one of the most significant events of the century, a delicate web of lies obscures the line between the casualties of war and of the heart, making trust a luxury that no one can afford.

www.mirabooks.co.uk

M304_TAD

An innocent pawn
A kingdom for the taking
A new dynasty will reign…

1415, Katherine de Valois, the jewel in the French
crown. An innocent locked up by her mother,
Queen Isabeau, and kept pure as a prize for
the English king, Henry V.

For Katherine, a pawn in a ruthless political game,
England is a lion's den of greed, avarice and mistrust.
And when the magnificent king leaves her widowed
at twenty-one she is a prize ripe for the taking.

This is the story of Katherine de Valois, England's
most coveted prize. The forbidden queen who
launched the most famous dynasty of all time…

HARLEQUIN®MIRA®
www.mirabooks.co.uk

An indecent proposal

Lady Lucy MacMorlan may have forsworn men and marriage, but that doesn't mean she won't agree to profit from writing love letters for her brother's friends. That is, until she inadvertently ruins the betrothal of a notorious laird…

Robert, the dashing Marquis of Methven, is on to Lucy's secret. And he certainly doesn't intend to let the lovely Lady Lucy have the last word, especially when her letters suggest she is considerably more experienced than he realised…

HARLEQUIN® MIRA®
www.mirabooks.co.uk

Your mother's killer is about to be released. Your best friend has died and left you guardian of her daughter

Lacey O'Neill suddenly has the power to give a convicted man back his life, but how can you forgive your mother's killer, the one man who destroyed your family…

Lacey is facing the biggest decision of her life, when her best friend Jessica dies in a car crash, leaving behind a grieving eleven-year-old daughter.

Two choices, two lives. How would you choose?

M325_HMS